KAYLEE'S GHOST

Kaylee's Ghost

Rochelle Jewel Shapiro

Dear Michelle,
May a beautiful
future shimmer
before you.
Sincerely,
Rochelle Jewel Shapiro

RJS BOOKS

First edition

ISBN 978-1481033268 (pbk. : alk. paper)

RJS BOOKS

ACKNOWLEDGEMENTS

Thanks to Simon & Schuster for publishing *Miriam the Medium* in 2004. *Kaylee's Ghost* would never have happened without fans such as Elena Wayne Shapiro and Brenda Gatti and so many others who reached out to me, asking, "So when is your next book coming out?"

I am so grateful to Caroline Leavitt, the *New York Times* bestselling author of Pictures of You and the award-winning author of eight other novels, for her editing and especially her friendship and Jill Hoffman, editor of *Mudfish Magazine*, who listened to me read and gave terrific feedback.

Thank you so much to my family: my husband, Bernie, my children Heather and Charles, their spouses Jesse and Karen, and my four grandchildren: Rebecca, Jacen, Eden, and Ari for their love.

And thank you to my Russian grandmother, my *bubbie*, from whom I inherited my psychic gift.

http://rochellejewelshapiro.com

"I can call spirits from the vasty deep."
—*Shakespeare* (1 Henry IV, 3,1)

"An idea, like a ghost, must be spoken
to a little before it will explain itself."
—*Charles Dickens*

part one

I

MIRIAM SQUIRMED ON THE DUSTY CARPET OF THE lying-in hospital in Baltimore, her bunched-up raincoat her pillow. Her only child, Cara, was in the labor room with her husband, Dan, having their first child, and Miriam was frankly going crazy. She had already walked her soles off in the four hours she'd been here, but her husband, Rory, was still pacing. His size fourteen shoes passed her line of vision every few moments. She should have been here three weeks ago. Cara was three weeks overdue. The doctor had urged Cara to let him induce labor, but she had refused. She wanted to be terribly modern, do everything naturally, even though Miriam thought modern was more like what her own grandmother would have done during the time of the tsar.

Rory looked down at Miriam. He hadn't slept either. He took off his glasses and rubbed his eyes, but they didn't look any clearer. She had lost count of how many cups of coffee he'd drunk.

"Mim," he said, "while you dozed off I checked upstairs. The couch there doesn't have wooden arms separating every seat. You can lie across it instead of on the floor."

"I want to be close by," Miriam said. "I want to be here for the first cry."

"You're always close by, Mim."

It was true. Nine months and three weeks ago, Miriam had bolted up in bed, an image rousting her from sleep. "Rory, I just saw a stork standing at the foot of Cara's bed. She's pregnant."

"Go to sleep," he'd mumbled. "Every image doesn't have to be a premonition," and he pulled the covers back over his head.

After that, Miriam was so giddy that it was hard for her not to immediately phone her daughter. She hadn't wanted to let Cara know that she knew anything. Having a psychic as a mother was, as Cara had so often said, "a spoiler." For weeks the image had come back, erupting when Miriam was doing the dishes or going to sleep, always the same, a stork looking quizzically at her as if to say, What are you waiting for? But Miriam knew her daughter, and she knew the pregnancy wasn't hers to announce, but Cara's.

Six weeks later Cara had phoned to say, "Don't you dare tell anyone this, not even Dad. I don't want to get everyone worked up until I'm sure." Cara had been married four years and had been focusing on her business designing hats that she manufactured to sell in boutiques around the world. It killed Miriam when people had begun to look at Cara's stomach, and say, "Well, anything in there yet?" It reminded her of when, at sixteen, Cara had shot up to 5'10" and people felt compelled to ask her, "How's the weather up there?"

"Oh, I shouldn't dare tell anyone about what?" Miriam had said, forcing a yawn.

"I just took a pregnancy test and passed with a plus sign."

Miriam couldn't help the way her heart rocketed in her chest, the way her mouth flew open. She had known Cara was pregnant all along, but sharing it was something different. A child! A child! Every time she heard it, it sounded like music. "Cara, I'm so excited," she said.

"I don't want you to be excited until I know for sure."

Miriam didn't want Cara to be anxious. Anxiety had a negative effect on a fetus. "Be sure, honey," she blurted.

"You knew!" Cara said, accusingly.

Busted, Miriam thought, wrapping the phone cord around her wrist. "Yes, I knew."

"Well, please wait until I go to the doctor before you jump to any more conclusions," Cara said, her voice tight.

"Of course," Miriam answered, and right away, like a future sonogram, she saw a pink bud in Cara's womb. A little girl was on the way. A girl! She could take her shopping and to the park. She thought of her own bubbie, who had taught her to see spirits in mirrors and puddles, to sense the colors around people and what they meant. Bubbie had taught her how to look to the right to see the past and the left, the future. Oh, they'd had had the most wonderful times together. "I won't say another word," Miriam told Cara.

Well, that had been a long time ago. Throughout Cara's pregnancy, Miriam had known when Cara was going to have morning sickness, when she would stain and panic. Miriam had also known it wouldn't be anything, but she kept her mouth shut, because the more silent she was, the more Cara opened up to her.

Now Rory reached his hand down to Miriam. "Come

on," he said, wagging his fingers. "Lying on the floor like that, you look homeless. I'll get you as soon as I hear anything."

Miriam took his hand and let him pull her up. "Ow," she said. One of her long red curls, now threaded with white, had managed to wind its way around a button of her raincoat. Rory unwound it and pulled her to her feet. Her knees creaked.

She took her rumpled raincoat and went upstairs. There was the couch Rory had told her about, just waiting for her. She felt a pang for abandoning her clients, especially her weekly one, Kaylee, who Miriam could sense was filling up her voicemail with urgent messages to get right back to her, even though it was the middle of the night. But Miriam was too immersed in Cara's labor and too exhausted to do one thing about it.

She lay down on the couch, too antsy to fall asleep. The waiting room was clean, but she felt like vacuuming the carpet, dusting the end tables. Was she getting the nesting instinct? A volcano of sympathetic labor erupted in her lower back. She had had back labor with Cara. Before three weeks ago, when Cara should have given birth, Miriam had worried about whether her granddaughter would be psychic. Her own mother had worried about the same thing when she was born. Her mother hadn't wanted a daughter who was a "babushka lady" from the Dark Ages like her father's mother.

When Miriam was pregnant with Cara, her mother had told her that Bubbie had predicted Miriam would be born with a caul. Miriam's mother had been scared it was a disease.

"A caul," Bubbie had explained, "happens when the

water sac doesn't break and you see the baby's head right through it."

"See, I was right," Bubbie had said after Miriam was born. "My granddaughter had the caul."

"Who knows?" Miriam's mother had said. "I was happily knocked out with twilight sleep," but Bubbie still maintained that her vision was accurate, and Miriam had believed her.

Miriam had wondered whether Cara would be born with a caul as well, but her daughter, with her green eyes, took after Miriam's mother's side of the family, the side who had only used tea leaves to brew tea. When Cara became pregnant, Miriam obsessed over whether or not Cara's baby would be born with the caul. She wanted it so badly, she couldn't tell if what she was seeing—the thin veil over the baby's face—was really there, or if she were wishing it so. A caul didn't just mean that the baby had a gift; it was a connection, just as Miriam had been connected to her bubbie.

Now, though, all Miriam could think about was whether something terrible could have happened as a result of her granddaughter being in the womb too long. Each week that Cara had gone back to the doctor, he had tried to talk her into inducing labor. He had even made her sign a form saying that he wasn't responsible if she didn't let him induce the baby, but Cara was stubborn. She had been so determined that she would go to Cornell that she hadn't even applied elsewhere. And when she'd spotted Dan walking on the Triphammer Bridge over the falls on campus, saw his brawny build, blond hair, hazel eyes, the cleft in his chin, she'd said, "That's the guy I'm going to marry." Maybe Cara was psychic after all.

Maybe she was the sort who only got information for herself instead of "sticking her nose into other people's business," which was how Miriam's mother had described Miriam's gift. Maybe some inner knowing had directed Cara to not listen to her doctor.

"The doctors and the undertakers are partners," Bubbie used to say.

Miriam wished she hadn't thought of an undertaker. Her worry about whether or not her granddaughter would be psychic now seemed better than worrying that something had gone wrong with the baby or with Cara. Even if her granddaughter had Miriam's pale blue eyes, it didn't necessarily mean that she'd be psychic. But Miriam's Aunt Chaia, who had been psychic, had had those same eyes, and her life had turned out so miserably that now Miriam spit three times to ward off bad luck.

She got up from the couch and dug her palms into her low back, but the volcano of pain kept erupting, as if she were in the last stage of labor.

Suddenly she heard a commotion and heard Rory call her name. She dashed downstairs without her raincoat. Nurses and doctors were running into the birthing room. She grabbed a nurse.

"My daughter's in there," she said, her heart in her throat. "Cara Sachs. What's happening?" But the nurse shrugged her off and hurried through the swinging doors. Miriam wanted to go in too, but she had street clothes on instead of scrubs, and worse, she'd been lying on the dirty carpet.

"Mim, what's going on in there?" Rory asked, mopping

his brow with his hankie. "Did something happen to Cara? To the baby?"

She tried to take deep breaths. Psychic information came in with oxygen, but her chest was tight with panic. Nothing, she got nothing. Time was ticking through each of her nerve endings. She clutched Rory's hand so hard that her own hurt.

"If we don't hear anything soon," Rory said, "I'm going to knock at the door."

No! Miriam gripped his hand harder to prevent him from disturbing the medical team. When he'd had a hernia operation just after they got married, his mother, who had wanted to be the only "Mrs. Kaminsky," had been so nervous waiting to hear how he was that she'd paged the doctor during the operation. The doctor, thinking it was an emergency with another patient, left Rory to answer the call. Did he ever tell Rory's mother off!

Two nurses came out of the swinging doors. "I've never seen anything like it," one said softly to the other. "That shining veil over her face. But what a cutie."

Miriam's hand flew to her chest. She had her answer. "Rory, Cara's fine. And the baby's not only fine, she was born with a caul. She's going to be psychic." Miriam could see the storm cloud of an argument brewing in his head, but at that moment, the doors swung open again. This time Dan came out, wearing blue scrubs and an ecstatic grin, and handed them pink bubblegum cigars.

"You can come in now and meet Violet," Dan said.

"Violet," Miriam repeated. "Such a lovely name." Cara hadn't wanted Miriam to know the baby's name in advance.

Since Miriam wasn't good at getting names psychically, Cara hadn't even given her a hint. "You think you know everything, but you don't," Cara had said, the dimples deepening in her cheeks.

"She's named for my grandmother, Vivienne, who played the harp," Dan said.

Miriam had wished that they would name her Sara after Bubbie. But a harp player was good too. A harp player who was psychic, that is.

With a hand on each of their shoulders, Dan ushered them into the birthing room. There, on the bed, lying stomach-down on Cara's belly that still rose like a hill, was Violet. Her face, turned toward Miriam and Rory, was a pocket mirror of Cara's, but even though her eyes were closed, Miriam could see that they pointed up in the corners, like hers and Bubbie's and she knew, just knew, that they would be the same pale blue and stay that way. It had been almost thirty years since Miriam had nursed, but she suddenly felt the tingle of the let down reflex in her breasts. *Violet.* She heard Rory weeping softly.

"Our little girls," Rory said.

For a moment, just a moment, Miriam's worries were cotton candy dissolving in her mouth. And then all the burdens of being psychic bumped into her brain. Miriam promised herself to take her vitamins, exercise, and lower her cholesterol. She had to be here to protect Violet so she didn't suffer as Miriam had after Bubbie died, leaving her alone in the world with her gift. When Miriam had heard that a girl from her third grade class, Fern, had drowned over the summer, she had had nightmares for weeks of her with fish in her eyeballs and seaweed hanging from her nose. But nothing had been scarier than when Fern's spirit walked right through Miriam's bedroom wall, looking just as she always had, with her long dark braids fastened with bows. The only difference was that you could see through her. "You ate my bologna sandwich," Fern complained, which had been true, then walked out through the wall again. There was no one Miriam could talk to about it. And in fourth grade, when she saw in her mind her teacher, Miss Curtis, kissing Mr. Wallbaum, the principal, and asked her if they were getting married, how could Miriam have known that Mr. Wallbaum already had a wife? How Miriam's cheek had stung when Miss Curtis slapped her face! And Miriam couldn't have gone home to tell her mother, who would only have slapped her even harder for saying it. No, Miriam was going to be needed to guide Violet through her early years, to teach her to hone her skills and safeguard herself from others, just the way Bubbie had with her. But how could she ever get through the barrier of her own daughter to do it?

II

"MIM, THAT CAUL-THING IS JUST AN OLD WIVES' tale," RORY said, bonking his palm on the steering wheel. They were in their Honda Civic, crawling along in the eternal traffic on I-95 toward their house in Great Neck, Long Island. "I'll buy that a baby being born with the membrane intact is a good thing because it might protect it from infection until the membrane ruptures, maybe ensure survival for a couple of weeks, which was especially important before antibiotics, but that's it."

"You always think like a pharmacist," she said.

"Look, just don't go promoting our granddaughter as a psychic," he said. "Could be with her pharmacist grandpa and her geneticist father she'll be a woman of science someday. Or she might take after your mother's side like Cara does and end up the next Coco Chanel."

"Hey, I thought you were proud of my gift."

Miriam remembered how scared she'd been to tell him about her abilities, given his science background. When her previous dates had found out, they'd all asked her for the answers to their next exam. One had wanted to take her to the track with him so she could pick him a winning horse. But Rory had kissed her and called her his "Live Wire."

"You know I'm proud of your gift," Rory said now, "but I don't want you to type-cast Violet while she's only talking spit bubbles. Violet's birth is one of the brightest things that ever happened to us. Do you have to make it into a thunderstorm?"

Miriam knew he was right, but still turned away from him. In the night window, she thought her face looked like a "Just Say No to Botox" ad. In Great Neck, even some of the residents at the Grace Avenue Nursing Home had gotten facelifts. But as Miriam was aging, she had begun to look more and more like Bubbie and didn't want to change that.

They had stayed at Cara and Dan's the two days that Cara was in the hospital. Shortly after Cara got home, she'd said, "Dan and I don't want you and Dad to feel hurt, but we need this time alone to bond with Violet."

"Oh," Miriam had said, "sure. Well, we can come back next weekend."

"Dan's parents are flying in next weekend."

"Dad and I will stay in a hotel and give Hillary and George the guestroom," Miriam said. "It will be so nice to see their reaction to Violet. Our joy will quadruple."

Cara had bitten her lip. "Mom, really, it's too much company for us at one time right now. And this is Dan's parents' first grandchild too. They deserve the time to be with her the way you and Dad have been."

It killed Miriam to think of Dan's mother, Hillary, holding Violet: Hillary, the speech therapist with the sleek hairdo and foundation makeup face and perfect diction; Hillary who became rich in her own right from designing an electronic device that worked the jaw muscles to help people stop stuttering. When she'd learned that Miriam was a psychic, Hillary had wrinkled her bobbed nose as if she'd smelled a sweaty armpit.

"No offense, but George and I don't believe in psychics," she'd said. "It's not actually a profession. It's, well…" Her voice had trailed off and she'd done a dismissive flick of her wrist.

Hillary looked down on anyone who didn't have a Ph.D., and even then they had to be the most accomplished, the most famous. She never had little stories about Dan growing up, just how well he'd done on exams and at science fairs. Hillary had insisted that she didn't want to be called "Grandma" and wasn't the type to enjoy kids. Miriam worried that Violet would love Hillary more. Bile rose in her throat. Grandmotherhood was turning her into just the kind of person she couldn't stand.

The car had a moldy smell because Miriam had left her damp raincoat in the back with the windows closed, but now she smelled the unmistakable sweetness of the lavender powder Bubbie had puffed on her creased neck. Miriam looked from the corners of her eyes, left, right. There on the dashboard, like a little magnetic statue, stood Bubbie with her ocean blue eyes, her white hair braided and coiled on her head like a crown of challah. She had on one of her black dresses with a white lace collar and her marcasite brooch, all in miniature.

"Don't you worry," Bubbie said. "The baby will love you like nobody's business. The baby will love you like you love me."

After Bubbie disappeared from the dashboard, Miriam

drifted. She was a child again in Bubbie's kitchen with its shelves of dried herbs. She and Bubbie were sitting at the metal table with the red and white checked oilcloth over it so their elbows wouldn't get cold while Miriam helped Bubbie shell peas from their pods. It was a summer day. Miriam knew it because there was no radiator hiss. Bubbie's window was open. Through the screen came the cooing of pigeons.

"Mrs. Kransky is out there again, feeding those pigeons," Bubbie said, shaking her head.

Mrs. Kransky used to come out at noon every day with a bag of breadcrumbs. She wore a slicker to feed the pigeons, but pigeon doo still got on her gray bangs, the frames of her plaid glasses, and on her black laced-up shoes.

"A wild creature has got to know how to find its own food to live," Bubbie said. "Kransky feels like a big shot feeding the pigeons, like a regular St. Francis of Assisi. But white bread, even challah, swells up inside a pigeon's belly like yeast and makes it easier for a cat to eat him."

"How do you know the bread swells inside a pigeon's belly?" Miriam asked.

"I can see inside."

"You can see inside a pigeon's belly?" Miriam felt her eyes popping.

Bubbie threw her head back and laughed, the bowl of pea pods wobbling in her lap. "I can see into anyone's belly, into their heart, their lungs, even their *tuchases*."

"Like the x-rays Dr. Bardel reads," Miriam said.

"Dr. Bardel," Bubbie scoffed, blowing out air through her teeth. "What does he know?"

"He knows Mom pencils a beauty mark on her cheek," Miriam said. "He told Mom that the spot could be skin cancer. His face got as red as borscht when he rubbed his finger across it and it smeared."

Bubbie laughed again.

"Bubbie, could you show me how to see inside someone?" Miriam asked.

Bubbie's brows knit over her round silver glasses. Miriam knew why Bubbie worried. Before her mother had left her with Bubbie to go shop at B. Altman's, she had made Bubbie promise not to teach Miriam any of her *bubbeh meisehs*, superstitions from the Old World.

"I won't tell," Miriam told Bubbie.

"When you have the gift," Bubbie said, "you got to learn to carry secrets anyway. So why not? I'm making a nice roast chicken for tonight. I can show you what's inside the chicken so you can start learning."

Miriam had seen her mother take off her rings and clean out a chicken, but she hadn't watched closely. She hadn't even been able to stand the sucking sound when her mother pulled the insides out. But if Miriam wanted to be like Bubbie someday, she knew she'd have to start looking at all these things.

"All right, Bubbie," she said, her voice shaky.

Bubbie put down the bowl, got up, took the chicken out of the refrigerator, and set it on the counter. Miriam stood on a chair to watch. The goose-bumped chicken skin was cold and shiny. Bubbie reached into the cavity and pulled out the insides.

"This is the heart," she said, and handed it to Miriam.

It hadn't looked like any valentine Miriam had ever seen. It had grayish gristle on it and had tentacles coming out of its head like a sea monster.

"This gray egg is the most delicious part," Bubbie said. "And this dark ball is the spleen. Most of what you see is the *pupik*." She showed Miriam a flattish sac. "The gizzard is where the chicken keeps her teeth."

"Grandma Ada keeps her teeth in a glass of water," Miriam told Bubbie.

Then Bubbie showed her the neck bone with its sharp edges.

"And here's the chicken's *loch* where the *pishechtz* come out," Bubbie said.

The chicken's peepee was curved and it didn't have hair like Miriam's mother's.

A knock sounded at the door. Bubbie looked at the clock. "Your mother," she said, shoving the parts back into the chicken.

"Mamma," Miriam's mother called through the half-opened door. "May I come in?"

"Sure, what are you, a stranger now?" Bubbie said, washing her hands at the sink.

Miriam's mother came in carrying a shopping bag, a big smile on her face. She'd taken the subway into the city for a day alone. She had on her blue and white checked spring coat with a small blue hat that tipped to one side.

"Hi, Mommy," Miriam said as innocently as she could.

One look at Miriam and the smile went off her mother's face.

"What's in your hand?" she demanded.

Miriam had forgotten to give Bubbie back the chicken heart.

"I was showing her how to clean a chicken," Bubbie said.

Her mother frowned. "Mamma, you're always scaring people half to death."

"I'm not scared," Miriam insisted.

"You're too young to understand," her mother answered. "Mamma, you always want a whole day with Miriam and then you go and ruin it with your voodoo."

"It's not ruined," Miriam wailed. "It's not." But she knew it really was, though not by Bubbie. It had been ruined by her mother.

"What can I say?" Bubbie said with a sigh. "I try my best with everyone, but I'm never right with you, Dorothy."

"Give Bubbie back the chicken heart and wash your hands," her mother said. "We're not staying for dinner."

Tears stung Miriam's eyes. She could see by the tremble of Bubbie's chin that she was fighting back tears too. "Do what your mother says," Bubbie told her.

Going down the flight of steps, away from Bubbie, with her mother's high heels clip-clopping angrily on the tile floor, Miriam felt as if she were being pulled into an undertow. Her throat burned as if she had drunk saltwater. They didn't stop into Miriam's father's butcher shop downstairs to say goodbye to him. They just kept walking so fast that her mother's shopping bag swung on her arm like a pendulum. After four blocks, her mother slowed down.

"I know you want to be just like Bubbie, that she's your

hero, if you can call a woman that," Miriam's mother said. "I keep thinking that you're too young to hear the truth about your bubbie, but if she thinks that when you're six years old you should be handling chicken guts, well, I can't hold back anymore. I know Bubbie can help people, but those superstitions that she carried with her from Russia along with her featherbed and candlesticks can do real harm."

Miriam set her mouth in a straight line. "Bubbie can't do harm," she said.

"Oh, yes she can," her mother said. "When I was pregnant with you I was so happy and so was your father. It had taken us two whole years to conceive. He was so grateful that he didn't even care if you were a girl or a boy. "

Her mother was talking to her as if Miriam were her age, and Miriam wished she'd stop.

"Bubbie told me that if I stepped over a snake, the baby would be strangled by the umbilical cord," her mother went on. "I laughed. 'Where are you going to find a snake in Rockaway Beach?' I asked her. But it was hard not to believe Bubbie. After all, she had looked into my eyes and told me I was pregnant before I knew it myself."

Miriam had seen Bubbie do that with a lot of ladies. The only one who had gotten mad about it was Barbara Schmully because she wasn't married.

"Your father and I went for a walk on a nice spring day just like this," her mother said. "We were holding hands and we were so excited, so in love. All of a sudden I noticed something green curled at my feet. A snake! I thought. I was so startled that instead of backing away, I tried to jump over it. I had your father's hand, but I still belly-whopped to the ground and landed on the garden hose. I started staining."

Miriam didn't know what that was and didn't think she wanted to either.

"The doctor prescribed a week of bed rest with my feet up," her mother said. "But at the end of the week, I was still terrified that something had happened to the baby. All the joy of my pregnancy was gone. I stayed in the apartment, watching out for snakes in the bathroom, beneath the kitchen sink, under the beds."

"But what if it had been a real snake?" Miriam said. "Then you would be happy Bubbie had warned you."

Her mother shook her head. "If you weren't a girl, you'd make a good lawyer. But for your own good, I can't let you win this case.

"After I felt you kicking inside me," her mother went on, "I began to feel better. I went out to see a revival of *The Hunchback of Notre Dame*. When Charles Laughton pulled the rope in the belfry and the church bells rang, an alarm bell went off in me. 'If you see a hunchback when you're pregnant,' Bubbie told me, 'the baby will be born with a *hoiker* on its back too.' I almost fainted. I picked up my maternity blouse and stuck my thumb down my girdle and spit three times, Bubbie's antidote to a hex. But it didn't stop my nerves. My blood pressure shot up. It looked like I was wearing doughnuts on my ankles. Even my nose swelled. I couldn't relax until you were born and I could run my hand over your back. So I want you to keep all this in mind when you glorify Bubbie. Do you understand me?"

"Yes," Miriam said, but as they continued on toward

80th Street, where they lived in a big Victorian house that had been carved into apartments, Miriam went over in her mind all the chicken parts Bubbie had shown her. *Gizzard,* she thought, and pictured the sac with the teeth inside. *Pupik,* she silently said, and she saw the slimy tubes again. *Loch,* where the peepee comes out.

"Mim, you're not still sulking, are you?" Rory asked softly.

She turned back to him, smiling. "Of course not." She began to think about her and Violet cleaning a chicken together someday so that Violet could learn the names of the parts. She pictured herself teaching Violet to read tea leaves and the lines on the palm of a hand.

"I'm pulling into the next rest stop," Rory announced.

When they got there, as Miriam waited on the ladies room line, she counted the grandmothers ahead of her. *Violet,* she said to herself, and felt the elation of immortality. Someday she would be speaking to her psychic granddaughter from the dashboard of Violet's car.

In the stall, she balanced herself over the bowl. The woman next to her was farting, but Miriam still smelled Evening in Paris. She looked up. Her mother, wearing a red hat with a veil and a black feather stuck in the black hatband, was looking down at her, wagging her finger.

"Oh, no you don't," her mother said. "You're not going to turn Violet into a babushka lady like you and Bubbie, not as long as I'm alive."

"But you're not," Miriam said.

"Says you!" her mother said. "Don't be fresh."

III

Kaylee Fiorelli slammed the receiver down. She'd been calling Miriam for like a week minimum and she wasn't there. She had left a ton of messages without one answer. She'd been Miriam's client for four years and had readings at least twice a month, sometimes more. Miriam could at least have given her a courtesy call to say, "I'm away." Even if Miriam was in Bermuda, she could call back. Everybody had unlimited long distance calls now. What would it have taken for her to call Brooklyn to say when she was going to be back? Being a medium, Miriam probably could even call to say, "I'm dead." Kaylee liked cracking herself up, but now her heart started to bang against her t-shirt with one of her anxiety attacks.

The phone rang. *Maybe it's Miriam,* she thought.

"Kaylee," her mother said like a long sigh.

Kaylee was afraid to ask her what was wrong, but she had to. Her mother had no one else to tell anything to. "What's the matter, Mom?"

"My sinuses are all plugged up. I tried steaming them over the kettle like Aunt Shinead, may she rest in peace, used to, but I put my face too close and scalded it. I didn't want to bother you and Tom, so I took a taxi to the emergency room.

They gave me some silver cream with sulphur in it. Now I can't even blow my nose."

Kaylee cringed. She thought of her mother's heavy face with a red scalded circle over it like Aunt Shinead after her years of steaming under a tent towel. Uncle Finn had gone back to Ireland four times to take the pledge, but his face hadn't had any red on it or busted capillaries and he had out-lived Aunt Shinead and her sinuses.

"Oh, poor you," she told her mother. "Do you want me to come over?"

"No, you'll only catch my cold and then we'll both be sick. Stay home with your Tom."

Kaylee was glad not to have to go. Her mother would want her to watch a soap opera with her. The actors always had so much more doing in their lives than she did that it made her feel worse. Still, she didn't like her mother to be lonely. "Okay, Mom. I'll call you later." She didn't want to, but her heart started bonging again. "I love you, Mom," she added quickly.

"You're a good girl, Kaylee. Other mothers, they aren't so lucky. Their daughters don't listen to them, but you, you always listen."

I'm twenty-seven years old and I still always listen, Kaylee thought. She pressed her hand against her chest as if she was willing it to keep her heart inside. "Bye, Mom."

Tom was in the bedroom reading *The Post* in the easy chair he'd brought from his dead mother's house when he and Kaylee got married eight years ago. He would have brought everything if Kaylee hadn't had a big fit.

She sat down on the four-poster bed with the angels' faces

carved into the mahogany headboard. "Don't you think it's weird that we sleep in my parents' bed?" she asked.

He didn't put the newspaper down. "Nah. Your mother said to me, 'Tom, what do I need with a big bed when my husband has been dead for eighteen years?' We did your mother a favor taking it. It was depressing her. She says she's so much happier sleeping in her new twin."

"I wish I had never told Mom that we were looking to buy a new bed. I feel like our bedroom is haunted now."

Tom peered at her momentarily over the paper. "Kaylee, where do you get your ideas from?"

She grabbed her hair in a bunch at one shoulder and studied it. "Yesterday, I found a gray hair." Tom's hair was still thick and dark brown; his eyebrows, too, on his thin face. She'd married a man almost twenty years older than she was and she was the one who was getting gray. "I plucked it out," she said.

"Jesus, it says here how much teachers get each year for their pensions," Tom said through his newspaper. "I should have been a teacher. Before you know it, retirement will be on me. We better start seriously saving. You better cut back on talking to your psychic."

Tom was always griping about how much she put on the credit card to talk to Miriam, but she didn't care. She and Tom never went on vacations. He was always saving for retirement. Kaylee fluffed out her hair and leaned back on her extended arms.

"Tom, if we had a baby and it was a boy, do you think he would be skinny like a frankfurter?"

Tom put down his paper. "Hey, what're you saying about

my physique?" His dark eyes glared, but his lips twitched with a laugh.

"I'm saying, Tom, that I want to have a baby. I'm twenty-seven now. I'm not getting any younger."

"What about me?" Tom said. "I have eighteen years on you. You have to think about that, Kaylee. You lost your father when you were nine. I grew up without a father too and I don't want any kid of mine growing up without one."

"Why do we always have to live our lives by death?" She felt like a hypocrite. Most of her calls to Miriam, she'd ask, "Please contact my father? I want to know what he thinks I should do about whatever..." She started to cry. "Tom, most days I hate to go outside because I see all the women pushing baby carriages, and all the kids skipping ahead of their parents and getting yanked back. Sometimes I want to just take a kid and run."

Tom came over and sat next to her on the bed. He took her hands in his and kissed her fingertips. His lips were wet. She wanted to pull her hands away, but maybe this time he'd agree to have a child.

"Kaylee, Kaylee, you know how much I love you. I love you to death."

She groaned. There it was again, death.

"Look, I told you from the get-go, no kids, and you agreed.

"I was nineteen then. What did I know?"

"It's not just the age, Kaylee, even though it's a big part. You're kind of delicate. You know what I mean, with your heart and all? I don't know what I'd do if anything ever happened to you."

"The doctor said my rapid heartbeat is just nerves. You know that. You were right there and you heard him."

"Yeah, but if you have nerves with no baby, think of how much nerves you'd have if you had a baby screaming and getting fevers and pulling down everything from the shelves like I did. I probably was the death of my mother."

She put her hand over his mouth. "If you say death one more time, Thomas Frances Fiorelli..."

"I'm sorry, I'm sorry," Tom said, his repentance vibrating against her palm. He took her hand from his mouth. "Your mother had that preclampsia when she was carrying you and she almost died, you along with her."

"You said it again," she shouted at him.

He blinked. "What'd I say?"

"*Died.* You said my mother and I almost *died.*"

"I just don't want anything to happen to you, Kaylee."

"I wish my mother never told you about her preclampsia. I wish she never told me."

"You know, once you have a baby, you can't take it back," he said. "You hate to clean, you hate to cook. How are you going to feel about diapers and spit up?"

"I don't need to worry about any of that with my mother coming to cook and clean. She loves to do that. And she'd babysit, too, any time. "

"Yeah, well, your mother's getting up in years and so am I. Don't fibrulate your heart with worries." He put his arms around her and tried to draw her down on the bed, but she couldn't do it now. Even though it only took five minutes, she just couldn't.

"I'm walking over to my mother's," she said.

"I'll come with you."

"No, I want to see her by myself."

Tom shrugged. "Okay. But sometimes I wish that your mother lived farther away so you'd need me to drive you there."

Her mother, Kaylee thought, would have an asthma attack if she heard Tom say that. Her mother adored him. She had been the one who had encouraged Kaylee to marry him, even though he was Italian. "I'm warning you, Kaylee O'Brien, you'll never find another man like him," her mother had said. "If I were younger, I'd go after him myself."

Now Kaylee went out, slamming the door behind her. As soon as she did, doors opened all along the hallway and little old ladies peered out.

"I thought it might be Tom," Mrs. McEnroe said. "The batteries in my hearing aid died again, and I can't hear a thing."

Then how did you hear me slam my door? Kaylee wanted to know.

"Kaylee, when you get a chance," Mrs. Gluck said, "tell Tom the light bulb in my bathroom is out."

How about you ask the super for once? Kaylee thought.

There were four more requests by the time the elevator came. The old ladies all loved Tom as much as her mother did. He did everything for them, and they didn't have to give him a tip. Kaylee knew she was just being mean. Her booming heart told her so. "I'll tell Tom," she called out.

Her mother was four blocks west on Ditmars. Kaylee walked six blocks east, looking up. The palm reader was over a deli. She wished she'd written down the address when she saw it the first time. Her neck was starting to hurt.

"Palm Readings, Five Dollars," the sign said. The hallway was dark and smelled like pickles. She was afraid to go up. She remembered what Miriam had said about Tom. "He's a good man, just afraid of life." That made her take one step and another. She didn't want to be like Tom anymore.

She stopped at the door that said, "Reader Inside. No Appointment Necessary." She thought of the long wait there always was to get an appointment with Miriam and Miriam charging thirty times what this reader did. Kaylee was sweating. Her mouth was a desert. But she knocked at the door.

"Come in," a woman with a Spanish accent called.

The room smelled like Tabu and fried plantains. Kaylee knew the smell of fried plantains from Mrs. Rosario in 5C, who had also kept a live chicken in her apartment until someone reported her to the Board of Health.

"I'm Lena," the woman said. She was heavy, like Kaylee's mother. She could hardly put her arms at her sides. "Sit down." She gestured to a folding table with a plastic lace tablecloth over it. Her hoop earrings wiggled as she talked. After Kaylee sat down, Lena said, "Five dollars for a palm reading, but I do a whole life card reading for twenty."

"Palm," Kaylee said.

"Put your palm and your money on the table."

Kaylee did what she was told. Lena just looked at her hand without touching it, like she was scared of germs.

"I see you have a secret, one you don't want your husband to find out," she said.

"He doesn't know I'm here," Kaylee confided.

Lena nodded, her earrings swinging.

"And I see you have losses."

Kaylee thought of her father, dying for years from kidney troubles, sleeping on a hospital bed in the dining room when he could no longer make it up the steps. Her father, with a long face, pale, with dark smudges under his eyes, her father who hardly said two words to her. "I don't want Kaylee to get close to me," she'd heard him say to her mother, "because I'm dying. I don't want her to miss me." But since her father was already on the other side, Kaylee was sure that he missed her and would want to help her figure out what to do.

Lena seemed to know everything and she was such a bargain. "Yes, I have had losses." She hoped Lena would tell her what her father saw for her. He had died before he could guide her, but she hoped it was never too late.

"I see miscarriages," Lena said.

"It can't be," Kaylee said. "I never got pregnant."

Lena looked her in the eye. "I receive the past, present, and future," she said.

Kaylee got up so fast that one of the legs of the folding table tipped. She felt as if she'd been cursed, that if Tom ever did change his mind, she would only have a miscarriage and not a baby. As Lena tried to right the table, Kaylee flicked her hands against her T-shirt and jeans, as if this could get Lena's prediction off of her. She ran downstairs, crying. Why had she tried to go to anyone but Miriam? She would go right home and call her and keep calling her until she reached her, no matter how long it took.

IV

Miriam's body was back in her house in Great Neck, but her mind was in Baltimore, where she had thought she would be spending time with her granddaughter. And why not? Dan and Cara had a three-floor row house in Fells Point. Apparently, the round-the-clock doula that Cara and Dan had hired to help them with Violet wasn't any trouble, as Miriam herself would be. Miriam had wanted to do the laundry and tidy the house and be part of that wonderful chaos she remembered from when Cara was an infant, but Cara had also hired a housekeeper who came in three days a week. Miriam had planned on helping Cara breastfeed and had even bought a special breastfeeding pillow. Miriam had nursed Cara until Cara was two and knew just how you teased the nipple across the baby's lips to make her latch on and how to make sure that you've emptied the breast so you didn't get an infection. But Cara went to a breastfeeding counselor instead. What was the role of a grandmother these days anyway, psychic or not?

She hadn't even checked her voice mail. Never had she found herself so detached from her work. Whenever she'd been away before, she'd always phoned clients. But this time Miriam didn't have the heart for it. She wanted to be upbeat for them. They deserved it.

She had to get out of the house. It was spring, but when she opened her parasol there was still enough wind to blow it inside out, never mind that it was guaranteed not to. From having grown up near the beach in Rockaway, where she'd anointed her pale skin with a mix of iodine and baby oil and used a reflector, sunscreen alone was enough to protect her from getting more basal cells. She would buy a tiny pair of sunglasses for Violet and a bonnet with a huge brim. But Cara and Dan had probably bought that for her already.

"Mom, thank you so much, but we don't need anything else," Cara had insisted when Miriam had given them a plastic halo so shampoo wouldn't get into Violet's eyes, just like the one that Cara had worn. True, Violet was too young for it, but Miriam had thought that it would be nostalgic for Cara, a reminder of all the baths Miriam had given her. Before Miriam had come up with that gizmo, Cara used to cry, "The shampoo stinks my eyes."

Miriam tried so hard not to upset Cara. She had never told Cara how shut out she felt. Miriam's own mother had spoken her mind, no matter what was on it. She had even complained about Miriam nursing. "You should be a modern woman and give Cara formula," her mother had insisted. "It's measured out. At least you can see how much the baby is taking in by the numbers on bottle. You might be starving my granddaughter," she accused, despite Cara's round, rosy cheeks. And the baby carrier enraged her. "You'll end up with a dowager's hump and you could smother her."

When Miriam had become pregnant, she and Rory had moved to Great Neck. Her father had already died five years before, and Rory's parents hadn't even lived long enough to see their only son married. Her mother, no matter how querulous, had been and still was precious to her, but Miriam knew she couldn't have her mother on top of her. Her mother had hated Miriam being a psychic, hated it so much that she purposely mispronounced it, calling her a "physic," which was like the Phillip's Milk of Magnesia that Grandma Ava used to drink to move her bowels. The corners of Grandma Ava's mouth had always been white from it. Miriam's mother used to send Miriam articles saying that psychic ability might be associated with a brain tumor and that Miriam should go get her head examined right away. After Miriam's mother had died, her spirit had forgiven Miriam for being psychic, but while her mother had been alive, Miriam's gift was like stitches her mother needed to rip from a crooked seam. Yet Miriam hadn't moved out of state to get away from her. Twice a week she'd driven Cara to her mother's in Long Beach, where she'd moved after Cara's father had died. Miriam would sit back and watch the two of them cutting out material with pinking shears and her mother allowing Cara to put her foot on the sewing machine pedal. Miriam's mother had taught Cara to cast on her first stitches to knit and now Cara was manufacturing knitted hats.

Look around you, Miriam chided herself. *Take in the season.* The azaleas and rhododendron hadn't bloomed yet, but Miriam's tulips and narcissus proudly edged the flowerbeds. A blue jay flitted from the honey locust tree, an oriole from the gingko. *Breathe in the spring,* Miriam told herself as the honeysuckle and wild onion made the air as sweet and sour as Bubbie's meatballs. She remembered sitting next to Bubbie on milk crates in the small yard behind her father's butcher shop when a butterfly had fluttered around Bubbie's head, then landed on her white lace collar, resting there like a second brooch. All living things felt safe around Bubbie because of her vibrations, and Miriam had that inside herself too. So why was her own daughter so ill at ease with her that she'd had to move to Baltimore and hire a retinue of helpers to keep her mother away?

Miriam kept going, passing the other Tudor houses on Grace Court where she lived, then round the corner and up Grace Avenue toward town. *I should have taken a different route,* she thought as she approached Grace Park. It was punishment to be here and see all the children while her granddaughter was so far away. But most of the kids were attended to by nannies rather than nanas. Still, her heart ached from missing Violet. She went into the park and sat down on a bench, making sure that she was a certain number of feet from the playground. Adults could no longer go near playgrounds unaccompanied by children.

She heard a throat clearing and smelled piney Old Spice shaving lotion. She slid her eyes to the side. Her dead father was next to her. He had on a yellow nylon short-sleeve shirt with a couple of pens stuck in his pocket protector as if he were still ready for business.

"This is what happens when you send children away to college," he said. "A diaspora. They get used to not being with their parents and never come home again. You only send an unmarried child away to escape a country."

"Daddy, Cara got into an Ivy League school," Miriam explained. "I couldn't very well say 'No, you have to stay in Great Neck and commute to Hofstra.'"

"Hofstra?" her father said, shrugging as he faded off.

Being dead, he was as out of the loop with his grand-daughter as Miriam, alive and in Great Neck, was with Violet. Maybe what her father had said was true, that once kids get a taste of being away from their parents, they lose the need for them. Once they had dropped Cara off at college, her conversations with her and Rory began and ended with two words: "Gotta run."

The first time Dan had come to the house, Miriam had seen pink light pulsing between him and Cara. Cara had had one bad boyfriend in high school, but after that the boys had been so gaga over her beauty that she could boss them around, and that made her tire of them quickly. When Cara had made plans for her and Dan to go out with friends the following night without telling him, Miriam had overheard him say, "Hold on, here, Cara. I'd appreciate being asked first next time." Cara had apologized, something Miriam knew she hadn't been used to having to do with guys. *Perfect,* Miriam had thought. *This is the guy Cara needs to temper her, a guy she respects.*

Before dinner, Dan had walked into the kitchen and asked, "May I help you, Mrs. Kaminsky?" She knew from the way his words moved toward her in even waves that he wasn't just being polite, that he meant it in a larger way. If she were lucky enough to have him as a son-in-law, he'd be a loyal support to her always. After dinner, he'd played *Moonlight Sonata* on their out-of-tune piano, not like he was showing off, but like he couldn't resist. And then he went off with Rory to talk about genome mapping and the Yankees. He was brilliant, but a regular guy. Rory called Cara "Kitten" and loved her dearly, but Miriam had never thought until then about how much he had missed out in not having a son. And Dan would be able to fill that empty spot.

Dan never complained about his parents, but when Miriam had gotten her first psychic image of Hillary and George, they had their hands behind their backs, a symbol of withholding. When she met them, she found out how right she'd been. Dan had been sent off to boarding school at eleven because his mother had wanted to travel on business with his father. Their house was stark Scandinavian without even drawer pulls on the furniture. If you left one thing out of place at Hillary's house, you'd look like a murderer. Dan, she'd realized, needed her and Rory, too.

Miriam had foreseen Dan putting a diamond ring on Cara's finger, but she was afraid that it was only her wish and not a true psychic vision, the way she had foreseen Cara moving back to Great Neck after she had a baby.

When Dan had told Cara their first Valentine's Day, "Cara, I love you," she'd tapered to calling Miriam twice a week. But Miriam had gotten such pleasure out of how close Cara and Dan were that she hadn't minded. Aside from having pulsing pink in their auras whenever they even thought about each other, Cara had told Miriam that they ran things by each other, confiding, advising, and they even read to each other at bedtime. *When Cara has a baby, she'll need me and we'll be close again,* Miriam had thought. But now, with Dan and Violet and her work and the doula and breastfeeding counselor, Cara mostly emailed.

Well, many of the Great Neck women she ran into had grandchildren in Latin America or Europe, one even in South Africa. *I should count my blessings,* Miriam thought.

Then a blonde woman about Miriam's age walked into the park pushing a pricey pram and making kissing sounds to the baby inside. Definitely not a nanny. All of the nannies were on their cell phones. The woman looked up from the carriage at Miriam. It was Barbara, the mother of Darcy, one of Cara's high school friends. After Darcy had gone off to Stamford, she and Cara had lost touch.

"Miriam, just look at Alexander, my grandson," Barbara chirped, turning the pram to give Miriam a full view.

Alexander, blond and blue-eyed like his mother and grandma, gave Miriam a goofy grin that made her chest feel like a hearth. She wanted to reach out and shake his tiny hand, but she didn't have Purell with her. Purell, Miriam had learned at Cara's, was the liquid key to the modern kingdom of baby-touching.

"Is Darcy visiting you for a bit?" Miriam asked.

"She and her husband, Roiphe, just bought a house on my block," Barbara said, grinning. "Darcy didn't want me to miss out on even one day of Alexander."

See, Dad, Miriam thought silently, some kids do come back. Just not my only child.

Barbara rattled off all of Darcy's accomplishments, implying how much money Roiphe made in currency trading and Darcy in corporate law. "So, what's Cara up to these days?" she asked before Miriam could fully recover.

Miriam told her about Cara's degree from Cornell, her business, Dan's Ph. D. in genetics, and of course she showed a picture of Violet.

"And where do they live?" Barbara asked.

"Baltimore."

A frown came over Barbara's face, as if Miriam had done something very wrong to deserve this, which was just what Miriam had already been thinking.

"Well, I'm sure Alexander and I will see you around a lot," Barbara said.

"Yes," Miriam said. *Sans Violet,* she thought.

Miriam went right home, climbed the back staircase to her white office, and sat at her white desk. The crystals hanging on fish line at the windows cast shimmering rainbows. She couldn't wait to show Violet her office someday. Would Violet think it was as magical as Miriam had found Bubbie's parlor, where Bubbie had seen her customers? Miriam remembered Bubbie sitting in a big wooden chair with ball and claw feet, telling her customers what was wrong with them and how to fix it. They gave Bubbie pots of Chinese ferns and little ivory figurines and once even a mandolin in thanks for her wonderful readings. Miriam took Visa or Mastercard.

Now she checked her voicemail. There were nineteen messages from Kaylee, all in her little girl's pleading voice.

Although Miriam had never met her or seen a picture of her the four years Kaylee had been calling, she knew Kaylee had long black hair and a pale, fragile face. People always wanted to talk to Miriam on Skype, but who needed it when she could visualize them fine like this? Anyway, she wouldn't be able to concentrate with a 2-D head talking on the screen. Also, she'd have to wear makeup, and at fifty-five that wasn't easy. Your eyelids and lips suddenly had all this topography.

Miriam dialed Kaylee's number, but her line was busy. The image of a cat's cradle always came to her for Kaylee, the string game that she saw in her mind for over-involved mother/daughter relationships. Kaylee and her mother were classics. Her mother was a short round woman, getting shorter and rounder all the time. Kaylee was married, but couldn't do a thing without her mother's say-so. The relationship was a trap for both of them. They were keeping each other from moving on. On the other hand, Cara was so independent that Miriam felt abandoned. Wasn't there a happy medium? Well, this medium wasn't happy, Miriam thought. She felt so unappreciated.

To cheer herself up, she went through personal notes from clients that she kept in cookie tins. There was a letter from a man thanking her for warning him that he was about to lose his job. He had been able to line up a new one before he was left unemployed. Another was from a businessman, thanking her for telling him that the strip mall he was going to invest in would stand empty. "I bless you every time I pass it," he said. "It looks like a stage set for a ghost town." And then she read one from a woman whose husband had wanted to move his girlfriend into their apartment.

Dear Miriam,

You were the one who told me that Veronica was Nestor's girlfriend and not a housekeeper like he claimed. What a fool

I would have been to go off to work while they stayed home
and did what I don't want to think about in our bed during
the baby's naps. I know I got mad at you for telling me the
truth, but now that I'm rid of Nestor, I'm glad.
    Thank you,
    Lolly

When Miriam finished the letter, the only thing that stayed with her was the baby napping. Right away she could see Violet napping in her bassinette set up on Cara's side of the bed, her eyelids fluttering, her tiny lips dream-sucking, a lacy cap on her head. She wondered if Violet was aware of her. She wondered if Violet had seen her while she was still in utero and even before. Bubbie had always said that a soul waiting to be born knew its whole future, but the Angel of Forgetfulness put its finger to its lips to make it forget, and that's why there's an indentation below the nose, an angelic fingerprint.

"Mim, can I come up?" Rory called. "I've got something great to show you."

"Sure," Miriam said. Now that the business was sold, Rory only worked forty hours a week instead of sixty.

Miriam heard him taking the steps two at a time. With a big grin on his face, he showed her his iPhone.

"Look at the great pictures of Violet that Dan emailed me," he said. He had to hold the iPhone. Miriam didn't know how to do one thing on it. Cara had bought it for him on his birthday and wanted to buy her one for her birthday. But Cara must have seen a look of fright on Miriam's face, because she bought Miriam an antique Victrola instead, like the one Miriam's maternal grandma had had, the grandma who wasn't the psychic, of course.

There were pictures of Dan lying down with Violet on his stomach, just as Miriam had first seen her on Cara's right after she was born; Violet in her baby bath, her long legs hiked up; Violet swaddled in her pink bath towel with bunny ears; Cara nursing Violet; Violet wearing one of the knitted berets with the rhinestone patterns on the front that Cara had designed for grown women—or rather the cap wearing Violet. Rory and Miriam billed and cooed over each of photos, but when they were finished, Miriam just missed Violet more.

"It's been over a month since we've seen our grand-daughter," Miriam complained. "I don't want a virtual relationship with her. I want to hold her in my arms."

"Well, we can't very well barrel in on them," Rory said. "Dan emailed that he took an extra week of paternity leave. Maybe after he gets back to work we can go up and see Violet."

"I keep wondering why they moved all the way to Baltimore," Miriam said. "I mean, Baltimore. Dan's parents are from Michigan and they retired to Florida. Dan could have gotten a job at Columbia Presbyterian, North Shore Hospital, anywhere. Who is in Baltimore that they should have to live there?"

"Johns Hopkins," Rory said. "In Dan's field, you don't need to know any other names."

Rory was still standing. He didn't like to sit in the only other chair in her office, the big wicker one with the white cushions where clients sat when Miriam saw them in person. He was afraid she'd read his mind if he sat there.

"You want to come down and watch *Law & Order* with me?" he asked. "I taped the last episode."

Suddenly Miriam heard a click in her mind and knew it was Kaylee at last getting off the phone with her mother.

"I can't," Miriam said. "I have to call a client back right now, before she calls her mother again. There's only a small window of time before they're on the phone again."

"Okay, I'll have to watch someone getting murdered all by myself," Rory said with a shrug.

As soon as Miriam reached her, Kaylee asked, "Are you mad at me?"

"Of course not. Whatever gave you that idea?"

"I went to someone else," she said, her voice a whisper. "I went to a palm reader. She told me there were miscarriages in my future."

"What a horrible thing to say!" Miriam said. "It's absolutely not true." She wound the phone cord tightly around her finger, afraid that Kaylee would ask her again if she was ever going to have a baby. "Am I ever going to have a baby?" Kaylee asked.

Miriam didn't see any pink or blue cigars in Kaylee's future, but couldn't say no. She just couldn't. "A baby could just fall into your lap somehow."

"Like a foundling on my doorstep? Miriam, come on."

"Like a miracle," Miriam said. "Miracles can always happen." She needed one right now to get Kaylee off the topic of babies.

"I keep having these nightmares," Kaylee said, "where I'm wandering the streets, lost. It's a no-brainer that it means I have to have direction. I have to know what my purpose is in life."

Miriam felt so sad that Kaylee had no one in her life but her mother and her husband, Tom, who were like a team keeping her stuck. Kaylee's whole world was her apartment, her mother's, and some local stores she frequented. She had never even taken the F train from Brooklyn to Manhattan. Miriam tried to see something for Kaylee that would put her on a path, but the future yawned out as listlessly as Kaylee's present. Then the liberty bell came to Miriam's mind.

"Your purpose in this life is to learn independence. You've got to get out there, meet people. If you don't want to take a job, just volunteer. What a help you could be to others!"

"Me?" Kaylee said. "I always seem to be the one who needs help."

Miriam got an image of Kaylee's mother in her size 22 black widow's dress, limping, leaning on Kaylee's arm as she walked.

"It looks like you're good at helping," Miriam said. "Has your mother developed a problem with her leg?"

"You name a part of the body and my mother has trouble with it. It scares me. I get scared I'll have hemorrhoids and ulcers and polyps and lumbago and rheumatism too."

"Can't you ask your mother to stop talking to you about her ailments?"

"How can I? My poor mother has nobody else to talk to since my father died. And she's always there for me. She's my best friend."

Whenever Miriam heard that, she knew whoever said it was usually calling from an eating disorder clinic or the psych ward at Payne Whitney. A woman had to break away from her mother to grow up. But did they have to become enemies to make that happen?

"Mom and I spend every day together," Kaylee said. "I don't know what I'd do without her."

Plenty, Miriam thought. She wished that she heard some fire in Kaylee's voice, some inkling that Kaylee could see how destructive her mother was to her. But she couldn't tell Kaylee that. You couldn't upset someone's world without giving him a new future and she just couldn't see one for Kaylee, not yet anyway.

"Tom says I am so lucky to have a mother and I should always be good to her."

Miriam could also see Tom. He had a large nose, big brown eyes, and a dark pompadour. He was tall, but narrow. He was more like a father to Kaylee than a husband. And he had lost his own parents young, so Miriam could understand him feeling that way. "It's a balance," Miriam said. "You have to be careful that you're not limiting your own life too much to accommodate to your mother's fears about her life and Tom's about his."

"That's not what I'm worried about," Kaylee said with an edge.

Kaylee was always unnerved by anything that suggested she should make changes. Miriam had urged her to see a therapist, but she said, "My mother says therapists turn you against your mother." Kaylee's mother could burst into tears in a blink and would gasp as if she'd drawn her last breath if she didn't get her way. How could Miriam blame Kaylee for succumbing to the tyranny of the weak? Since Kaylee had lost her father to kidney disease when she was only nine years old, of course she was terrified to lose her mother, too. And Tom was so afraid he'd lose his beautiful young wife to illness, or possibly another man, that he encouraged her to stay home and do nothing.

"Is my father around?" Kaylee asked.

Miriam took deep breaths and tried to see him, just as she had every other reading, but she had never succeeded and wasn't seeing him now. She felt terrible, as though she was keeping Kaylee from her father's ghost.

"I'm a fine medium," Miriam said, "but that doesn't mean I can contact everyone on the other side. Sometimes I'm trying too hard or the spirit feels as if all his work on Earth has been done." Or, Miriam thought, the person had been so burdened in life that whenever he drove by a cemetery, he'd think, *Those lucky stiffs.* Miriam was pretty sure that Mr. O'Brien fell into that category.

"So you're telling me my father will never make contact with me?" Kaylee said in a high-voltage voice.

"No, not at all. What I'm saying is that your father's spirit might come through with a different medium. I know I've suggested this before, but this time I've asked around and found someone who has a good reputation."

"After I went to that palm reader, I'm through with going to anyone else," Kaylee said. "I feel safe with you. Anyway, I'm sure it's not your fault. My father didn't want to get close to me, because he thought I would be hurt more when he died. He never asked me how my day was at school. He never read me stories. Figures he'd keep away from me after he died, too."

"Wait," Miriam said. "I see something. A man. He has a pointy chin, but a nice smile and a scar on his forehead, right above his eye."

"That's Uncle Finn," Kaylee said with delight. "Does he have a message for me?"

Miriam listened hard. She couldn't understand what he was saying, but she repeated it as best she could. "Cushla Machree," she said.

"That's what he used to call me. It means beat of my heart. He used to swing me around and sing, 'Cushla Machree, you're a darlin' to me.' But Aunt Shinead was always sending him packing because of his drinking, so I hardly got to see him."

Miriam could hear Kaylee weeping softly. Uncle Finn's spirit drew out a flask and swigged ghostly spirits. "Cushla Machree, you're going to be playing someday like a child ought," he said, and then he faded away as quickly as the head of foam on a beer sipped by greasy lips.

When Miriam repeated what Uncle Finn said, Kaylee said, "That would be like heaven. My mother didn't let me to go to the playground because I got my knees scraped. She even sent a note to my teachers to keep me on a bench at recess."

Miriam could sense Kaylee's heart tomtoming through the phone, like it did whenever she admitted anything negative about her mother.

"My mother just wanted to keep me safe," Kaylee added quickly. "You can't blame her for that."

Miriam tried to build on the joy that Uncle Finn had brought Kaylee. "Maybe you can do volunteer work with children. There are so many who need help and there's a New York City volunteer website. I know you don't have a computer, but I could look it up and..."

"My other phone," Kaylee said. "I have to get it."

Kaylee's mother didn't like hearing a call-waiting beep, so Kaylee kept another line in case her mother had one of her emergencies.

"Couldn't you wait until the reading is over?" Miriam asked, but she was already put on hold and could feel the energy that Kaylee had gotten from the reading leaking out like air from a pin-holed balloon.

V

"IT WOULD HAVE BEEN OVER THE TOP TO PAINT
Violet's room violet," Cara said. She and Dan stood in the
center of Violet's Victorian bedroom with its lace shades and
big dollhouse. Cara had hand-painted nosegays on the pink
walls of Violet's room with striped ribbons around the green
stems and sewn her own floral bumpers for the crib. The
overhead light in the center of the ceiling was a cluster of
rose-colored tulips with tiny electric bulbs inside.

"I know Violet is going to move out of our bedroom
soon," Dan said, "but I'll miss her snuffling noises, her little
cries."

"Me too," Cara said.

"Your parents are champing at the bit to see her again.
And I'd like to see them too. How about they come for a week
or so?"

"You know my father can't get away from the pharmacy
that long," Cara said.

"He can certainly get away for a couple of days, and your
mother can arrange her appointments to stay longer."

Cara plunked down on the rocking chair in the corner of
the room and covered her face with her hands. "You really
don't know what it's like to have my mother around all the

time, do you? It's like she inserted a microchip in me and can track me anytime. I know how sweet my mother is. I love her. She always put me first before anything. When I started driving I knocked a hole in her front right fender, and all she said was, 'Thank God you weren't hurt.' She let me go to Heavy Metal concerts. 'Just promise you won't become one of those violent noshers,' she said. She always cracked me up. 'Moshers,' I told her. 'Moshers.' But the psychic part of her ruined everything. She could see me making out with my boyfriend."

"I'd rather not hear about that," Dan said.

Cara winked at him. "Here I am," she said in a sultry voice, "nearly as big-bellied as I was before I gave birth, and I can still make you jealous."

"You're right," he said. He sat down on the toy chest, took her hand, and held it against his heart. "Feel how it's beating for you." He moved her hand lower.

She laughed. "Let me warn you, my mother might be watching."

"That put a damper on things," he said, letting go of her hand. Then he shrugged. "If Miriam's going to be watching us from faraway, then she might as well be here enjoying Violet."

"It's just too much to have her into everything. It's like the umbilical cord was never cut. When I finally convinced my mother to let me go to sleep-away camp, there was an announcement over the loudspeaker: 'Cara Kaminsky, your mother called and said that you have poison ivy and you have to pick the jewelweed that grows near the ivy, and make a tincture of it, and rub it on.' I felt so humiliated."

"But did it work?"

"Yeah, but everyone began calling me Itchy."

"While Miriam is visiting," he said, "I could arrange for her to give a talk to one of my classes about natural cures."

"Don't. It will only encourage her. I used to be terrified to tell her when I got sick because she never rushed me to the doctor for antibiotics like a normal mother. Instead she'd give me Bubbie's cures. For bronchitis, she made me drink hot milk with goose grease in it and put mustard plasters on my chest. It was like child abuse. I'll never let her do any of that to Violet."

"But Cara, it's grandparent abuse not to let your parents come. You know my parents aren't the grandparent-y type. My mother already said that she wants Violet to call her Hillary and my father, George."

Dan was trying to be breezy, but Cara noticed his shoulders slacken. Whenever George and Hillary phoned, their first question was about how Dan's research was going. She could just imagine Hillary chasing Violet around her house with a wet cloth to wipe away fingerprints. George and Hillary were so stiff and formal. Sometimes Cara thought that Dan missed her parents more than she did.

"All right," she said. "I'll invite my parents."

"I was thinking," Dan said, "we could buy a bigger place so that when our parents visit, they won't be on top of us. Sure, my parents aren't wrangling to see Violet that much now, but love often skips a generation."

"Is that scientific fact?" Cara asked.

"A hope," Dan said quietly. "But your parents will definitely come often."

Cara threw up her hands. "You haven't been listening to me. I want privacy from our parents. I want our own life. I don't want Violet to have to skip kindergarten and go straight to third grade to get your parents' approval. And I want to raise Violet to be a normal, modern kid without my mother's knocking on wood, throwing salt over her shoulder, spitting three times. I don't want Violet to be burdened by knowing what's happening to everyone else before they do."

"Slow down," Dan said. "We have no idea if Violet even has your mother's gift."

Cara sighed. "I guess you're right."

"Call your mother now and invite her."

She took her iPhone out of her smock pocket and punched in her mother's number. When her mother answered, Cara lost her nerve and handed the phone to Dan.

"Hi, Miriam," Dan said. He put the phone on speaker.

Miriam's voice came across loud and clear. "I've already got my bags packed," she said.

Cara rolled her eyes, but she couldn't help laughing.

An hour later Dan had gone to the lab to work on his project, and Cara was alone, thinking, *Oh, God, my mother is coming.*

She remembered the exact day she had learned to hate having a psychic for a mother. She was eight years old. Before then, she had wanted to be just like her. Her mother had seemed magical to her, everything about her: the whisper of her long skirt on the wooden floor, the flowers she knew the names of, and the birds. But most of all, Cara had wanted to be able to see the future like her mother could. She had wanted to know whether or not she'd be invited to Jenny's birthday party before the invitation didn't come. She had wanted to be able to see Grandma Dorothy after she died. Cara had loved her the way her own mother had loved her bubbie. Cara had adored Grandma Dorothy, with her tins of beads and sequins, her collection of old-fashioned buttons with women's faces on them, the manicure kit that she'd bought when she was sixteen to give manicures for a nickel. Grandma Dorothy would buff Cara's nails with Crème Rouge and make lunches that looked just like what you'd see in a magazine: radish roses, Tomato Surprise—the surprise being that there was egg salad inside when you lifted the cunningly cut top of the tomato. Cara used to love sitting at Grandma Dorothy's black Smith Corona typewriter, pressing the ivory keys that were ringed with silver. Grandma Dorothy wore Evening in Paris cologne and used to dab some on Cara's neck and wrists. Cara had missed her so much and longed to see her again.

The day Cara had decided that she wanted no part of any of her mother's practices, she 'd asked her mother if she could teach her to see Grandma Dorothy's spirit. Cara remembered how happy and upset at the same time her mother looked, because her mother always got the business from Grandma Dorothy. Once, Cara had overheard Grandma Dorothy say, "Cara should have been my daughter instead of yours." Cara remembered her mother crying and was sorry, but she had also been glad that her grandmother had wanted her as a daughter. In physics, Dan had told her, matter could only occupy one place at a time, but Cara knew that opposing feelings could creep through the chambers of your heart and nest there and there wouldn't be a thing you could do about it.

Her mother had lit a candle on the dining room table. Turning out the lights, her mother told her to gaze at the candle's flame because that's what an aura was like and seeing auras was the first step to lifting the veil between worlds. Cara sat in the dining room watching that candle, hardly blinking, her eyes burning. After awhile, she felt like she just had to wiggle, like that song Grandma Dorothy used to sing to her. "I've got ants in my pants and I just gotta dance." But no matter how restless Cara was, she stayed put, not daring to risk an interruption in watching that candle glowing out into the darkness in ribbony waves. The flame wavered as if Grandma Dorothy were breathing next to it. Cara imagined her with the beauty spot penciled on her right cheek, her eyelashes curled, and her eyes like green pools. She'd wondered what Grandma Dorothy would be wearing. Grandma Dorothy always surprised her by wearing something new she'd sewn: a sheath dress with a jungle print sash across the hips or a pink blouse with black rickrack on the collar and cuffs. Cara remembered her grandmother's hands guiding her when she let her sew on her sewing machine. Cara's eyes brimmed with tears at the thought of seeing her again, not just looking at her pictures, but really seeing her.

Her mother turned up the dimmer switch and let more light into the room, then stood up against the wall. "Look at me, but not right at me," she said, pointing to a spot about a foot from the right side of her head. "Keep your gaze soft. Don't stare. And if you don't see anything, it's all right. We'll try again another time," but there was excitement in her mother's voice. Cara had felt pressured to be able to do it, as if this was an initiation into the most wondrous club you could ever hope to be in.

Cara had stayed there, watching that spot, watching and watching. She'd stayed there for as long as she could. She didn't see anything but the white stucco wall and a flyaway strand of her mother's curls. She felt her bottom lip tremble. She wasn't going to see an aura. She wasn't going to learn how to see her grandma's spirit, and her mother would know the truth even if she lied. Just like Grandma Dorothy, her mother would wish she had a different daughter, one who could see what she saw, who could talk to the dead as easily as to the mailman. Instead, her mother would be stuck with her.

"I hate this," Cara cried out that day. "I hate watching candles and worse, I hate watching walls. This is stupid. Just plain old stupid and I never want to do it again."

"It's all right," her mother said. "I told you that you might not see anything this time. Bubbie and I used to practice over and over."

Cara didn't want to practice that or anything else that would make her psychic. It wasn't any fun. It was worse than practicing scales for Mrs. Benson's piano recitals. It was worse than flash cards with multiplication tables on them, worse than doing pliés and relevés at the dumb ballet school in Great Neck where the teacher had no kids of her own because she hated all children.

And who would want their child to live the life my

mother does? Cara thought. Who would want her child to go to a restaurant and have some woman tear her sleeve in her zeal to find out if her thirty-eight-year-old daughter would ever get married? Who would want her child to be such an oddball that no one could be her friend, except other psychics who wanted to steal all her business? Who would want their child to look as if she were talking to herself and when you looked carefully, there was no Bluetooth in her ear? Who would want a child to go to a four-year college and end up doing something an illiterate could do? Besides, it was unethical to know private information about people that they haven't told you and it was weird talking to the dead. You could make yourself sick like that. The whole business gave Cara the willies.

Now something welled up inside her, something floating up from the darkness like a drowned body in a night river. She remembered her mother driving her to the state hospital, the tall metal fence circled on top by barbed wire. Cara had been a senior at Great Neck High, already accepted to Cornell, and had insisted on going. She had thought she was old enough to finally meet the only living relative her mother had left in the world. On the dandelion-studded grounds, the staff led groups of patients who were all together, but so alone, talking out loud, shouting at something or someone only visible to themselves. Cara almost asked her mother to take her home right then, but it wouldn't have been fair, that long drive for nothing. The windows of the yellowish brick building were barred. Inside, the hospital smelled like Lysol and pee. And when the elevator opened onto Aunt Chaia's floor and Cara heard shrieks and jackal-like crazed laughter, she pressed her back against the elevator wall.

"We could go home," her mother said. "I won't be mad. I feel like going straight home myself."

But stubbornness and curiosity had pulled Cara forward. Aunt Chaia was in a fetal position in a railed bed, shrunken, her arms and legs like sticks, with just a few patches of reddish gray curly hair still on her head. Her eyes were closed. She looked as if she'd already died and they were keeping her above ground.

"Aunt Chaia," her mother said, "it's me, Miriam, and I brought Cara with me, my daughter."

Great Aunt Chaia's mouth began glubbing like a fish's mouth over her toothless gums. Then she opened her eyes. They were the same pale blue as her mother's eyes, the same shape, and deep set, too. Cara was so scared she could hardly breathe.

Chaia looked at her for a moment and then began to scream and kick the rail of the bed with her feet, punch at it with her hands. Her mother had pressed the alarm for the nurse's station, and when no one came she ran out into the hallway calling for help so Aunt Chaia wouldn't break her bones. Cara, left alone with her, stood gaping in horror but unable to look away. Her legs didn't remember how to run. Although Aunt Chaia was so frail, two big orderlies had to hold her down while the nurse gave her a shot.

"It would be best if you two left now," the nurse said. "The patient needs to sleep."

Her mother gave the nurse the cookies that Chaia probably couldn't eat anyway. In the car, her mother said, "I'm so sorry you saw this, honey. I don't know what got Aunt Chaia so agitated. Maybe they missed a dosage of her medication. Do you want to talk about how you feel?"

"Why did you name me after her?" Cara said through her teeth.

"I didn't. You're named after your father's mother, Clara. Ashkenazi Jews only name after the dead. I named you Cara because it means 'dear' in Italian."

"My name is too close to Chaia's. It's just too close."

Her mother pulled the car to the shoulder of the road and took Cara's hand. "Mental illness isn't catching," she said. "This isn't going to happen to you, I swear. You have to understand. Aunt Chaia didn't have a normal childhood. Her father, your great grandfather, had left for America to earn money to bring his family over, and in the meanwhile there was a pogrom. The Cossacks attacked their village and did terrible things to people. Chaia saw it all, but Bubbie had thought that because she was so young, barely two, she didn't remember any of it. Bubbie never spoke of what they went through. 'The past, it should stay in hell where it belongs,' Bubbie used to say. She didn't know how important it was to talk over distressing things like we are right now."

Cara burst into tears. "Why did Aunt Chaia get so upset when she saw me?"

Her mother sighed deeply. "Aunt Chaia doesn't get to see young people. I think she was remembering herself at your age. From pictures I saw how beautiful she was back then, with long red curly hair, softer curls than mine, waves really, and skin like a porcelain doll. But she had a breakdown when she was about your age and by nineteen, she had to be put in that hospital and never was able to get well enough to come out."

Cara had so many questions, but she just wanted her mother to start the car and drive home. She just wanted to get to Darcy's house so they could practice their dance routines for the talent show at school. Cara had been sewing the skirts they would wear: red satin with a slit up the left side. They had already bought the tops: black bustiers that she was going to add material to in some way so they would be allowed to wear them. Cara took out a pad and began to sketch the little black bolero she'd make for each of them. Madonna, watch out!

Both her mother and Aunt Chaia had been encouraged by Bubbie to wallow in the supernatural, where anything could happen instead of reality, which was bound by natural laws. Cara wouldn't let her mother put Violet in danger by filling her head with spirits and telepathy. She had to shield Violet from her mother. It was her obligation, and Dan would stand by her.

VI

"LOOK AT THE WAY SHE'S LOOKING AT ME," MIRIAM said on their next visit as she held Violet in her arms. Violet's eyes had remained blue instead of turning green like Cara's or brown like Rory's and Dan's. Violet's eyes were the color of Miriam's and Bubbie's. "She's an old soul," Miriam said. "I can feel it by the way she locks eyes with me and by the cute little worried furrow between her brows."

They were in Cara and Dan's living room, Miriam and Cara on one couch, Dan and Rory on the other, a coffee table with hummus and pita chips and salsa dip separating them.

"She's worried that you're going to give her ginger water for colic and make her wear a necklace of garlic cloves," Cara said. "She's worried that you're going to tell her that she was Madame Curie in another life or that you're going to teach her how to read a tarot deck. Or she's scared you'll sneak in and tie red ribbons all over so she won't get the evil eye."

Miriam felt a sudden change in Violet's vibrations, a tingling that spread outward from Violet's body and permeated Miriam's arms. Violet's lips began to open and close. Her head didn't turn sideways as if she were rooting for the nipple. She looked as if she were trying to form words.

"Shh," Miriam said. "I think Violet is trying to tell me something. What is it, Violet?"

Rory was shaking his head at her, but she couldn't stop herself. She had to know what the baby was trying to say. She listened hard.

"Bub-ba," Violet suddenly uttered and pointed her tiny damp fist toward the corner of the room.

"Bubbie," Miriam said. "Violet just said Bubbie. Did you hear her?"

Cara rolled her eyes. "You're imagining it," she said. "Violet is just making sounds. She does it all day and all night. It's speech preparation, not real speech."

"We had to move her to her own room because she kept us up at night with her gurgling," Dan said. "But now I can't sleep without it."

"Bub-ba," Violet said, waving at the corner again.

"What did I tell you?" said Miriam.

Rory chuckled. "I sound like that after I eat too much pot roast."

But Miriam knew what she knew. Violet had said Bubbie and pointed to the corner of the room. Miriam got a whiff of Bubbie's lavender powder. The air began to shimmer, then take on a definite shape. Now Bubbie was sitting on the occasional chair next to the Tiffany lamp in the corner, her face a mosaic of glowing stained glass.

"Don't listen to them," Bubbie said. "Your *ainekele*, your darling granddaughter, she sees me all right."

Miriam was happy to bursting, but she clamped her teeth hard. She didn't want to cause any trouble on this visit.

"I'll take Violet, Mom," Cara said, but when Cara reached for her, Violet began to bawl. Her little fingers gripped Miriam's finger. Her face turned red. She could barely get out another cry.

"Mom, you're not letting her go," Cara said.

"Of course I am. She's just holding onto me."

"I'll take her," Dan said. He got up, but he couldn't get her free from Miriam either. Violet kicked her little legs like a baby kangaroo.

"This isn't a joke," Cara said. "She's crying because she's hungry. I have to feed her."

Miriam tried to hand Violet over, but Violet turned her little body into Miriam's, pressing her weight against her.

"This is certainly odd," Dan said.

Cara tried to take Violet again, but Violet curled herself up into an unwilling ball.

"Mim, carry Violet up to her room, why don't you?" Rory said. "Cara can take her from the crib."

Miriam rose and walked up the steps with Violet. Violet calmed down and grabbed one of Miriam's curls that had come undone from a beret. She set her down in the fancy crib and watched her for a moment. "Violet," Miriam whispered, "we're going to have to be careful around them. Do you know what I mean?"

"Bub-ba," the baby cried, and now Miriam saw Bubbie wind the Little Bo-Peep mobile hanging over the crib. "Little Bo-Peep has lost her sheep," tinkled in the soft pink air.

Miriam threw Bubbie a kiss and then one to Violet. Violet was so relaxed that her eyelids began to droop. "Sleep tight,

Neshomelah," Miriam said softly. As she turned to walk away, she saw Cara in the doorway, glowering at her.

"I don't like this, Mom. I don't like this a bit."

"What do you mean?" Miriam said, batting her eyelashes to try to appear innocent.

"How did the mobile begin to play? I didn't see anyone wind it."

"Things like that happen," Miriam said. "Springs can pop, clocks stop or start ticking, a piano can suddenly play a note or two spontaneously."

"Not in my house," Cara said, tight-faced with anger. "Come out before you wake Violet."

Miriam touched Cara's arm. "Cara, I love you," she said, but Cara jerked her arm away.

"Do you know that before I got pregnant with Violet I insisted that Dan and I go to a genetic counselor, one who didn't know us well and could be objective, so I could find out if mental illness is inherited?"

Miriam felt slapped in the face. "Cara, what are you implying? Are you talking about me? Aunt Chaia?"

Without answering, Cara turned and stomped down the steps, not looking behind her.

Miriam stayed in the hallway a few moments, leaning on the banister, trying to compose herself. She felt Cara was pushing her away on the deepest level by not being proud or even admitting that Violet had a gift. Not only was Cara not admitting the gift, she thought anyone who had it was insane. *Cara has inherited my mother's aversion for psychics,* Miriam decided. She wished she could apply a hot ginger compress to the ache in her soul. She put a brave smile on her face and went downstairs. She didn't have to worry about keeping up a breezy conversation. Cara was brooding and Dan was clenching his jaws against his yawns.

Rory got up. "You two must be exhausted," he said. "You can expect this for about two years if I remember right."

"Thanks for understanding," Dan said, his yawn escaping this time.

They all said goodnight, Cara giving Miriam just a quick peck on the cheek. Then Rory and Miriam went off to the bedroom vacated by the Jamaican doula. After Miriam put on her nightgown and Rory his pajamas, he took up Cara's cause.

"Mim, you're going to get us barred from the house if you keep this up. Cara's hormones aren't even settled from the birth yet and you're aggravating her."

"What am I doing? What?" Miriam demanded.

"You're trying to get Violet to be just like you. You're interpreting everything she does to make that innocent baby sound like a precocious psychic."

Miriam hung her clothes in the spare closet. "I keep reading those websites of parents who swear that their kids are indigo," she said.

"You mean they're blue?" Rory asked.

"Indigo children are what they call kids who are supposed to be psychic. Some parents swear that their kids are the next stage of human evolution as if they're sci-fi creatures. How awful for those kids. I saw this video of a little boy, about four, who his father said was transmitting messages from spirits.

That child was skimming—making unintelligible sounds and rocking his head. He's suffering from autism, and his parents refuse, absolutely refuse, to get him help because they think it will interfere with his paranormal abilities. A lot of those kids have severe learning disabilities, but their parents won't let them get resources from the school or state because they're wishing that their children are misunderstood psychics. Those are the people who are interpreting everything their kids do as proof of psychic ability—not me. Violet said 'Bubbie,' pointed at her, and then Bubbie appeared, but I'm not allowed to declare that Violet has my gift!"

Rory put his hands on her shoulders and turned her around to face him. "Whether Violet is psychic or not, and I'm not saying she is, she's not our child. She's our grandchild. That's one step removed. We can't just say and do anything we want in Cara's house. It's her house, her life."

"Where was this argument when your mother wanted to bar our friend from coming to our engagement party over a fight she had with his aunt? Where was this strong voice of yours when your father said, 'Your girlfriend, this Miriam,' after you had already put a diamond on my finger, 'she's aggravating your mother and if you were a man you'd tell this Miriam off'?"

Rory threw up his hands. "Do you always have to bring up the dead?"

"That's my job."

"Why can't we learn how to enjoy being grandparents together, given the situation as it is, instead of pressuring for the way you want it to be? Don't you think I would love to have Violet come to the pharmacy and listen to the pills pinging down in the pill counter? Don't you think I'd love to take her to Grace Avenue Park where we used to take Cara? 'I swung your mother on this very same swing,' I'd tell Violet, even though the playground looks nothing like it did back then, with its newfangled plastic bucket swings and those slides that twist around. Sunday afternoons, my father's only day off from his dry cleaners, he'd read me the funnies. You should have heard him do *Gasoline Alley*, 'Golly gee, Miss Molly,' in his German accent. I wish I could read those funnies to Violet every week, but I don't even think they exist anymore. And I used to dream of all the things I would have done with my grandfather if he hadn't been killed in Auschwitz. Did I ever tell you that my grandfather once built a boat in his basement with his brothers and it turned out that it was too big to get out of the house?" He sighed deeply. "Mim, I know you'd love to have the same connection with Violet that you had with your grandmother, but we can't have it our way, and if you keep this up, we'll have it no way. You must butt out." He paused, his chin jutting. "You just have to, or it will not only affect our relationship with our kids, but our relationship together."

It was hard for Miriam to take his threat seriously, since he looked so vulnerable in his striped pajamas. Besides, she still had arguments rattling inside her. But from the next room, she heard Cara and Dan raising their voices at each other.

"Do you hear them?" Miriam asked.

"Who?"

Miriam wasn't sure whether Rory's hearing was getting

worse or whether she was hearing Cara and Dan psychically, but she stood very still and listened.

"I told you," she heard Cara say. "Didn't I tell you that my mother was going to try to make Violet into her own image? She couldn't do it with me, so now she's going to try with my daughter."

"You're talking as if your mother is an enemy," Dan said. "She means well. She loves Violet."

"Dan, this isn't your family, it's mine. I don't tell you to tell Hillary to stop correcting my hard New York r's or to stop pressuring you about your career, so don't tell me what I should and shouldn't do with my mother."

Tears leaked down the corners of Miriam's eyes. She had wanted Dan to be family to them, and now Cara was putting a wall between them. Rory was right. Her excitement over Violet's psychic gift was causing trouble. Miriam brushed the back of her hand along Rory's bristly cheek. He grabbed her and held her tight and kissed her. But when they got into the trundle bed, she rolled away from him. She was in Cara's house, she reminded herself. If she could hear Dan and Cara, maybe they could hear her and Rory.

Miriam couldn't sleep. Eventually she got out of bed, put on her shoes, threw her coat over her nightgown, and let herself out the side door into the small garden behind the house. It was early November, but a cold snap had brought most of the leaves to the ground. Cara's bed of impatiens had keeled over in a frost and lay there, headless, without their blossoms. The sky looked like a glossy calendar photo, all oranges and purples.

"Bubbie, I know just what you went through with my

mother, how she hated your gift and wanted to stamp it out of me. But she was your daughter-in-law. I never expected this from my own daughter."

She smelled lavender and saw Bubbie floating a little above the dead grass, her eyes like daylight, her brooch twinkling like a star. Miriam thought of all Bubbie had been through, her five sons, all of them except Miriam's father murdered in a pogrom, and then the sadness of her youngest, Chaia, having a breakdown from which she never recovered.

"*Neshomelah*," Bubbie said, "there's no trouble too small for you to tell me."

Even though Miriam was sure that Bubbie already knew the whole story, she began to tell her how angry Cara and Rory were with her, and how Cara had thrown Aunt Chaia's illness in her face. And Bubbie listened quietly, nodding.

DAN COULDN'T SLEEP. HE HATED DISHARMONY IN THE house. He never thought that this would happen between him and Cara. It had been so easy before Violet was born. He went to the window. Miriam was in the yard, talking to the sky. She was like a cat that had been locked outside. Quietly, he slipped a pair of jeans over his boxers, pulled on a sweatshirt, and went downstairs. He stuck his bare feet into his loafers and went out in the yard.

"Miriam, are you okay?"

She turned to him, tears running down her cheeks. "Sure. I just needed some air."

"Me too," he said. He had already wrapped up the garden furniture in plastic or he would have offered her a seat. "When I saw you from the window, you looked like you were talking to someone."

"There's no one here," she said defensively. Then she looked into his eyes defiantly. "If you must know, I was talking to my bubbie."

"It must be so comforting to imagine that she's with you."

"I'm not imagining Bubbie any more than I'm imagining you. I know that you're worrying about a fellow scientist. He has a Swedish name."

"Ingebord," Dan said. He felt as if his eyeballs could spring out like a cartoon character's. "I just was at a conference with him and he has been on my mind. Miriam, I've always known you were psychic and I've seen you read people's minds, but it's still startling to have it happen to me."

"Sorry," Miriam said. "Cara warned me never to 'psych you out,' as she says."

He looked down at his loafers. He didn't want to get into the whole thing with Miriam, start making it look as if he was taking sides between her and Cara. But he couldn't stand that she was made so miserable in his and Cara's home and how much anger there was between Miriam and Rory after a visit. Didn't he have something to say about that? "I should talk to Cara...."

Miriam cut him off. "Thank you, Dan, but the most important thing is for you and Cara to get along."

She looked so nervous with her shoulders hiked that he couldn't go against her wishes. "I understand," he said. Then he noticed that she was shivering. "Hey, you're getting cold. We'd better go in."

Miriam looked up at the sky. "Good night Bubbie, good night Dan, good night moon."

Dan laughed. They went inside quietly.

When he got into bed, Cara stirred. "You've brought the cold in," she said. "Where were you?"

"The backyard."

"What were you doing out there?"

"I got up and happened to look out the window and your mother was out there, so I went to see if she was all right."

"Was she?"

He didn't want to step on a landmine. "Yes, we chatted a bit."

"About what?" she asked.

"Stop grilling me."

"Oh, Dan, you can tell me," she said.

"Well," he said, then paused, "she knew I was thinking about Ingebord."

Cara's face went from pleasantly dreamy to attack dog. "So you were having a reading with my mother?"

"Kind of. I didn't ask her. She just knew. It was interesting."

"Judas," she said.

"I'm sorry I told you." He pulled the covers over him and made a great show of falling asleep.

The next morning the blueberry pancakes and hazelnut coffee were hot, but the conversation was frosty.

"Do you want more syrup, Mother?" Cara asked

"No, thank you," Miriam said. She could tell by the little

snuffled snore that Violet was just dozing at Cara's breast, and still Cara kept Violet covered by the nursing shawl that hung around her neck. Violet was so elaborately hidden beneath it that it looked as if Cara was trying to protect her from the evil eye, which is what Cara seemed to think about being psychic—that it was a curse, as Miriam's own mother had thought. No one spoke. Miriam could hear everyone chewing and swallowing. Dan, who usually had a he-man appetite, picked at his food. Rory just drank cup after cup of coffee, which he wasn't supposed to because of his reflux. Who knew when she would see her granddaughter again?

VII

Miriam was grateful for Thanksgiving, when families got together and acted happy, no matter how they really felt about each other. Cara had set the dining room table with her wedding china and silver. Violet, in her brown velvet dress, was passed around the table like a gravy boat.

"Remember how tiny Violet was?" Rory said, "and now she's sitting in Dan's lap at the head of the table, smiling at everyone. Just listen to her cooing."

"Dad, you're in danger of becoming a boring grand-parent," Cara said, laughing.

"Papapa," Violet babbled, leaning forward.

At the sound of Violet's words, the vines of the William Morris wallpaper behind George's chair began to stir. And then Miriam saw who Violet was talking about. Miriam's father, glowing like the flame in the glass candlesticks, appeared. He took off his felt hat, as he always did when he came inside.

"My great-granddaughter," he said, his blue eyes spar-kling in his misty face.

"Papapapapa," Violet crowed again, looking right where Miriam's father stood, her dimpled hand opening like a starfish.

Oh, my God, Miriam thought. My father didn't just appear on his own. Violet is already calling forth the spirits.

Miriam's father nodded, as if in agreement with Miriam's thoughts. Then he looked at the table.

"Nice spread. Is it kosher?"

"Papapapa," Violet called again, and Miriam's father blew Violet a kiss.

"*Pushelah,*" he called her, the nickname he'd given Miriam when she was little, derived from *pushkeh,* the tin charity box that used to hang on Bubbie's wall. He had said that Miriam made him feel like a rich man even though he would become poor paying her dowry someday. Miriam was in danger of blubbering.

"Violet is calling George 'Papa'," Hillary said. She had on a dark blue Armani suit and hadn't taken off the jacket, even though the dining room, just off the kitchen, was well-past room temperature because of all the cooking. Each layer of Hillary's chisel-cut, frosted blonde hair was as distinct as a step on a staircase. Miriam would have felt out of place in her white, puffy angora sweater and her hair drawn back into a low frizzy ponytail if Violet hadn't called forth Miriam's father. This miracle lifted Miriam out of her worldly insecurities.

Miriam's father, not one to hang around if he couldn't eat, faded off into the William Morris vines.

"I had wanted Violet to call me George," George said, "but Papa has a surprisingly nice ring to it, coming from her."

Miriam wasn't about to announce that Violet had spoken to her great-grandfather and not to George, especially since Dan looked so happy. The trick to being included in family occasions, Miriam realized, was to remain a boring grandparent.

"Yes," George went on, "Papa makes me sound less like a fogey than Grandpa."

George had at least a decade on Rory, but because of his full head of white hair, he looked younger and was determined to keep up that illusion. He had had laser surgery on his eyes so he wouldn't have to wear glasses, but it had caused dark floaters to zip through his vision that distracted him. Right now Hillary grabbed George's arm to stop him from trying to flick away a nonexistent fly from the air.

"Cara, you look gorgeous," Hillary said. "No one would know that you gave birth just five months ago."

"I thought Cara was just as gorgeous when she was nine months pregnant," Dan said with an edge.

Miriam noticed Dan's irritation as he watched his mother poke at her one slice of gravy-less turkey and teaspoon of cranberry sauce with a small hill of peas. Hillary kept herself so chic-svelte that her chin looked as if she'd stuck it in a pencil sharpener. Whenever Miriam had had dinner at George and Hillary's house, she'd been struck by how little Hillary served them. Had she measured out everyone's portion on a Weight Watcher scale? Dan had admitted that after eating at his mother's house, he'd stop for pizza. Remembering that Dan had made Cara promise that she'd never diet, Miriam loaded up her plate even more.

"Dan, your father and I have been wondering, when do you think you'll be ready to finalize your research?" Hillary said.

"When it's finished," Dan said with a tight smile.

"What exactly are you working on?" Rory asked.

"I'm close to creating a virtual gene that can replicate itself and be used for testing the effects of viruses, vaccinations, environmental toxins, and uses that I haven't even been dreamed of yet."

"Don't forget," George said, "the early bird catches the worm."

"Keep your eye on the prize," Hillary chimed in. "You have to be a winner in this world. Don't forget, you're our son."

Dan choked on a slice of turkey. Rory patted him on the back. Miriam couldn't stand George and Hillary pressuring Dan like that, when he was already under so much pressure. Dan's work was like a marathon, with all the other scientists of the world bearing down on him to the finish line. Sometimes she felt their collective breaths on his back.

"Violet is quite a prize," Miriam piped up.

"She is," Hillary said. She ate a few more peas and asked, "Cara, how's your business going?"

A flicker of worry passed over Cara's face, which Miriam was glad not to have caused for once.

"I'm trying to keep a mind of gratitude, today especially," Cara said, "but Katharine, the production manager I hired, was supposed to do all my traveling for me. I gave her such a high salary to ensure she'd commit that she decided to renovate her apartment. Now she's stuck with no-show workmen she has to chase, and if they do show, she can't take her eyes off them or they'll botch everything."

Miriam got a psychic flash of Katharine Kyo, sunning herself on some tropical island far from her Upper West Side apartment, where she was supposedly held hostage by workmen. "Oh, dear," Miriam said. These days she gave no psychic insights, not even regular opinions. Instead she'd developed a repertoire of "oh's" in different octaves, sometimes embellished with a "dear" or a "my," which seemed to sand the rough edges in her and Cara's relationship. Cara would find out the truth in her own time and her own way. Insight, Miriam reminded herself, had to come from within or it was a kind of assault.

"I think you should get rid of her," George said, voicing what Miriam had held back. "I would never have been able to retire at fifty if I had relied on employees."

George had gotten into computers in the days when they were still huge and had to be kept in dust-free, air-conditioned rooms.

Hillary speared another pea. "Yes, get rid of that manager and fly to Korea and take care of everything yourself."

"Mom," Dan said, "Cara and I discussed this already, and we've decided that she wouldn't travel for business while Violet is still young. Parents should be with their children," he added pointedly.

Miriam could see how much Dan resented that Hillary and George had placed him in a boarding school when he was fourteen, even though it was a top prep school.

"Nonsense," Hillary said. "You have two sets of grandparents eager to take care of Violet."

Dan stared at her for a few moments. Miriam could hear

his thoughts. Is this woman really the woman who raised me? Does she really want to risk getting her suit spit up on?

Miriam's heart suddenly warmed towards Hillary. Who would ever have thought that Hillary would be responsible for giving me what I have been longing for? she thought. Time alone with Violet. She heard snatches of George and Hillary going on about Korea, and George speaking a few words in Korean, and Cara telling them what a relief it would be to oversee things herself once again. But all Miriam could think of was spending hours and hours alone with Violet. She would bundle her up and bring her to Grace Avenue Park, show her off to Darcy's mother. Better still, she'd take Violet up to her office and show her the crystals hanging at the windows from fish line. She would sway the crystals so that Violet could see the rainbows shimmer against the white walls. And when Violet grew up, she'd have memories, however dim, and every time she saw a crystal, she'd see Miriam's face in it. Or maybe Cara would want Miriam to stay in Baltimore. Miriam would sit in the rocking chair in Violet's room with Violet in her lap and call forth the spirits of relatives to bless her.

"But I'm still nursing," Cara told George. "Besides, I couldn't bring myself to leave Violet."

"Whenever we travel," George said, "there's always a baby yowling, even in first class. Why not bring Violet?"

"What?" Miriam said. "Bring the baby? Doesn't Korea have dengue fever? "Didn't the hantavirus originate there?"

Cara rolled her eyes. "Mom, I'm not going to North Korea. South Korea has great hospitals. Americans line up there to get cheap hip replacements and facelifts."

"Can't we all go?" Miriam asked desperately.

"You know I can't get away from Mirror that long," Rory said and next he said "Ow," because Miriam stepped on his foot under the table.

"Dan, would you mind?" Cara asked.

"I would miss you and Violet like hell," Dan said, "but as long as you and the baby are together, I'll cope."

"I would miss you, too," Cara said.

"Hillary and I are the logical choices to go with you," George said. "After all, I know their currency, their customs. I still have business contacts there."

It took a few moments for Miriam to register that she had been excluded from the travel plans. She had a Korean client who always thanked her for her reading. *"Go mab seum ni da,* Miriam said to George.

"Thanks for what?" George asked.

For nothing, Miriam thought.

"I've been saving this until after the meal, but I can't wait anymore," Hillary said. From a shopping bag she'd put under the table, she drew out a hand-knit sweater and hat edged with tiny violets. "I knitted this for Violet," she said.

"The violets look so real," Cara exclaimed.

"I didn't even use a pattern," Hillary said.

"Hey, could I make a pattern from those violets?" Cara said. "I could use that design for my business. Maybe even a violet for a logo."

Miriam looked down at her plate. There was nothing she could do for Cara these days. She couldn't even knit a blanket for the baby, let alone a hat. She felt her fantasy of taking care of Violet unraveling. Her only grandchild would be on a jet, flying to Korea, her mother's breast milk soon to be tasting like red pepper paste.

IN MARCH, MIRIAM SAW PICTURES OF VIOLET IN Cara's arms in front of the Gyeongbokgung Palace, George and Hillary on either side of them like grinning bookends. She brewed herself a cup of Valerian tea, the Russian tranquilizer, gulped it down, and waited, but the soothing feeling didn't come. She closed her eyes and tried to see what Violet was doing right now. Instead, she saw a wild print, like a jungle paisley. Slowly, she made out Violet's little face coming from a pouch that Cara was carrying her in. Cara was talking to a Korean woman, gesturing and holding out a hat. Violet was in a factory! Surely that couldn't be good for her: the noisy machinery, the smells. Then Miriam remembered how much she had wanted to see her father at his butcher shop and her mother telling her, "You could get a disease from being around dead cows and sawdust."

Miriam imagined her own eyes like zoom lenses. She saw the dimples on Violet's plump cheeks, a spit bubble on Violet's little lips. Even with this intimate vision, Miriam had the same terrible hollowness that clients reported after she made contact with their loved ones who had died.

"I wish I could touch my husband," a widow had wailed. But because Miriam couldn't arrange that, she was often left with nearly as much sorrow as the client.

I'm getting morbid, she warned herself. *If I could knit something for Violet,* she thought, *it would relieve me and connect me to her.* Miriam even had some knitting needles and wool left over from her mother that she hadn't been able to bear throwing away. Her mother had loved knitting so much that she even knitted on the toilet. Miriam had heard the clicking of her mother's needles from behind the bathroom door. She fetched the materials and tried to cast on the first stitch. Before long she had filled the whole needle with stitches and even knit a few rows, but she didn't know how to follow a pattern.

The next morning, she went to The Knittery in town.

"I'd like a knitting lesson," she told the woman sitting at the long table, whose overly bleached hair looked as if it had just been shorn from a sheep and her veneered teeth like a set of pearl buttons.

Peering over her half-sized glasses, the woman said, "That's not the way it works here. You buy the wool, the needles, and the directions from me, and then you get the lessons free."

"Sounds good," Miriam said. "I'd like to make something for my granddaughter, who is five months old."

"You should make a sweater and a hat for an eighteen-month-old so she doesn't outgrow it right away," the woman said. She showed Miriam silky wool—pink flocked with magenta that cost $40 a skein. "If you're going to put time and effort into it, you should only work with the best."

"But I'm just experimenting. I don't even know if I'll be able to learn how to do it yet."

"Any idiot can learn to knit," the woman said. "And I'm selling you my easiest, but most beautiful pattern."

"I already know how to cast on stitches." Miriam proudly held out her needle.

The woman twisted her mouth. "You'll have a mess on your hands if you work from this." After she ripped them all out, she said, "You need to make a slip knot, and then..." The woman made her fingers as if she were pointing a gun and began casting on stitches in a way that Miriam couldn't follow at all. It was like the time she and Rory had decided to take tango lessons at Arthur Murray and stumbled all over each other for six weeks.

The woman handed the needles back to Miriam. "You try now."

Miriam's hands shook as she tried to follow the slip knot and gun method, but she couldn't do what the woman said any idiot could.

The door opened and a young woman came in with her little girl, who seemed to be about four. The child had on a matching hat and sweater that Miriam could see was lovingly hand-knit.

"Grandma," the little girl said, running up and throwing her arms around the knitting teacher's neck while the woman's daughter watched with a glowing smile, just the way Miriam wished Cara would.

Miriam got up. "I'll come back tomorrow," she said.

"Six skeins of wool will be needed for this outfit," the woman said. "That's $240, and the pattern is only $3.86. Lucky you, you can use the same needles you brought in."

Lucky me, Miriam thought as she handed over her charge card.

Miriam found a video on YouTube of disembodied hands casting on stitches, knitting and purling to a twangy beat. Miriam played and replayed that video until she got it. She kept knitting, her needles clicking like a metronome. "Only an idiot couldn't learn to knit," the woman had said, and Miriam was becoming a fool for knitting. She knit in bed until Rory pulled away the needles.

When she had all the parts of the sweater and hat finished, she spotted holes from dropped stitches and rows billowing out like waves. Her fingers felt like broken twigs. She tried to unravel the wool so she could at least make herself a scarf, but she'd knitted so much of it tightly that the wool was knotted and frayed like her life.

part two

VIII

"ONE, TWO, THREE, FOUR, FIVE," VIOLET COUNTED off on her fingers. "I am five years old and I can do my own hair." She pulled it back and put a band around it, once and twice, flicking her head to feel her ponytail swish. Her hair wasn't as curly as Grandma Miriam's. She wished Grandma Miriam didn't live so far that she had to drive a long time or take a train. Grandma Miriam must live as far as Korea, she thought.

Grandma Miriam had told her, "If you ever want me, just call out and I'll know it. Before long, you'll see me or hear from me."

"Grandma Miriam, I want to see you now," Violet called softly so Mommy wouldn't hear. She waited. She didn't see Grandma Miriam, but something strange happened. The air became twiddly and the flowers on her wall waved around like in a windstorm. "Who has seen the wind?" Violet recited. "Neither you nor I." Grandma Miriam had taught her that poem. "But when the trees bow down their heads, the wind is passing by." From faraway and close, she saw Grandma Miriam right on her wall. She could always see her inside her own mind, but now Grandma Miriam was outside Violet's head, as if the wall had become a TV screen. Violet was so surprised that she stepped back and stumbled over her Flower Fairy, but not once did she take her eyes off Grandma Miriam. One look away and Grandma Miriam might go poof. But even with looking at her, Grandma Miriam was getting cloudy.

"Grandma," she called out. "Don't go, stay and play with me. I'll share my Flower Fairies with you."

Mommy walked in. "Who are you talking to?"

Violet hesitated. "My Flower Fairies."

"Funny," Mommy said, "I thought I heard you say grandma."

Mommy was looking hard at Violet, so hard that Violet's hands were getting sticky. Still Mommy didn't look away. Violet stared down at her socks. When she chose them off the rack, the sticker said they were made of cotton and clearance. She felt the prickles of Mommy's stare. "I was talking to Grandma Miriam," Violet admitted. "She misses me. I want to go to her house. Please don't bite your lip, Mommy. I want to go."

"But Grandma Miriam still works. She doesn't have much time."

"Grandma Miriam didn't hurry when she saw me just before. She would have stayed a long time but you scared her away like a monster." Violet shut her eyes tight when Mommy bent to look into them.

"Violet, you couldn't have seen Grandma Miriam," Mommy said softly, kissing Violet's cheek. "She's in Great Neck. You must have been thinking about her and then imagined you saw her. Great Neck is hours from here by car or train. With the long lines at the airports, it takes hours by plane, too. Grandma wasn't really here."

Violet heard Mommy's almost-crying voice and opened her eyes. Mommy's forehead was all crinkly and her bottom lip trembled, even though Violet could tell that she was trying to not let it. She loved Mommy. She didn't want to see her so sad. "Grandma Miriam wasn't really here," she announced.

Mommy smiled and patted her on her purple shirt, right on the pink and red heart with GAP written across it. Violet had known that spelled *gap* since she was two years old. She had made Mommy smile by telling the lie that she didn't really see Grandma Miriam, but her throat felt like she had swallowed a Fred Flintstone vitamin without chewing it. What if Grandma Miriam could still hear and thought that Violet didn't want her to come when Violet always did? And Mommy had told her not to lie. Violet felt a ping-pong ball ponging and pinging in her head. "Grandma Miriam had white all around her," she blurted out. "She was in a white room with big diamonds hanging in front of the windows. And there was a big white desk, bigger than mine, and a white telephone on it."

Mommy gasped. "That's Grandma's office all right. She didn't take you up there when we went for Passover, did she? I told her not to, but she did, didn't she."

"No, she didn't, Mommy, even though I begged her and begged her. Why can't I go up there? I go into your office and sometimes to Daddy's office. Why not Grandma Miriam's?"

"I guess it's silly of me to make such a big deal over it," Mommy said. "I'm only making you more curious. It's just that your grandma was always going on about Bubbie's parlor where Bubbie used to do her work. I was worried that Grandma's office would make the same kind of impact on you when you're too young to think about where that would lead."

Violet felt questions pressing against her forehead.

"I see that all I've done is confuse you," Mommy said. "I mean I want you to have choices when you grow up. I don't want you to get trapped in Grandma Miriam's life the way she got trapped in Bubbie's."

"But Grandma Miriam has lots of fun and she helps people. She showed me her appointment book. It has wire curls on the edge like my Hello Kitty notebook, but her cover is dark red. When I grow up and do what Grandma Miriam does, I'm going to have Hello Kitty on my cover."

Mommy's lips got tight. Violet didn't want to get Grandma Miriam into trouble and make her get time out and she didn't want Mommy to be angry. She wished she could suck all her words back into her mouth like spaghetti. She shook her head again, really hard, her ponytail dingling. "I'm not going to do what Grandma Miriam does," she announced. "I'm going to be a ballerina and a archeologist."

Mommy smiled. "Wonderful choices," she said. "Anyway, I spoke to Grandma last night. She had an emergency dental appointment this morning. She got a seed from the health food store stuck in her gums, so she wasn't in her office like you said. That's one of the troubles with what Grandma Miriam does. It's so iffy. You never know if you're right."

Mommy was happy now and Violet wanted her to be,

but words flew out of Violet's mouth like blackbirds from a king's pie. "Grandma Miriam was in her own office and that's where she still is. Call her, Mommy, and you'll see."

"Grandma's phone will be off while she's at the dentist," Mommy said.

Violet pouted. "Please call Grandma."

"Okay, okay, I'll leave a message."

Mommy took her phone from her big pocket pants and called. "Back from the dentist already, Mom?" She was quiet a moment. "You should have gone. Getting something caught in your gums can be serious."

Violet reached for the phone. "Can I talk to Grandma?"

"Say please," Mommy said.

"Please....Hi, Grandma," Violet sang out.

"Violet, my darling, only a few minutes ago I was up in my office and I couldn't stop thinking of you. I think I saw you. Are you wearing a purple GAP shirt?"

"That was me, Grandma," Violet said, bouncing on her toes. "I'm wearing my purple GAP shirt because my name is Violet. My best friend has the same one in green, but her first name isn't Green. It's Lisa."

Grandma laughed like a bell ringing. "I love you so much, Violet."

"Grandma, when are you and Grandpa Rory coming to see us? It's been sooo long."

"I'll ask Mommy when she and Daddy are free."

"I saw you like you saw me, Grandma. I knew you weren't at the dentist. Did you tie your tooth to the doorknob with string and slam the door like Bubbie used to?"

"No," Grandma said. "I took the seed out with eyebrow tweezers."

"What are eyebrow tweezers?" Violet asked.

"Oh, she didn't!" Mommy said.

Mommy's face got pale and she started to sway. Mommy was having her low blood pressure. The air behind her began looked like it was being mixed with a spoon, and the small, white haired woman with Grandma Miriam's twinkly blue eyes peeked out.

"*Dahling,* you remember your *alte bubbe?*" the woman said.

Violet nodded.

"Tell your mother to sniff white vinegar," Bubbie said.

Violet knew better than to mention Bubbie to Mommy, but Mommy was sick. "Bubbie said you should sniff white vinegar," Violet said.

"How lovely that Bubbie is there with you," Grandma Miriam said into the phone.

"This isn't happening," Mommy wailed. "Bubbie's remedies coming back to haunt me through my own daughter? Violet, say goodbye to Grandma," she said sharply. "I have to talk to her."

"Goodbye, Grandma." Violet wanted to send her special birdy kisses because Grandma might really need them after Mommy talked to her. "Twee, twa, twee, twee," she said.

"Mom," Mommy said when she put the phone to her ear, "it creeps me out that you took tweezers to your gums. I don't care that you sterilized them. Please don't tell Violet such things. What if she tried it? I know I get my eyebrows threaded, but still, she might find tweezers somewhere in the house."

Violet felt thumpety. She had gotten Grandma in trouble again.

"How should I know what impressions she's gotten of Bubbie?" Mommy said. "I'm only Violet's mother. No, please, don't send me candied angelica. Violet, take your fingers away from your mouth and stop chewing your cuticles. You'd better go downstairs and watch for the bus. I'll be right down."

"But the bus isn't coming today," Violet said.

"Hold on, Mom," Mommy said. "Yes, there's school today."

"No, it—"

"Violet, you'll be late for the bus if you keep arguing."

"But when is Grandma coming?"

"The bus," Mommy said. "I'll talk to Grandma later about visiting, but you have to get your backpack and watch out the door. Bye, Mom." She clicked her phone closed.

Still Violet didn't budge.

"Hurry, we have to be by the front door so Mike sees us waving and stops the bus," Mommy said.

"No, we don't, Mommy. The bus isn't coming today. School is closed."

"But it's not a holiday."

"School is closed today," Violet insisted, stamping her foot.

"Stop telling stories," Mommy said.

Daddy came upstairs, a mug of coffee in his hand. "I got

a call from the school," he said. "There's an outbreak of an early flu. They're being proactive. They've closed school for today."

Mommy slumped down on the floor, her head in her hands. "I'm going to faint," she cried.

"Daddy, hurry, get the white vinegar," Violet said.

AFTER TALKING TO VIOLET, MIRIAM COULDN'T BRING herself to hang the phone up right away. She held it to her heart until the raucous phone-off-the-hook reminder began. As soon as she set the receiver in the cradle, the phone rang. Miriam saw Kaylee's number on her caller ID. Then she saw pink roses.

"Happy birthday, Kaylee," Miriam said as soon as she picked up the phone.

"I can't believe that I'm thirty-two and my life is still the same old, same old," Kaylee said, sighing.

Miriam thought about turning sixty-five and loving it because Violet was old enough now to phone her and write her letters and read the ones Miriam sent to her. She wondered how she'd feel about aging if she didn't have Violet. But one of her single clients had taken up comedy at fifty and at fifty-five appeared on Leno. Her eighty-five-year-old childless client was just as ecstatic because she'd recently published a biography of Nat Turner with a major publisher. And her ninety-three-year-old client was thrilled because he'd managed to outlive his ex-wife. "Kaylee, if you can't have what you think you want, you need to create something else."

"I've been going over the notes from all my readings with

you. Five years ago you told me that a baby could fall into my lap, and Uncle Finn said I'd be playing like the child I never got a chance to be. So I went to a playground and sat there, just watching kids, hoping for a miracle. The mothers didn't talk to me, but they started looking at me funny. And then one of them made a call. Before I knew it, a cop came over and asked me, 'Are you accompanying a child here?' I told him that I hoped to be someday soon and he told me to move along."

"Oh, I'm so sorry, Kaylee. But you have to make a new dream to tide you over." Miriam could see a dam in the stream. Kaylee wasn't going to go with the flow.

"I didn't call for a reading," Kaylee said. "I just wanted to tell you it was my birthday."

"Well, happy birthday again," Miriam said.

When she got off the phone, Miriam remembered that if your energy was high when you visualized, you would be more likely to make what you wanted come true. She pictured herself at Cara and Dan's, playing with Violet. With that bubbly energy coursing through her, she now pictured Kaylee with a big smile on her face. Miriam wasn't sure if it would help Kaylee, but at least she felt better.

THAT NIGHT VIOLET WATCHED HER WALL, BUT SHE didn't see Grandma Miriam even though she called out to her. "Who has seen the wind?" she recited again, but her wallpaper didn't get swirly. "Grandma Miriam," she whispered, and still she didn't see her.

She got out of bed, opened her door, and listened in the

hallway. Daddy and Mommy were asleep. She tiptoed down the stairs and into the kitchen, her way lighted with little nightlights here and there. She pulled the stool to the counter so she could reach the land line. Land line, land line. She liked saying the words. And this phone was too big for Mommy to carry around, so she couldn't be in charge of it. Grandma's number was in Violet's head. She dialed all ten numbers.

"Grandma!" she said.

"Violet, what time is it?"

"Your throat sounds froggy, Grandma. Did I wake you up?"

"It doesn't matter, Violet. I just want to know if you're okay and everyone there is okay."

"Everybody is sleeping and I tried to call you and you didn't answer until I called you on the land line. How did I see you today in my room and not just in my mind?"

"That must have been my doppelganger," Grandma said.

"Doppelganger?"

"That's when the ethereal body slips out of a living person and travels through the air like dandelion fluff, but keeps the form of the person, and sounds and looks exactly like him or her."

"I like that word, Grandma. It's like bubblegum."

Grandma laughed. "Sweetheart, you'd better go back to bed. You'll be so tired in the morning."

"But how do you get your doppelganger out of you?" Violet asked.

"I'll tell you some other time," Grandma said. "Go to sleep. I don't want Mommy to get upset."

Too late. Violet heard footsteps. Then Mommy switched on the big light.

"It's five o'clock in the morning," Mommy said. Her cheek was creased from her pillowcase. "What are you doing in the kitchen making phone calls?" She narrowed her eyes. "And I don't have to guess who you're talking to. Who else could you talk to about doppelgangers in the middle of the night besides Grandma Miriam? Give me the phone."

Violet held it behind her back.

"Well, I'll have to disconnect it. You can't be making phone calls before dawn."

"But I want Grandma Miriam. I want her to come to our house. I don't just want her doppelganger. I want Grandma Miriam to come to my room and play with me."

Grandma was shouting through the phone. "Violet, I don't want any trouble. Just hang up the phone and listen to Mommy." But Violet didn't care about trouble. She was mad that she had to see Grandma's doppelganger instead of Grandma. "And I miss Grandpa Rory, too."

"This is so awful," Mommy said, shaking her head sadly. "So awful. A case for King Solomon." Mommy took the phone. "Mom, when can you and Dad come?"

Violet threw her arms around Mommy's legs. "Thank you," she said. She hoped Mommy's blood pressure wouldn't be high or low except the way it was supposed to be.

IX

"You packed way too much, Mim," Rory said. They were in the car again, on I-95. "How are you going to manage all those suitcases coming home by yourself on the train? I swear I can feel the back end drag when I accelerate from all the stuff you loaded into the trunk."

Miriam pressed her lips together so she wouldn't yell at him. Ever since Violet was born, Rory had been blaming her for everything, as if he had no issues with Cara either, as if he had been the prize dad. "Rory, don't start with me. I'm so happy that Cara wanted us to come and even have me stay on for two whole weeks. Can't you let me have that?'

"All right," he snapped. "I was just saying that you over-packed."

"But I'm going to leave a lot at Cara's," Miriam said, "so whenever I come by myself from now on, I won't have to schlep so much."

"This wouldn't all be so complicated if you would only stop interfering with Violet, pushing her to be psychic against Cara's wishes. You know I still have to be at Mirror, even though I sold it. It's part of the contract. You can work from anywhere or take off whenever you want. I can't be in Baltimore more than a weekend or maybe a couple of weeks a year. If it weren't for all the trouble you cause, Cara would let Violet stay at our house where I could see her more, too." His jaw clenched.

Miriam knew it was true, but how many times could she say she was sorry to him for something she couldn't help? How could she hide being psychic? It was like an elephant trying to hide its trunk. And how could she hide being psychic from Violet, who could already see the images forming in Miriam's mind? Even if she never said a word to her, Violet would know just as much about what Miriam was thinking, maybe even more.

"By the way," Rory said, "did you ask Cara about whether she wants you to keep your things there? She'll probably think you're trying to move in."

"She will not." Miriam had brought a book along with her, a skinny Pulitzer Prize winner. It made her nauseated to read in the car, but it also made her sick to hear Rory shooting down her hopes. She couldn't wait to be with Violet and she knew that Rory was just as eager. But did he think if he kept zinging her, she could somehow stop herself from being herself around Violet?

Miriam had left a message on her voicemail that she would be away and answer all calls when she got back, but she didn't have to be psychic to know that Kaylee had called and left a bunch of messages. Miriam didn't want her to feel abandoned again. She got out her cell phone and called Kaylee.

"I just tried to call you," Kaylee said. "I need a reading."

"Like my message said, I'm not home," Miriam told her. She didn't want to say that she was going to visit her daughter.

She tried to keep her personal life personal. Also, she didn't want Kaylee to start feeling sorry for herself again about not having children.

"Couldn't you please give me a reading anyway?" Kaylee pleaded. "I'll pay you for a partial reading if you don't have a lot of time."

Miriam mouthed to Rory, *A client.*

He nodded and turned off the radio.

"All right," Miriam said. "I can only stay on a little while. No charge though."

"Thank you, thank you," Kaylee said.

"I left a number on your voicemail of an after-school center where you can volunteer to help kids with their homework," Miriam said. "It's within walking distance from you."

"I was thinking of calling them, but my mother, with her asthma, gets so sick if she gets even a little cold. She said, 'Children are bioterrorists. One of them sneezes on you and we'll all be sick.'"

Miriam stifled a groan. She felt more urgently than ever she should contact Kaylee's father to help her get out of her mother's snare. She took deep breaths and said silently, *Please, please, Mr. O'Brien, your daughter needs you.* A car swerved into Rory's lane and Rory blasted his horn, but Miriam still tried to focus. It started to rain. The ticking of the windshield wipers helped her go into an open-eyed trance. Slowly, Mr. O'Brien drifted into her mind like a plastic bag coming toward her in a draft. He had dark, smudged eyes and his horsy face was pale.

"Mr. O'Brien, do you have a message for Kaylee?" Miriam asked out loud.

She heard a catch in Rory's breath. He had never gotten used to having ghosts in his car.

"My father's with you?" Kaylee said breathlessly.

Miriam couldn't answer her. She had to concentrate. This was Kaylee's ghost, the one she'd longed to contact. A spirit could leave in a blink.

"Who is the man sleeping in my bed?" Kaylee's father asked.

"I don't know if I should repeat this," Miriam said.

"What? What? Tell me."

"Your father wants to know who the man is who is sleeping in his bed."

Kaylee burst out laughing. "A few years ago my mother gave Tom and me their bed. Tell my father that it's my husband, Tom."

Kaylee's father's spirit lifted his brows dubiously. Kaylee was still laughing when Rory drove into a dead zone and the call was dropped.

"Rory," Miriam said, "I just had a miracle. I've been trying to contact Kaylee's father's spirit for years and couldn't. And now, sitting next to you in the car, I finally made contact with him."

"Nice, Mim, but if I were you, I wouldn't share it at Cara's, okay?"

She humphed. "All right, but you just made my miracle into *schmutz*."

"I'm just worried that you'll go head to head with Cara and our visit will be spoiled."

"Rory, trust me. I know how to handle myself with Cara."

"Oh, sure," he said.

Five hours and fifteen minutes later, they were parked in front of Cara and Dan's. Miriam flung open her door before Rory had fully stopped.

"Take it easy, Mim," he said.

He popped open the trunk just as the front door opened and Cara came out to greet them. She'd gotten her hair cut to her shoulders and she was wearing a pair of red Capri pants.

"My God, it looks like you plan to move in," Cara said.

Rory shot Miriam a look. "I told your mother she went overboard,' he said.

Miriam felt as if Rory was pulling the sidewalk out from under her, especially when Cara jumped into his arms. "Daddy," she said, "I'm so glad you're here."

"We're so glad to be here, too," Miriam said, loudly, hoping Cara would remember her.

Dan came toward them. "Hi, Rory, Miriam," he said.

She remembered how she had called her in-laws Mom and Dad as soon as she got engaged, and Rory had called her parents Mom and Dad as well. It didn't matter whether you all got along or not. It was just what you did. Sometimes she wished she could turn back time, but then Violet wouldn't be born yet, and Miriam's world wouldn't feel the same.

Violet was at the window, her lips puckered against the glass. Miriam let Rory and Dan carry the luggage, but she took the Uncle Wiggily board game. She couldn't wait to play it with Violet, because it was a game she'd played with Cara when Cara was Violet's age. Anyway, it would distract Violet from wanting to play psychic games.

"Grams," Violet said, opening her arms when Miriam stepped inside. "Grams, you came."

Miriam laughed. "You call me Grams now?"

Violet looked at Rory and nodded. "It's you and Grandpa together," she said.

"That's wonderful," Rory said. "You already understand plurals." He kissed her on the top of her head.

"I've brought you an old-fashioned game that I used to play with my mommy when I was a little girl," Miriam said, even though it wasn't true. Miriam's mother used to knit, sew dresses from Vogue patterns, and try to make meals that looked just like pictures in *Good Housekeeping*. She didn't like actually playing with Miriam. "You play with your friends, not with your mother," she'd say.

Violet took the box and tried to open it herself, but soon Rory took over. Then Violet settled herself on the family room floor, opened the board, and sounded out the directions.

"I pick red because that's my favorite if there's no violet or pink," Violet announced.

Miriam sat down cross-legged, tucking her long skirt around her.

"Why do you always wear long skirts, Grams?" Violet asked, wiggling her front tooth, which had loosened.

"I just like them. They remind me of the old-fashioned days when families all lived nearby."

Violet picked a Mr.Wiggily card from the pile. "I get to move ten times," she said, and hopped her Mr. Wiggily to spot ten. Miriam pulled a twelve. She began trying to psychically find low cards to pull so that Violet could win, but her Mr. Wiggily kept hopping ahead of Violet's.

"You look worried, Grams," Violet said.

Miriam smiled. "I want you to win."

"Don't worry, Grams. I will. It says if you land on the rabbit hole, you skip and hop to 83, and that's just what I'm going to do." On her turn, Violet picked a nine and hopped her rabbit straight to the rabbit hole, then to 83. "I told you, Grams, didn't I?"

Miriam was more overjoyed than she ever thought possible. For the last three years, whenever she had the chance and no one else was around, she'd been playing guessing games with Violet. When Violet was only one, Miriam began with "Which hand am I hiding the penny in?" When Violet was two, Miriam went to more complex things such as "How many fingers am I holding up behind my back?" Violet would hold up her own fingers to show her. By three, Violet could get the image of pink roses and know it was someone's birthday. When she called out "Happy birthday!" to some stranger, the person would blink at her and ask, "How did you know?" At four, she could guess the color of the crayon Miriam held behind her back and could even draw a picture with the colors of what someone would be wearing that day before she'd seen them.

At five, Violet talked about her dreams to Miriam and tried to see if anything in them would come true. She was good at it. Once she dreamed that her nursery school teacher would tell that she was getting married, and the next day the woman showed the class her diamond ring. Another time she had a dream that their neighbor from across the street was moving away. Soon a "For Sale" sign appeared on a sign stuck in their lawn with the name and number of the realtor. Best of all, since Violet had learned to read and write, they wrote what Mark Twain called "letter crossings" that he'd done with his friends, where Violet tried to write to Miriam just what she would be reading in a letter that Miriam would be sending her. Usually, the letters came the very day she sent hers out. Violet was truly psychic and had such confidence about it, while Miriam often still second-guessed herself.

Now Miriam said, "Violet, you won." Forgetting herself, she said, "You saw the future. You told me what card you'd pick and where that would take you and you were right."

"Mom," Cara said loudly, startling Miriam, and her Uncle Wiggily fell over. "It's a game, just a game."

Miriam had meant to be careful, but she'd only been here twenty minutes and had already made trouble. When she was with Violet, it was as if everything and everyone else went out of focus. It was like a moment of eternity. She could feel her DNA spiraling like ribbons of destiny. But now she could also feel each mental dart Rory was shooting at her.

"For statistical purposes," Dan said, "Violet would have to repeat this at least a hundred times to be proof of anything at all."

"Let's play again," Violet said.

Miriam shuffled the deck thoroughly, first with the cut and shuffle method, then making a bridge between her palms and letting the cards sandwich between each other.

"No matter how much you mix them," Violet said, giggling, "I'm going to land on Rabbit Hole." Violet drew a ten. With a twelve, Miriam's Uncle Wiggily hopped past Violet's. They kept going, Miriam's rabbit well in the lead.

"I'm still going to get on Rabbit Hole, Grams. You'll see."

Being with Violet was no longer a private moment of eternity. Miriam felt everyone's eyes on the two competing rabbits. Her underarms got damp. It was a terrible race, so much hanging on it. If Miriam won, Violet would be disappointed in her own psychic ability. But if Violet won as she'd predicted, Cara would be angry at Miriam.

"You have to let Grams win sometimes."

Violet shook her head. "Never," she said, laughing.

By her fourth turn, Miriam was eight points ahead of Violet and only two points from the Rabbit Hole. Nervously, she chose a card. "Hop back three," it said. With delight, Violet moved Miriam's rabbit back for her. And on her turn, Violet landed in the rabbit hole once again, which let her move all the way to 83. On her next turn, she landed on 97.

Reading from the directions on the box, Rory said, "Violet, how many spaces would you have to go to get to 100 and win?"

"One, two, three," Violet said.

"Well, you'll have to be patient then," Rory said, "because the directions say that if you pull a card over three, you'll have to stay put."

"I only have to stay put...." Violet rolled her eyes toward the ceiling..." two more times and then I'll win."

The backs of Miriam's knees were damp too. She wanted Violet to be right. She didn't want her to lose confidence in her psychic ability and second-guess herself the way she herself sometimes did. But she also knew she was risking Rory and Cara's wrath.

"I'm going to get a two and then a one," Violet said. "You'll see."

Dan was watching intently.

"When I was in college," Miriam told him, "there was a notice in the bookstore that a parapsychologist needed subjects for a study. He was paying $1.39 an hour. Who could resist? I remember it as if it were today. I went to this room where the parapsychologist tested me with Zener cards."

"Karl Zener invented them in the thirties," Dan said. He lowered his eyelids as he always did whenever he used his photographic memory. "The symbols on the cards are a hollow circle, a hollow square, a Greek cross, a star, and three vertical wavy lines." He opened his eyes again. "How did you do on the test, Miriam?"

"Unremarkably. I wish they had used Uncle Wiggily cards instead."

"So, would you say that emotional connection influences results?" Dan asked.

Cara gave him a nudge in the ribs with her elbow. "Let's put away the game now," she said sharply.

"But we're not finished," Violet complained. "Grams has to have her turn."

Miriam picked a card telling her to hop back one.

"Too bad, Grams," Violet said, and picked up a card. "Two," she called out, wriggling excitedly and holding the card up so everyone could see.

Miriam was so nervous that when she hopped Mr. Wiggily five times as her card said, she knocked him over. It was Violet who remembered what space he'd been on.

Violet drew her card. "One, one, hah, a onesie one," Violet sang out, popping up and down.

Everyone was quiet for a moment. Miriam was agog. "Maybe we'd better play something else," Rory said.

"One more time," Violet insisted. "I can win Grams one more time."

"Well, I'm shuffling the cards this time," Cara said. She claimed the deck.

"Cara, you're shuffling so long that you'll scratch off the words and pictures," Dan said.

When the board was set up again, Violet closed her eyes and waved her hands over the board like Bubbie used to wave her hands over the *shabbes* candles. "This time I'll win regular, without landing in the rabbit hole," she announced.

Miriam became aware of her own pulse beating in her wrists. She could feel Cara's tension, her wish that Violet would lose rather than have her grandmother's gift.

Violet picked several threes and then a four. Miriam was way ahead of her. And then Violet picked a twenty and her rabbit hopped ahead, while Miriam picked "Hop back three's" four times in a row. She was almost back at start when Violet yelled, "I won, I won."

Miriam heard a long sigh from behind her and knew it was Cara's without having to look or use the eyes in the back of her head. She could feel Rory's anger spiking.

"Mom, I want Violet to relax now," Cara said, so wound

up herself that her voice squeaked. "Maybe Violet can watch some TV with you and Dad."

Miriam understood the subtext. Long ago she'd told Cara that TV watching cut down on psychic impulses.

"Is Dora your favorite program?" Miriam asked Violet.

"Yep. Dora even went to Korea like I used to."

"I can't wait to see the show," Miriam said, even though she would have liked nothing better than to keep playing Uncle Wiggily to watch the evidence building that Violet was psychic.

"I'll catch up on the dishes," Cara said.

"Daddy, you come see it, too," Violet said, taking Dan's hand.

Dan scooped her up and put her on his shoulders. "Giddyap," Violet said, holding his ears like reins. "Giddyap, Daddy."

Violet had refused to go to Korea anymore with Cara. "You can go alone, Mommy," Violet had said. "Daddy and me can take care of ourselves."

Rory's eyes looked sad and faraway. Miriam could see him remembering himself as a young man, tiptoeing into Cara's room at night with his pharmacy jacket on to see her asleep in her crib. She saw him remembering himself showing up at Cara's basketball game just as the opposing teams were high-five-ing each other right before the visiting team got back on their bus. He saw himself weeping in the stadium at Cornell while Cara took off her mortarboard and threw it in the air. "I wish I'd spent more time with her," he'd whispered to Miriam. "Where did the years go?"

"Listen," Dan said, "while you're watching Dora, I have to catch up on my work. Rory, Miriam, if I don't get back before you leave, thanks for coming and have a safe trip home."

"No, Daddy," Violet said, clutching his hand. "Stay and watch Dora with us."

He kissed her on both cheeks. "Don't you want Daddy to get a gold star at work?"

Violet shook her head hard. "I want you to stay right here."

"Dan, why don't you stay?" Rory asked. "I wish I had watched more TV with Cara when she was little."

Dan sighed. "Really, Rory, I would much rather stay, but I found out that a scientist named Ingebord is working on the same thing that I am. I have to get going."

Miriam saw the meaningful look he gave her with a nod, as if he was giving her credit once again for the night in the garden when she'd told him that he had been thinking of a Swedish scientist. But Dan was in distress now, so it took the luster out of having been right.

Dan was already heading toward the door. 'Keep your eyes on the prize,' as my parents would say," he said. "At least I won't feel guilty while Violet has so much great company."

Miriam could see Rory gearing up for another pitch for Dan to stay, so she gave him a don't-interfere grimace. Anyway, it would be nice to have Violet to themselves for a little while.

As soon as Dan left, Cara came into the den, her eyes narrowed and watchful, as if Miriam couldn't be trusted with Violet, as if she'd turn her into a voodoo doll.

After Violet went to bed, Miriam couldn't stop thinking about the sour looks Cara had given her from practically the moment she'd arrived. Miriam was shaking with anger. She had tried to keep her mouth shut and back off, but the older Violet got, the more belligerent Cara became to Miriam. How could it get any worse? Miriam had had to take Mylanta because her stomach lining felt so raw. She was in the guest bedroom with Rory. He had decided to read the classics and was now in the armchair, nodding off over *Moby Dick*.

"Rory, you never stick up for me with Cara. If she were after you like that, I'd say something. I'm going to have to confront her myself about how she's treating me."

"Don't you dare," he said, slapping *Moby Dick* closed. "You'll not only upset Cara, you'll have me to reckon with. We're already in a vulnerable situation here, thanks to you, Miriam."

Miriam liked her full name, but not when Rory said it. Mim was his term of endearment for her, and the way his back was pressing against the chair, he might have called her bitch. It sounded the same. "All right," she said. If she hadn't already flossed her teeth, she would have taken another dose of Mylanta.

When he dozed off and even *Moby Dick* falling on his slippered foot didn't wake him, Miriam left the guestroom and went looking for Cara. She had to defend herself. She just had to. She found her alone in the den at her computer, working on her business.

"Knock, knock," Miriam called into the open door.

"Come in," Cara said.

Miriam stood at Cara's desk, too nervous to sit down. "Cara, what would be so terrible if Violet did have my gift? I don't get it. In fact, I feel hurt that you don't want Violet to be like me. It feels as if you reject me."

"Mom, did you ever wonder what you could have done with your life if you weren't psychic?"

A geyser of hot anger rushed through Miriam. Despite herself, she thought about how lovely it would have been to have a daughter who could see Bubbie and her parents and all the beloved souls who had left the earth. She thought how lovely it would be to have a daughter who could send her messages that weren't in text, but projected from her mind. She thought of how she and this psychic daughter of hers could entertain themselves by trying to guess each other's thoughts. What fun it would have been, and Miriam would know that when she was a spirit, she could pop into her daughter's kitchen and have tea with her. "It is what it is," Miriam said.

"Mom, listen," Cara said, "if Violet has your gift, I'll have to accept it somehow, I guess." She spread her palms on the desk and stood up, chin jutting forward. "But I'm going to do everything I can to fight it. It's okay, I guess, for someone to dabble in it, but I don't want Violet to be cornered into being psychic."

Miriam wished she could take Cara's hand and show her how the ethereal body separated from her earthly one, how it was possible for the starlit soul to travel up above the narrow rooftops of Fells Point and into the ethers, where the spirits floated like figures in Chagall paintings, the lightness of it all.

But there was no way to describe all of this to someone who could never experience it. And besides, this conversation was off limits. Miriam resorted back to her safety mode. "Oh," she said. "Oh, I see. Oh."

X

VIOLET WAS AT THE EASEL IN THE CORNER OF HER kindergarten class, painting a purple tree. Trees could be purple if you wanted them to be. Violet had seen purple trees in the museum with Mommy. She liked them better than brown trees. Brown wasn't her favorite color. She was wearing a plastic smock, but purple dripped down onto her shoes anyway.

Even though Violet had her back to Kimberly, she could tell that Kimberly was upset. In her brain, she could see Kimberly pressing her lips together to stop herself from crying so Kevin and Peter wouldn't say, "Yah, yah, crybaby" to her. Violet was glad that she didn't cry so easy as Kimberly. She would hate anybody saying crybaby to her.

The bird in the purple tree was yellow, but some of the green leaves got into it and some of the purple too, so it wasn't really a yellow bird like Violet had wanted. It was a smushy bird. The bird got smushed because Violet couldn't stop seeing Kimberly trying not to cry. But Violet could see that Kimberly had dark squiggles in the spaghetti—what did Grams call it?...The intests? Testins?—she couldn't remember. Grandma Miriam had said, "If you get a picture in your mind of some part of a person's body and see something strange, no matter how silly it seems, it might be a sign that that person is sick and you are meant to help him or her." Grandma Miriam had drawn her pictures of parts of the body: the heart, the liver, the stomach, and all the spaghetti below it. "If you see dark spots anywhere, that also shows there's a problem." Those were squiggles, not spots, but Violet knew she had to do something to help Kimberly. She had to tell Mrs. Oliver.

Mrs. Oliver was at the window watching so Lisa Green didn't feed the turtle too much so it would die. Lisa Green was Violet's best friend. She liked Kimberly, too, but Kimberly really and truly was a crybaby like they said. Violet could, if she wanted, do two paintings, because you could. If she left the easel now, Peter, who was tapping his foot, would take her turn. But she put her brushes in the water can and went over to Mrs. Oliver.

"I have to tell you something," Violet said with her hand covering half of her mouth so no one else would hear.

Mrs. Oliver had hair like a hat, all puffed around her face, and eyeglasses with plaid frames. She wasn't tall like Mommy, but she bent way down to listen.

As Violet started to talk, more words came to her, as if someone was whispering in her other ear. "Kimberly has dark squiggles in her spaghetti," she said. "She has to poop, but she hates to poop at school. If she doesn't soon, she's going to be called worse than a crybaby. She will be called a Poopy Baby." Violet wrinkled her nose so Mrs. Oliver would get the idea.

Mrs. Oliver glanced over at Kimberly, who was wriggling in her seat now. She called a teacher in from the hallway and took Kimberly to a bathroom that wasn't in the classroom where everybody could hear what you were doing in there. Tinkle, tinkle or anything.

When Mrs. Oliver left, Lisa Green took out her Polly Pockets that you weren't supposed to bring to school. You were only supposed to play with the kindergarten toys in kindergarten. If you brought other toys, Mrs. Oliver took them and kept them in a locked drawer for one whole day before giving them back. But the teacher from the hallway didn't know Mrs. Oliver's rules. She just stood there with her hands at her elbows. Gregory took out a little high-bouncing ball that you could get from the machine in the front of the diner and bounced it high. Violet wished she had something with her that she wasn't supposed to. And then she remembered that she had two oatmeal raisin cookies with her for lunch and she gave them to Michael, who wasn't supposed to have any sweets, even healthy ones, because his mother said so. It was fun doing what she wasn't supposed to. You didn't have to do everything grownups said.

Quick, quick, she saw Mrs. Oliver coming down the hallway. "Mrs. Oliver's coming," she whispered loud, and Lisa Green put away her Polly Pocket and Gregory his ball and Michael stuffed both cookies in his mouth at once.

When Mrs. Oliver came back with Kimberly, who didn't look like she was going to cry anymore, she gave Violet a curious glance, curiouser and curioser.

The next day Kimberly wasn't in school. In the playground, Violet huddled in the tube that led to the slide and peeked out the holes in it. That morning she had insisted that she didn't need her wool tights and now her legs were cold.

Mrs. Oliver came over to her. "Violet," she said through the hole, "you really helped Kimberly yesterday by telling me what was upsetting her. I think that when she comes back, she'll be happier in school from now on, thanks to you."

Violet felt warmer, even without her tights. She wanted Mrs. Oliver to say more nice things about her. "Kimberly's mother sits on the toilet for a long, long time," Violet said. "She has consternation."

Mrs. Oliver covered her mouth as if she had wanted to laugh. "Do you go over Kimberly's house often?" she asked.

"I never went there," Violet said. "Lisa Green is my best friend and I'm going to go to her house this week."

Mrs. Oliver's face lost its smile. "You shouldn't say that about Kimberly's mother."

Violet put her back against the roundness of the slide tube. Her eyes were no longer right up against the holes to look out. She didn't have to look at Mrs. Oliver if she didn't want to. It was mixed up to go from being good to being not good when she didn't even know how it happened.

The teacher from the hallway was in the yard too. Mrs. Oliver said, "Judy, thanks for spelling me when I had to take that girl out to the bathroom yesterday. Her mother called." Mrs. Oliver looked around to make sure no kids were listening. Violet stayed quiet as she peered out the holes in the tube. "The girl," Mrs. Oliver said, "has intestinal worms. We should watch for symptoms in the other kids."

The spaghetti is intestines, Violet recited to herself a few times. She wondered why Kimberly had eaten worms. Violet locked her lips and threw away the key to remind herself not to tell anyone, even Lisa Green, or Kimberly would be a crybaby again.

"Okay, class, line up, it's time to go in now," Violet said just before Mrs. Oliver said it, as if she was Violet's echo. Violet felt strong now, a big girl, but then as she came out the slide tube, she bumped her head. But she was no crybaby, she reminded herself as the tears started. No crybaby.

On the bus, she sat next to Lisa Green and gave her a piece of watermelon-tasting gum. It was Mommy's and Violet wasn't supposed to chew it. No child was supposed to chew gum on the bus either, because the bus driver said children could swallow gum and he didn't have time to get it out of their throats. But Violet knew how to chew gum.

"Gimme gum," Peter said, "or I'll tell the bus driver," but Violet gave the gum to Darshan instead, because she could see in her head that he was wishing he had some, and he didn't yell like Peter.

"Let's make bubbles," Violet said. When she and Lisa made little bubbles, they leaned towards each other and popped them like a bubble kiss.

"No gum," the bus driver called out. "I don't have time to take it out of your throats."

With their tongues, they moved the gum to the side of their mouths and kept it there without chewing.

CARA LAY IN BED, EXHAUSTED FROM HER PARENTS' visit, even though they had left a week ago. She hadn't wanted things to go this way, a constant fight, but her mother was giving her no choice by ramming this psychic business down

Violet's innocent throat. She glanced at the clock. Seven-thirty. Dan had left for work two hours ago.

"Dan, are you okay?" she'd said. "I mean with the research. Is it going well?"

He was looking at his Blackberry instead of her. "My mother just texted me one word: 'Well?' That's all she wrote, but I know what she means. She and my father think they have to check up on me, prod me to get me to achieve. Please, Cara, don't do the same."

Cara was miffed, but the matter was sidelined by her upset over her mother prodding Violet to be psychic. Mothers with cattle prods branding their kids—Violet the Psychic and Dan the Award-Winning Famous Scientist, she thought. At least she was nudging Violet away from something. But was that any better? She hoped so.

Now Cara got out of bed and called over the banister, "Violet, did you have breakfast yet?"

"Yes, with Daddy."

No matter how early Dan got up to go to work, Violet got up to eat breakfast with him. Otherwise Violet probably wouldn't see her father at all. *Dan is getting like my father when I was a child,* Cara thought. She had always known that her father loved her, but he was never home, never there.

She heard Violet laughing downstairs.

"What are you doing, Violet?" Cara called.

"I'm playing Virtual Schoolhouse. I put the CD in all by myself."

"Clever girl," Cara said, and her troubles seemed to lift. "I'll be down as soon as I get dressed."

Cara smoothed the duvet, plumped the pillows, took a quick shower, and put on her jeans and black Shakespeare-in-the Park T-shirt. When they'd first moved into the house, Dan had swabbed the bottom of her shoe and shown her under a microscope the bacteria that harbored there. From then on, no one was allowed to wear shoes in their house. But Cara had a brand new pair of sneakers she'd ordered online and had never set foot outside in them. They were navy blue with red rhinestones and red laces. They sold those sneakers in Violet's size, and if Violet liked them, she'd buy her a pair too. For the last year, Violet had to approve of the clothes Cara bought for her or she wouldn't wear them. Cara had thought that this wouldn't start until Violet was a teenager. She'd try not to show how excited she was to buy these for Violet. Still, as Cara laced her sneakers, she thought of the pleasure she'd have, walking into town in the same glitzy sneakers as Violet. They'd play kick the pebble or whatever they could find, Cara thought, and she felt the distress of her mother's visit and Dan's increasing absence leaving her. She had never wanted to wear the long skirts and clogs that her mother went around in. *Violet will think I'm hip,* Cara thought. *She'll want to dress like me.*

Just as Cara approached her bedroom door, Violet shouted up, "Mommy, I know what you're wearing."

"Oh, really?" Cara said. "What am I wearing?"

"The Shakespeare-in-the-Park t-shirt," Violet said.

Cara startled. How did Violet know?

"And Mommy, I don't want those sneakers with the red shiny things. And Mommy, could you buy me a skirt that goes all the way down to the bottom of my legs like Grandma

Miriam's so I can twirl and the skirt will go all the way out like a flower?"

Cara was tempted to change her clothes and tell Violet that she was wrong, that she hadn't been wearing that t-shirt and sneakers. But what if Violet could see her do it? What an example to set for her daughter, lying and cheating. Was there going to be no privacy in the house? Were they all going to have to live in a fishbowl?

Reluctantly, Cara came down, still wearing the outfit Violet had seen with her psychic eyes. Violet gave a big yawn. Cara could hear that little click in the back of Violet's throat.

"Maybe you should take a short nap," Cara said, "so you won't be tired during your play date after school with Lisa Green." She always said the full name because there was a Lisa Brown in Violet's class and a Lisa Gray.

"I'm not tired," Violet said, yawning again.

"Come, I'll tell you a story," Cara said.

"About you and Grandma Miriam when you were a little girl?" Violet asked hopefully.

Cara was sick of being asked about her childhood with her mother, but Violet needed a nap. "All right," she said with a sigh. They went up to Violet's room. Violet had already pulled her quilt over her bed, so she lay on top of it.

"Once upon a time, when you were a little girl and you lived with Grandma Miriam," Violet began.

"Wait a minute," Cara said. "Who's telling this story anyway?" She tickled Violet's tummy.

"Once upon a time when you were a little girl and you lived in Grandma Miriam and Grandpa Rory's house, ants bit you all over. I can see it, Mommy. I can hear you screaming and slapping your arms and jumping up and down."

Nothing like that had ever happened. Cara was relieved that her daughter was using her imagination instead of messing around with psychic visions. "That's a really good made-up story," Cara said.

"It's not made-up, Mommy."

"But Grandma Miriam and Grandpa Rory didn't have a single ant in their house. They never even needed an exterminator."

"Mommy, I see you crying," Violet said adamantly. "And you're saying, 'Why did you buy me this, Mommy?'"

Oh, no, Cara thought. *No.* She remembered the ant farm that her mother had sent away for. The ants came in a vial. Who knew they were red, biting ants? She was sure she'd never told this story to Violet. She hadn't remembered it herself until just now. "Did Grandpa Rory or Grandma Miriam tell you about the biting ants?" Cara demanded.

"No, I heard it in my brain. The story is here." She pointed to her forehead with one hand and to the right with the other.

Cara remembered her mother saying that psychics saw the past to the right of them, the future to the left. "What's the end of this story already?" Cara asked, eager to stop whatever process was going on inside her little girl.

"Calamine lotion," Violet said.

"Now let me tell you a story," Cara said. "It's about a little girl."

"What's her name?" Violet asked.

"Mimi," Cara said. "She told stories about people that

they hadn't told her themselves and she hurt their feelings very badly. They didn't want to admit these things about themselves, even if there was nothing so bad about them. You see, Violet, things in a person's mind are private until they want to tell them to you. So when Mimi told these stories, whether they were true or not, people got very angry at her. 'Go away, you big fibber,' they'd say, "and Mimi became more and more alone and unhappy."

"Is Mimi really Grandma Miriam?" Violet asked. "Is Grandma Miriam all alone and unhappy?"

Cara thought of her mother, isolated in that big house, up in her office most of the time, having intimate talks with strangers she'd never really see and maybe never even hear from again. Someone could go mad that way. Cara almost choked up. She felt like rescuing her mother, asking her to come and stay for as long as she liked, but there was Violet to protect. "No, Grandma is very happy," she said. "And I want you to be happy, and you won't if you tell people things about themselves that they haven't told you like Mimi did. No one would invite Mimi to birthday parties."

Violet's lips trembled. "Poor Mimi," she said. "Poor, poor Mimi."

Maybe I went too far and this is backfiring, Cara thought. She laid down next to Violet and closed her eyes, hoping that Violet would fall asleep.

"I won't tell anybody that those ants bit you and you were so angry at Grandma Miriam for buying them and you stamped on those ants and killed them dead," Violet said.

"Good idea," Cara said.

After Violet left for school, Cara threw herself into her work. She searched the web for new markets for her products and new sources for materials. Every now and then, she thought about Violet and the ant farm and Dan never being home anymore to help her deal with all of this. Then she thought about how Dan was probably never thinking about her as he did his research, so she wasn't going to think about him either. By the time she had to leave to pick Violet up at Lisa Green's, she had found three new boutiques, one in Hoboken, another in Colorado, and one right in Great Neck. They all were willing to take a big order from her, but she decided against the one in Great Neck. Summer and winter her mother walked to town with her parasol. The store was right along her mother's route. She was sure her mother would go in raving about how the hats were designed by her daughter or buy them all to "help out," even though her mother never wore hats. Cara had also called China to speak to a factory there. She'd even looked into making part of her business a charity to help indigent women. She felt excited, successful, fulfilled.

But on the way to Lisa Green's to pick up Violet, Cara thought about how she herself had been shut away in the house all morning, working like her mother. If you were working on your own, you needed to make friends you could get together with, not just Facebook and Twitter followers. You had to have people around you who you felt close to besides your family. She had counted on having lots of friends once she had a baby. She'd joined a Mommy and Me class, but the other women were already friends and it was hard to break into their circle. Allison Green, Lisa's mom, was a lawyer who had cut her practice back to twice a week to spend more time with Lisa. She probably had a need for adult female companionship, too. Wouldn't it be nice if they had a cup of coffee together while the girls continued to play?

When she pulled up to Lisa Green's house, Violet was waiting on the porch with her backpack on, and Allison Green was tapping her foot.

"Hi, I'm not late, am I?" Cara asked.

"No, no, you're not late," Allison said brusquely. She was wearing a dark green hoodie and her hands were jammed in the pockets. She looked like one of the angry kids she defended in family court. If they could just talk a bit, Cara was sure she could help Allison feel better.

"This worked out so well for me," Cara said. "Maybe tomorrow Lisa can come to our house and when you come to pick her up, you and I could have coffee."

"I don't think so," Allison said coldly.

Cara was puzzled, but she didn't want to say anymore in front of Violet. When they got in the car, Cara saw Lisa in the upstairs window, looking out sadly as if she'd just lost her best friend.

"Violet, did anything bad happen at Lisa's house?"

"We played with her Polly Pocket dolls all the time and we had S'mores."

"But Lisa's mommy looked upset."

"I told Lisa that her Daddy really isn't going to move out like he said and that he was going to come home in two days."

Cara pulled over to the curb so she could look directly at Violet, who still had to ride in the back in a child safety seat.

She twisted her head so quickly that she heard the ligaments in her neck snap. "Did Lisa tell you that her parents were upset with each other?" Cara demanded.

"No."

"Were you listening in on a phone call?"

"No, Mommy, I heard it in my ear. This one," she said, pointing to her right ear. "They had a fight because of Ashanti."

"Who is that?"

"Her father's yogurt teacher," Violet said.

Cara put her forehead against the wheel. She thought of her mother once again, who had no personal friends even though she'd learned to not spill people's secrets unless she was paid to do it. It was unnatural. People didn't want to be around someone who had that kind of power to know everything about them. Oh, some had tried to make friends with her mother, asked her to lunch. But really what they had wanted was a free psychic reading to ask if their daughter or son was ever going to get married or would get into medical school or would stay there instead of quitting everything. *How am I going to get through to Violet?* She didn't want her daughter to have to be alone. And she didn't want to have to be alone herself because of her psychic daughter.

"Violet, honey, didn't you remember the story I told you of Mimi? This is just like that story. You went and told things that you only heard in your mind, and now Lisa can't play with you after school."

"Yes she can," Violet insisted. "Lisa Green is my best friend and we can play and play whenever we want to."

"Her mother won't allow it now that you've told Lisa that tale."

"Lisa's mother makes S'mores. I like going there. She doesn't make carrot brownies like you do," she added, wrinkling her nose.

Violet is too young to understand, Cara thought, rubbing the knot in her neck.

"What is custard of a child?" Violet asked.

"Are you sure you didn't listen in while Mrs. Green was talking on the phone?"

"No, that was what she and Lisa's father talked about yesterday night when they were all by themselves in the kitchen."

Cara lost it. "Shut up, shut up," she yelled, and burst into tears. Violet gazed at her in shock. *Now I'm a bad mother on top of everything else,* she thought. When she got home, she called Dan. "I've got to talk to you. Could you come home early?"

"I can't," he said.

She hung up on him and sat there with her head in her hands, crying, trying to pull herself together before Violet saw her.

That night, a little after 1:00 a.m., Dan still wasn't home. His hybrid Toyota Prius was so silent that she often didn't hear him pull into the driveway. She went downstairs to see if he was standing at the fridge, finding a snack. He wasn't there. She almost passed him in the living room. He was on the couch with the throw pillow over his head.

"Are you planning to spend the night here?" she asked.

He didn't answer. She panicked. "What's wrong? Are you sick?" She pulled the pillow off his face and put her palm on his forehead.

"Oh, come on," he said. "Can't you cut me a break?"

"A break from what?" she asked. "Me? Our marriage? Violet?"

He looked up at her, his whole face trembling. "I was so damn close, but that Ingebord, whose been dogging me for years, beat me to it. You should have seen him last March when I gave my paper in Sweden. He sat in the front row taking notes like crazy."

Dan had been working on this project for six years. She felt sick for him. He looked completely defeated.

"You'll find a new topic," she said in a soothing tone, "an even better one, something that you're more excited about. You're like Joe Palooka. I was amazed when you got that concussion on the wrestling team at Cornell and you went right back to it as soon as you could."

He rolled over to bury his face in the couch. "Can't you just let me be?" he mumbled.

"Remember when we used to talk everything over and make each other feel so much better?" she asked. "Don't push me away,"

"I'm sorry. Just give me some time alone, okay?"

What else could she do but grant him that? As she walked away, she heard him mutter, "How am I going to tell my parents?"

She was furious. She had to stop herself from storming back into the living room and telling him that she had lost respect for him. You didn't kick someone when he was down. But when was he going to get over wanting his parents' approval? It was more than time, now that he had his own family. And then she thought about her own conflicts with her mother and understood that possibly it would never be over. How could she tell him her worries about Violet now, when he couldn't even comfort himself? She felt as single as Lisa Green's mother was soon to be.

XI

MIRIAM WAS DUSTING THE CURIOS ON HER WHATNOT shelf with one of those new-fangled microfiber cloths that was supposed to be electrostatic. Now the little bride and groom statues from her wedding cake were so dust-free that they looked as if they'd been bathed in the fountain of youth. She picked up the other bride and groom, the one she'd begged Cara to put on top of her wedding cake. "Mom, that's so kitschy," Cara had said, but she gave in. "You keep it afterwards," Cara told her. And Miriam had, right next to the statuettes from her own wedding. Now, as she touched Cara's wedding figurines, she felt a shock in her palms, like a joy buzzer that brought no joy. What if Cara's marriage was suffering? She held the figurines to her. At their wedding, Cara and Dan had recited some lines of *The Song of Songs*. "Set me as a seal upon thy heart, As a seal upon thine arm; / For love is as strong as death." Miriam began to cry.

She went to her phone, picked up the receiver, and put it down again. What if there wasn't anything wrong with Cara's marriage and she put beans up Cara's nose, got her analyzing and worrying over nothing? She thought of what Violet was going to have to go through with Cara being unsupportive of her gift. Miriam wanted to be there for Violet. Only a psychic could guide a psychic child. Violet needed her, especially if Cara and Dan's marriage was in trouble. Miriam shivered. Was that part of the reason Cara was pushing her away? Did she not want her to know? She threw her arms around herself as if to protect herself against a draft. *With adult children, you have to do nothing, nothing,* she reminded herself, her stomach squeezing.

Miriam was thrilled to hear her business phone ring. She could absorb herself in someone else's life and forget her own troubles. She went, lickety-split, up the stairs to answer it. Her clients saved her as much as she saved them. As she reached for the phone, she knew it was Kaylee.

"Miriam," Kaylee said, "that's all my father talked about after all these years was his bed? He didn't even tell me if I was ever going to have a baby. Doesn't he care about me?"

"Sure he does," Miriam said. "But sometimes spirits get caught up in minutiae just the way people do when they are alive."

Miriam heard Kaylee sniff back tears. "I thought he'd tell me that he loved me," she said. "I thought he'd tell me, 'Kaylee, you're going to have a child and be so happy.' Does this mean that I won't have a baby?"

Everything tightened inside Miriam. What right did she have to tell a woman that she'd never have a child? "Maybe he doesn't see it for now," Miriam said, "but destiny isn't written in stone."

"You don't think I'll ever have one, do you?" Kaylee said angrily.

"I didn't say that. You're putting predictions in my mouth."

"What should I do to convince Tom to have a baby?"

Miriam saw an image of Tom and Kaylee with their backs to each other, which meant that they didn't have the same aims in life. "I don't think there's anything you can do to convince him."

"So if I'm ever going to have a baby, I have to divorce Tom, right?"

Miriam felt as if she had one foot in boiling water, the other in hot oil. She didn't want to be responsible for anyone getting a divorce. "Kaylee, I don't think I can do this reading," she said. She could taste the vegetarian chopped liver she'd eaten for lunch. "This is something you have to work out with Tom."

"Will...will sex ever get better for me at least?" Kaylee asked.

In her mind, Miriam heard a sudden, throaty, "Yes, yes" and felt herself blush as she repeated it back to Kaylee.

"That's encouraging," Kaylee said. "But I can't imagine how. When Tom and I are, well, you know, I have to picture myself with someone else. Sometimes I can imagine myself with a guy who is tall and dark, but not Tom. Then Tom sinks his teeth into my lips when he kisses me and my dream lover disappears."

Miriam wanted to be anywhere else but listening to this. It was too sad, and it made her feel like a keyhole-peeker. Everything she heard became so real to her that she wiped off her mouth with the back of her hand as if Tom had kissed her. And then an image flickered into her mind. "I see a candlelit room with a beaded curtain and you're in the room. You're holding your arms out to the world and you look radiant."

"When?" Kaylee said. "When will this happen?"

Some visions arose with a date on them, like a post-marked letter. This one was blank. "I don't know."

"Well, it's a least something to hope for," Kaylee said. "Like I never thought I'd hear from my father and I did."

Just then, Kaylee's father appeared by the window, one of the crystals hanging from the fish line dangling right where his nose should be. His thin lips were moving. Miriam strained to hear him.

"Lots of money is coming to my Kaylee soon," he intoned, then faded off.

"Your father says that you'll have money," Miriam reported. "A financial windfall."

"Wow, wow!" Kaylee said. "Miriam, you and my dad have given me something to look forward to. I'll go out every day and buy a Lotto ticket and I'll stop at the church and light a candle for my father. That will probably help the money come sooner."

After the reading, Miriam felt confident enough to call her own daughter. "Sweetheart, how is everything?"

"Fine. We're just busy, busy, busy."

Miriam wanted to reach through the phone and stroke Cara's cheek. What if her girl was suffering alone? Miriam could never tell her own mother anything. "So you think you have troubles?" her mother would say. "That's nothing," and she'd go on to list hers in detail.

"Cara, I want you to know that you can tell me anything".

"What do you mean?" Cara said, anger seeping into her voice. "What is there to tell you?"

"Um, you could tell me how Violet likes school."

"She likes it."

There was nowhere to go from here, no opening, not even a hope of closure. These days it was harder to talk to Cara than to the spirit world.

"I just want you to know I'm thinking of you is all," Miriam said.

"That makes me nervous," Cara said.

"And that makes me sad. I love you, honey. You're in my heart always."

"Love you too," Cara said.

Miriam was sure that beneath the barbs, Cara did love her. *At least there's that,* Miriam thought. And in a moment, Cara said, "Gotta go," and Miriam was left with her worries.

THE CAFETERIA OF JOHNS HOPKINS WASN'T CARA'S idea of the most romantic place for her and Dan to meet for lunch, but it was the only way he could make time for her while he was trying to find a new research topic. Dan had finally pulled himself together enough to tell his parents that Ingebord had beaten him to the finish line. He had the phone on speaker so he could shave, and Cara heard George say, "Didn't Mom and I tell you that you should get a move on? In a field like yours, if you don't make a big name, what's the point? You should have gone into business where you would have at least made real money." Cara felt her stomach tense when she thought of it. Dan had gotten three nicks on his chin, one of them so deep she was afraid it would leave a scar.

The cafeteria was full. She recognized some of Dan's colleagues and smiled and nodded. She sat at the table, strangely nervous, as if she were waiting for a Match.com date and might be stood up. Had Dan forgotten? She checked her watch. He was only seven minutes late. She touched her wedding ring. *I'm waiting for my husband,* she reminded herself, *my husband.* Her eyes smarted with the beginning of tears. Dan had become like a ghost in the house. Every day his bath towel was damp, his coffee mug was upside down in the dishwasher, and he reset the alarm clock for her. She needed these concrete things to remind her that he was really there.

And then she saw him beneath the clock, looking around for her. He was wearing a pale blue button-down shirt with a blue striped tie and khaki pants. She noticed a streak of gray at the top of his blond hair. Time was passing, and her Dan was drifting from her. "Dan," she called out, waving madly. "Dan, I'm here."

A strained smile appeared on his face as he strode over and sat across from her. He took her hand over the trays that already held their lunches. She hadn't wanted to waste a minute of their time together on the food-court lines. She wanted to ask him when he was going to spend more time with her, but wouldn't that be like nagging? After all, he'd been the one to ask her to come here for lunch. He had taken a step.

"Good to see you," he said, squeezing her hand.

"I'm feeling shy," Cara said.

Beneath the table, he rubbed his foot against hers. "That better?"

"It's a start. How are you? I've been so worried about you."

"I've been better."

"I blame your parents," she said. "I could kill them for putting so much pressure on you. Every time we see them, you have to get quizzed on how soon your research will be finished when you haven't even started a new project yet. It's enough to trip someone up."

"My career is my responsibility, not theirs."

"Then you should tell them that," Cara said.

"Lay off my parents, all right?"

"All right, all right." *A misstep,* she thought. Even though Dan had problems with his parents, she shouldn't talk badly about them. It only set him her against her.

"I love the ways Violet looks like you," Dan said.

"But her mouth is just like yours." Cara wanted to remain bubbly, but she could feel her brows were tense. That frown line must be there. "Dan, I'm worried about Violet."

"Why? She's great."

She looked around, hoping that her words had been absorbed in the hum of the other conversations around her. She wouldn't want anyone at his work who would scoff at psychics to know that his daughter thought she was one. "You don't know the half of what's been going on," she said. "Violet has been barred from Lisa Green's house."

"What? Why?"

She told Dan about the yogurt teacher and the child. Dan threw his head back and laughed. She noticed people smiling at them as if they were such a happy couple. She was upset that he was taking her worries so lightly.

"You think that's funny?" she said with quiet fury. "Violet's heart is broken."

"This morning at breakfast," Dan said, "Violet was telling me about Dashan, who sits next to her on the bus and colors with her. Her heart sure didn't seem broken to me. In fact, I think she has a crush on this kid. I felt a little jealous. Anyway, she's better off without people like Lisa Green's mother. What mother would try to separate a child from her best friend? I don't think I want Violet around a woman like that."

"Don't you see?" Cara said. "This psychic thing is interfering with Violet's socializing. Socialization is a crucial part of a child's education. I know how smart Violet is, but I don't want her to end up all alone in a hut in the hills somewhere. We have to nip this in the bud. We can't let her go on thinking she's psychic a minute longer. This is drastic, but I think we really have to lay down the law to my mother. We have to stand together as a couple and tell her that if she ever even mentions anything about being psychic around Violet again, even hints at it, she'll be barred from seeing her. I know I sound harsh, but I'm frantic over this. I need you to back me up this time."

"That's ridiculous," Dan said.

"To you," Cara said. "But you're not there. You didn't see the look on Lisa Green's mother's face. You don't even know that Allison Green went up to school and demanded that Lisa's class be changed so she wouldn't be around Violet so much. Bubbie got my mother into this stuff. She taught her things like how to see what wasn't there in the mirror or how to guess what someone was thinking. Sometimes you'd have to be right. Like now, I bet you're thinking that I should just leave Violet as she is and not interfere."

"I guess you're psychic," Dan said with a half smile.

"No, I'm a concerned mother. My mother was pushed into this by her bubbie, and the more her mother protested, the more my mother set her heart on it. My mother has done the same to Violet as her grandmother did to her. Instead of me trying to change Violet's mind and possibly have it back-fire, I think I should bring her to a therapist who can help her drop this destructive behavior."

"In hermaphrodite children," Dan said, "it's been shown that if the male genitalia are removed, even if the child was never told, there will be lifelong gender confusion."

"This isn't the same thing. You're making this sound physical. It's an idea, an idea that needs changing. If we get Violet help now, her life will go so much easier for her. I'd rather our little girl be happy than have this terrible gift, if you can call it that. My mother has been thrown out of more places than most people have ever been invited to. When she was the Brownie leader, instead of making wishing wells out of Crisco cans, she had us play with the Ouija board. When the stylus spelled out the name of Augustine Gibb's dead grandmother, Eula, Augustine began to sob and sucked her thumb for months. The other mothers ousted my mother. Whose mother gets thrown out of the Brownies?"

"I don't want our daughter going to a therapist for this," Dan said. "Why should Violet think of herself as being ill in some way when she's the most perfect child anyone could ever have?"

"Dan, how could you be so backward about this? Violet wouldn't even have to know that the therapist is a doctor. They do play therapy and have fun."

"Still, you take a child to a therapist if you think she has something wrong with her. Violet doesn't have a psychological problem. You're always checking her for symptoms, even worrying about them before she was born. Keep it up and she'll develop them, and someday you'll be right."

Cara didn't want to fight. She didn't want to push Dan away. She was almost sorry she'd brought all this up, but when was she supposed to talk to him about Violet? When he came home after midnight? "Even if you don't agree," Cara said, "it can't hurt Violet. It's just another adult interested in her. What could be wrong with that?"

"The psychic faculties are in the right brain," Dan said, "the amygdala. That's the same area that makes a child more imaginative, more artistic. Who would want to stamp that out?"

"Artistic would be wonderful," Cara said. "But this psychic thing is making Violet a pariah."

"Being psychic is not something to try to extirpate," Dan argued. "If there are true genes for being psychic, it should be honored." Then his eyes widened and he sat straight up, as if the import of what he had just said struck him.

"You're not on my side," Cara said. "You're not even on Violet's side."

"Don't wait up for me tonight," he said.

"When will you be home?"

"Late, very late." Without another word, he strode away.

XII

"I WANT A READING," A WOMAN SAID TO MIRIAM OVER the phone, "but first you've got to tell me three things about me so I'll know you're for real. You know how many phonies there are out there. They take down people's credit card numbers and sell them to the Russian mafia."

Miriam didn't take on clients who started out with that mentality. If they didn't trust her right away, the reading wouldn't go well. She needed to be relaxed to do her best work.

"I'm not getting anything on you," Miriam said, "so I won't take the reading, but thank you so much for calling."

After she got off the phone, it rang again. "You got me off the phone so quickly," the same woman said. "If you can't read me, how the hell do you have the nerve to advertise that you can?"

Usually Miriam put on a mental coat of armor when she dealt with people like this, but since Cara had been so cool to her, she felt the woman's nastiness seep in through a chink. She was going to hang up, but she saw an eleven with a gold band broken in half and a tire with a forty-two on it.

"You have been divorced eleven years and your waistline is forty-two inches," Miriam said. She saw a red 3,000. "And you owe $3,000 on your credit card, so you're lucky I'm not doing a reading for you." She could tell by the silence that she'd been on the money. "Goodbye and thanks again for calling."

When she got off the phone, instead of feeling triumphant, she felt as if she'd just thrown a boomerang dipped in crap. She took a sage smudge stick out of her drawer, lit it, and waved it in all the corners of her office to clear out the negativity. She began to cough and sneeze from the smoke and had to open a window.

The phone rang again. Miriam checked the number to make sure it wasn't the same woman. It was Kaylee, Kaylee who trusted Miriam.

"It's good to hear from you, Kaylee," she said.

Kaylee was silent. Miriam only knew she was still on the line by her ragged breathing. Then Miriam got an image of the black lace circle that Kaylee's mother bobby-pinned to her gray bouffant for church, but not Kaylee's mother. "Something happened to your mother," Miriam said with a start.

"My mother is dead. She's dead. My mother is dead. She had a stroke and she's dead. My father said that money was coming to me. I was so excited. I thought I could change my life. Well, he was right. My mother had a lot of life insurance and money from when she sold her house. So after the estate is settled, I will have a windfall like you said, but who knew I was going to church and lighting a candle every day to make my mother die faster?"

The phone weighed a ton in Miriam's hand. "Kaylee, I

only know what the spirits tell me. Your father didn't specify where the money was coming from. I'm sure he didn't mean to be cruel."

Kaylee was sobbing.

Miriam's stomach did a cartwheel. Kaylee's mother had so many psychosomatic ailments that Miriam couldn't believe that Mrs. O'Brien had actually died. Rory said that the hypochondriac's epitaph should be, 'You see? I was right.'" Miriam tried not to foresee people's death, because what if she did and couldn't stop? She might see Rory's and her own. If she worked herself up, she'd be no use for Kaylee. "Is Tom with you?" she asked.

"Uh uh," she choked out. "He took off work for three weeks, but he had to go back." She sobbed some more. "Does my mother have anything to tell me? I miss her so much."

Miriam always tried to be a dispassionate medium, but she felt rage like a mouthful of hot peppers toward Kaylee's mother. Mrs. O'Brien hadn't wanted Kaylee to go to college. "The tests will be too hard for you and you'll catch cold waiting for the buses," she'd insisted. When Kaylee got a job with the phone company, her mother had convinced her that so much electricity running through her office building would result in cancer. The only thing Kaylee's mother had encouraged her to do was marry Tom. "He'll take care of you," she'd said. Whatever Kaylee's mother would say from beyond would probably be just as destructive as what she'd said on earth. Without even trying to contact her, Miriam said, "Your mother must be traveling to a different plane. She's unreachable right now."

"Oh, what am I going to do?" Kaylee said. "She was my

whole life. She was all the family Tom and I had. Is there anything I can do to help you contact her spirit?"

"Yes, you can meditate. It makes you a channel. It's always easier for me to work with people who meditate." Miriam heard *ashram, ashram,* like an echo. "You were just thinking of going to an ashram, weren't you?"

Kaylee blew her nose hard. "Not thinking of it...well, maybe I was. I was so torn apart that I couldn't remember your number, which I always knew so well that I could have dialed it in my sleep. Good thing I had a copy of the newspaper where you advertise. Anyway, on the same page as your ad was an ad for an ashram. It's up in Massachusetts and it has a guru who studied in India for ten years and knows the Dalai Lama, so he must be good. But I don't know if my mother would want me to go."

Suddenly, the coat rack in the corner of Miriam's office wavered. Miriam kept some of her mother's hats on the hooks. The one with the feather began to swing slightly. And then Mrs. O'Brien appeared. She was still in one of her black widow's dresses, which she'd worn since her husband had died twenty-two years ago.

"Tell Kaylee not to go if he isn't Catholic," Mrs. O'Brien said.

Miriam couldn't bear to think of Kaylee staying in her apartment all alone, but she couldn't go against a spirit either. It would be wrong. "Your mother just came to tell me that you shouldn't go if the guru isn't Catholic," Miriam admitted. Then the guru popped into her mind. He had intense black eyes and a face like polished marble, and a long, dark ponytail. As if he'd drunk an Alice potion, she saw him shrink to a little boy with a nun cracking a ruler over his knuckles. "The guru started out Catholic," Miriam said, "so I think your mother would allow it. And it would be great for you go up to the ashram. Maybe you could go during the week, when Tom is working. A change like that would be healing for you."

Kaylee's mother's spirit shook her head so hard that her double chin wagged. "A former Catholic isn't the same as a present Catholic," she said.

"It's too soon," Kaylee said. "I can't. I just can't."

Her mother's spirit broke into a satisfied smile.

Miriam felt like Jacob wrestling the angel. "Kaylee, you must go. You must."

"You mustn't," Mrs. O'Brien's spirit said. "Who knows what germs this guru brought from India?"

Miriam knew it would be a terrible breach of her mediumship if she didn't report exactly what Mrs. O'Brien was saying to Kaylee, but she was sick of Mrs. O'Brien and her germs and her keeping Kaylee back from living life. All of a sudden, from the corner of her eye, Miriam saw a gravestone. Staying at home would be the death of Kaylee's spirit. If Kaylee didn't get herself out of the apartment now, she never would. This was the moment where either a dam would be built against Kaylee's future or it would flow freely. "You must go," Miriam insisted. Mrs. O'Brien's spirit took it personally and began to break down into pixels, a tiny square of her here, another there. And then she was gone. Miriam felt powerful. "Do it, Kaylee," she said.

"I'll go," Kaylee said. "Thank you, Miriam."

When Miriam got off the phone, she felt as if every mistake that she'd ever made with Cara had been erased by the good she'd done Kaylee. If only Cara could know how Violet could someday change a person's life, get someone out of the darkness and into the light, she'd be proud of Violet's gift, and proud of her own mother's gift, too.

The hat with the feather wavered again, and in a blink, Miriam's mother was wearing it. "How dare you ignore a mother's wishes?" her mother said.

Miriam jumped up from her chair. "You were listening!"

"I'm always listening. You're a troublemaker. You're making trouble between this poor girl and her loving mother who sacrificed her life for her only daughter. And you're making trouble between Cara and Violet and even with Cara's husband, what's his name?"

"You still blame me for everything," Miriam said.

Miriam's mother batted her eyelashes. "How can you say that when I'm an angel now?" Then her feathered hat was just a hat again, hanging back on the coat rack.

XIII

Kaylee blasted the radio. Two and a half hours on the road with Tom complaining! It was Friday, and he'd taken off work at eleven so they could get an early start, and he couldn't stop about that either. Even with Carrie Underwood belting out *Because You Love Me,* she could hear him.

"You realize, don't you, that we're going to miss church on Sunday?" Tom went on. "Jesus, your mother is hardly even cold in her grave and we have to go to an assram?"

"Ashram," she said for the millionth time.

"Whatever. It's just not right."

"I told you I could take a bus or a train there, but you insisted on driving up with me, so stop complaining."

"I'm not letting my wife go away for a weekend without me. That's for sure. And your mother would roll over in her grave if she knew you were going to a place like that."

"For your information," Kaylee said, "when Miriam contacted my mother's spirit, my mother said I should go."

"Yeah, yeah," Tom said. "Like that psychic was really talking to your mother." He went into a long rant about psychics. The earplugs that she used to block out Tom's snoring were packed in the trunk. If she asked him to stop so she could get them, it would be another thing for him to complain about. His hands were white-knuckled on the steering wheel. He was biting his lip and leaning forward against his seatbelt. He was whacked to be out of his regular routine, but whether he liked it or not, he'd made himself do this for her. That was her Tom, faithful and loyal. She just wished she liked being with him.

She watched out the window. The leaves had changed to the color of Irish hair, except for hers, which was dark like her father's. He'd said he had ancestors from Portugal. She'd always wished hers was red like her mother's had been before it went gray. Men's eyes used to follow her mother, but she'd never give them a glance. There was a time she remembered her mother happy, a short time, when she smiled at herself in the mirror, and let her hips sway when she walked. But before long her mother's lips pinched again, and she reverted to her foot-dragging walk. The toll of caring for a sickly husband, Kaylee thought. Then her mother put on all that weight, as though she wanted to show her burdens on the outside. It was such a shock to have found her mother face down on her kitchen floor in her flowered housedress. Kaylee wondered if her mother had died suddenly and then fell to the floor or whether she had felt dizzy or nauseous first. Had her mother lain there, unable to move, knowing that she was dying? She should have had one of the alarms around her neck like they advertised on TV.

"Kaylee," her mother had said, "I'm feeling so poorly all the time that if I had one of those things, I'd be setting it off morning, noon, and night."

Kaylee's mother had gone for a complete physical the week before she died. Kaylee had gone with her. The doctor had said that her mother's cholesterol and blood pressure were under control and that she wasn't wheezing. On the way home, her mother, who read up on ailments, had told Kaylee that a person about to have a stroke could get anxious or have a sense of doom. Had her mother known?

Now Kaylee burst into tears.

"Jesus, Kaylee," Tom said, "we'll be at the assram any minute. Stop crying. Please. It breaks my heart to see you like this."

She didn't say "ashram, ashram." She just let him drive and drive.

FOUR HOURS AND TWENTY MINUTES LATER, THE greeter told them proudly, "I hope you know we're strictly vegan." She had on a white yoga tunic, like everyone else that Kaylee had seen on the grounds, and a gap in her front teeth that was big enough for a carrot strip to fit through. But Kaylee envied her self-assurance. Kaylee, who had nagged to come here, was now Jell-O-legged with fear.

"The men's dormitories are over there," the greeter said, pointing to a big cabin on the north side of the sprawling grounds. "A volunteer is inside. He will make sure you have a clean sheet and blanket. And the women's dorms are in that cabin." Now her finger pointed south. The two cabins were separated by a wide margin, maybe half a mile apart, where yoga-suited people raked leaves.

"If those rakers were wearing stripes," Tom said, "it would look like a prison here."

They must be in some shape, Kaylee thought, to be able

to just wear those yoga suits while she and Tom had on their fall jackets and wool scarves. She was getting less certain of her decision every moment. She would call Miriam as soon as possible to make sure she was doing the right thing.

Tom grabbed her hand. "I'm not sleeping separated from my wife," he said. "Couldn't I pay extra for a private cabin? I see you have them."

"Those are for the volunteer workers, not the guests," the greeter explained, "although we all help out as part of our spiritual commitment." Her hair was in a long braid down her back. Kaylee noticed that the women were either wearing braids or had haircuts shorter than Tom's, no in-betweens. She'd braid hers.

"Is there a motel somewhere close then?" Tom asked.

She could already see it, Kaylee thought. One night in a motel and Tom would talk her out of coming back. She was scared, but she had to give this a try. She just had to.

"Tom," she said, "I want to get the flavor of the place. You can't get that by staying in a motel."

Tom grumbled, but he wheeled the bags over the damp ground, first to her dorm, and then she watched him head toward the men's cabin with his shoulders slouched more than usual and his head so far down you could hardly see it. Her heart sunk to her stomach.

"Welcome," the women in Kaylee's dorm called out gaily. Kaylee was as startled as if someone had thrown her a surprise party. At least forty women occupied the long cabin. A wood-burning stove gave off heat, and everything was made of wood. A fire and she'd be toast. She had to have a bunk nearest the door, and not the doorway that said "Bathrooms." What if that door led out to a hole in the ground? And she'd never slept in a bunk bed before. What if she got a top one and fell out of bed onto the wooden floor and landed like her mother, face down, her arms straight out from her sides? She'd have to have a bottom bunk. Someone grabbed Kaylee's elbow.

"You looked like you were going to pass out," the woman said. "You all right?"

Kaylee nodded. She hadn't been close to so many people since high school graduation. Everyone was watching her. What were they seeing? She imagined that they could see what a baby she was, how she couldn't manage at all without her mother, without Tom. "I'm Kaylee," she said, and they all sang out, "Hi, Kaylee," like Uncle Finn had said they did at his drinking meetings.

I'm Lee-ay," said a sallow-faced woman. Her braid was still dark, but the front of her hair was all gray. She had big breasts and hips, but her waist, circled by the belt of her yoga suit, was tiny, and she looked strong from the upright way she stood. Kaylee was hoping she'd get strong like that from yoga.

"This should be perfect for you," Lee-ay said, drawing a folded yoga suit from a shelf.

Thanking her, Kaylee took the suit and went out the "Bathroom" doorway. Phew, toilets in doored cubicles, stall showers covered with white curtains, and ten sinks. But there were no mirrors. She changed in a shower.

"Where are the mirrors?" she asked a woman when she came out. "I want to see myself in my yoga clothes."

"We are each other's mirrors," the woman answered.

Kaylee wished she could become invisible. How were they seeing her? she wondered once again.

"You are the flower of a lotus waiting to bloom," said Lee-ay.

Kaylee's muscles unknotted. She felt herself smile. Lee-ay showed her to a bunk near the front door, just as she'd hoped. She was still scared, but if one thing worked out right, maybe something else could too.

AT DINNER, THEY SAT AT THE LONG WOODEN TABLE, elbow to elbow with the other guests, each with a serving of thin brown soup with seaweed and something that looked like tiny wagon wheels floating on top. Kaylee felt like Little Orphan Annie.

"Well," Tom said, sitting across from her, "you were the one who wanted to get a flavor of this place."

"Shh," Kaylee whispered.

Tom turned to the guy next to him. "Jesus, your coloring is off. You must be eating too many carrots or something."

Kaylee tried to look as though she didn't know who Tom was. The retreatants were mostly women, two to one, she figured. With her chopsticks, she poked at the wagon wheel thingies that bobbed in her bowl.

"Hey, you have some knives and real silverware around here?" Tom called out to the people who were handing out bowls of rice and beans and sprouts.

She kicked him. Now everybody would know that they were married.

Someone struck a gong, and the most handsome man Kaylee had ever seen walked in. His hair, coiled at the back of his head, was so black you could see blue in it. How long would it be if he let it down? she wondered. His dark eyes had the kind of lashes women would kill to have. They outlined his eyes, making them even more intense. His skin was dark and his lips curved widely on top instead of pinching up in sharp points like Tom's. He had one thick, dark eyebrow that went right across without stopping at his nose. She could smell him: spicy, exotic. His yoga top showed a long vee of his chest. His skin shone. Her hands twitched in her lap as she wondered if his skin felt oily.

No one spoke. No one moved. "For the newcomers," he said, "I am Guru Anjad." His voice poured slowly into the room, like blackstrap molasses from a jar. "We are not here by accident. None of us are. There is no such thing as an accident."

"Yeah, tell that to Geico," Tom said under his breath.

Tom probably thought that everybody around him would break out laughing like hyenas, Kaylee thought, the way they did when he was a weisenheimer at the warehouse. Didn't he realize that since he was the manager, they laughed because their promotions depended on him and because they were dumb and bored? Tom was no boss here. She was glad the guru didn't look at him. That would only encourage him.

"We're here because we've been together before in at least one lifetime and will be in many reincarnations," Guru Anjad went on, his eyes lighting like a raven on each person in the room, "so we have to get it right this time around. We have to cleanse ourselves spiritually and physically using the Ayurvedic principles. For newcomers, this will be the last solid meal you'll have for the next couple of days. You'll be fasting on a special herbal. "

"Sure," Tom whispered, "they get your money then starve you out."

"At night you will rub ghee, clarified butter, on your temples and the soles of your feet to relax you."

"Then you sue because you slip and break your neck," Tom yell-whispered.

Kaylee wondered if the guru rubbed ghee on his whole body and who did the parts he couldn't reach?

"You will lose weight, but you will gain courage," the guru said, "because through the intense meditations that you will do here, you will not only know in your mind, but in your heart, that there is no such thing as death."

Kaylee hoped Tom was listening.

"Now, before we eat, we will chant our mantra." He raised his long-fingered hands in the air. "*Om mani padme hum,*" he chanted. "The Supreme Reality is the Lotus of the Jewel of Oneness." Everyone joined in. Kaylee hummed along.

When the guru put his hands down, there was silence. "Amen," Tom piped up, looking delighted with himself.

Kaylee glared at him. If the others heard him, she was relieved that they didn't show it. Ignoring him, she watched the others for table manners, lifting her soup bowl to her lips just as they did.

Everyone picked up their bowls and drank down the soup except Tom. "I'm not drinking this," he said. "It looks like what you grow bacteria in."

She tried to pick up a wheelie with her chopsticks, but it landed in her lap. She tried again, leaning close to the bowl. The wheelie made it all the way into her mouth. She studied the schedule written on a blackboard on the wall: hikes, meditations, juicing class, yoga, massage. Her mother's death had given her more life than she could ever remember living. The wheelies didn't taste like much, but she ate another and another, smiling as if they were the greatest thing.

WHILE MIRIAM UNLOADED HER DISHWASHER, A glimpse of Kaylee came to her unbidden. Kaylee had on a white yoga suit and was sitting cross-legged in a half-lotus position, looking up at the moon, her lips curled in a soft smile. She was in a circle of other moon-gazers. Miriam felt a boulder lift from her heart. She'd always been so worried for Kaylee, and now Kaylee had found her own way, *with a little help from me,* Miriam thought. There was some discomfort left in her chest, as if her soul had to belch. Maybe it was because Kaylee, like Cara, didn't need her anymore. *Am I as grasping as Kaylee's mother?* Miriam worried. Her flowered mug slipped from her hands and broke right inside the dishwasher.

IT WAS SUNDAY, JUST AFTER THE DAWN MEDITATION. The sky was huge over the ashram. Kaylee could still feel the vibrations running through her from the meditation circle. Tom had skipped the meditation so he could pack and now he was wheeling his bag towards her, looking like a hostage who had just been ransomed.

"I can't wait to get back home," he said. "All those beans

and that dormitory of men. Two nights of smelling strangers' farts. And that guru guy talking like he was the pope himself handing out blessings."

Kaylee took a deep breath. "Tom, I'm not coming back with you."

He jolted as though she'd punched him in the stomach. "What?"

"I'm staying. I found out that you can volunteer to work here for free room and board. I'm going to be dicing vegetables." She felt proud just saying it.

"Get your things," he said. "You can dice vegetables at home."

"It won't be forever," she said. "Just four months, and you can come up every weekend."

"You kidding me? Four months separated from you? I'm not going home without you."

"Tom, it's my chance to work."

"You want to work for beans? You want to be away from me for a quarter of a year?"

She saw tears spring to his eyes. She felt her resolve pop like a bubble. How could she hurt him like this? Still, she couldn't just go back to Brooklyn. She knew the names of everyone who worked here already. The guests came and went, but Lee-ay had signed up to stay, and so had ten other women from her cabin. She was so alone all day in Brooklyn, especially without her mother.

"Tom, I'm not doing this to hurt you. But I can't go back right now."

"You've got your mother's estate to look after," he said.

"You've got lawyers to see, insurance companies to call. You've got to clean out your mother's apartment instead of staying here to rake leaves or whatever the hell they have you doing. You've got responsibilities, Kaylee."

"I can make calls from here," she said. "I can come home for a couple of days if I need to sign something. And my mother paid her rent six months in advance to get that discount her landlord offered her. I'll be home in time to see to her things. But I need to do this, Tom. You've got to understand."

"I'm not going to understand anything about this," he said. "If I could drag you home by the hair, I would, but that's abuse."

"I'm staying," Kaylee said, even though Tom's face was quivering. She had never really been able to stand up to his sadness before. And when her mother was alive, her mother had taken Tom's side in everything. Kaylee hadn't been able to stand up to the two of them, but now she said, "Have a safe trip home." She didn't watch as he rolled his bags away.

XIV

AT HER NEW BIG GIRL DESK IN HER BEDROOM, VIOLET finished the picture that she and Darshan had been drawing on the bus. It was a lady with a dress that wrapped around like Darshan's mother wore. Darshan's mother had come to school wearing a bright yellow one. The crayon wasn't shiny so she put sparkly sticker stars on it. She'd bring the finished drawing to Darshan tomorrow. Maybe he'd give it to his mother and his mother would like her, not like Lisa Green's mother, who didn't like her.

Violet liked having a friend who was a boy, but she missed Lisa Green. She closed her eyes and tried to see what Lisa was doing right then. At first she just saw dark. Then she started to see a picture like she would see on Mommy's phone. There was Lisa, all by herself, curled up on the couch in the den, watching TV and picking her nose. Her mother said, "Use a tissue, Lisa," but Lisa had told Violet that tissues didn't get the boogers out as good as her finger and that whenever she saw her mommy or daddy picking their nose, she'd yell, "Stop it! Use a tissue." She and Lisa Green told each other things that they didn't tell anyone else. Like Lisa Green had told her that her father didn't hold his farts in and that when nobody was looking she had peed in her aunt's potted Dieffenbachia because it was poison to cats and Lisa loved cats. And Violet had told Lisa that she could talk to her Grandma Miriam whenever she wanted without even using a phone. Now Violet tried hard to talk to Lisa the same way. *Lisa, Lisa, Lisa,* she thought, and watched to see what would happen. Whenever she thought hard about Grandma Miriam, she could see her in her brain, and her grandma would look toward her and smile a doppelganger smile. *Lisa, Lisa, Lisa,* Violet thought hard as she could, but Lisa was still just watching Nemo and picking her nose. "Lisa," Violet shouted. "Lisa, Lisa."

Mommy rushed into the room. "Violet, what's wrong?"

Violet began to cry.

"You can tell me what's wrong," Mommy said. "You can tell me anything and I'll always be on your side."

"I called Lisa," Violet said quietly.

"What do you mean you called Lisa? The phone is downstairs."

Violet hesitated, and then blurted out, "I called her in my mind like I do Grandma Miriam and Lisa didn't answer."

Mommy sank down in Violet's rocking chair and shook her head over and over. "Honey, you can't talk to people unless they're with you in person or on the phone or on the computer. It isn't possible. It's just in your imagination. You have a wonderful imagination." Mommy got up. "And you make such good pictures. Why look at this woman in a beautiful, sparkling yellow sari."

Violet wanted Mommy to understand. She wanted to be able to tell her anything like Mommy said she could. "It's not the same," Violet said. "This is Darshan's mommy. We know what she looks like. Especially Darshan knows. So we just drew her. But it's not the same as what I'm talking about. I'm talking about this." Violet scrunched her eyes closed. *Grandma Miriam, call me. Call me on the phone. Grandma, call me. Call me now,* she thought as hard as she could.

"Relax, Violet," Mommy said. "You're working yourself up. Your face is all red.

Violet saw Grandma going through her pocketbook, turning it upside down. "Oh, here it is," Grandma said, and her cell phone fell out onto the table.

"Grandma Miriam is going to call me now," Violet told Mommy, "because I called her first in my mind."

"Sweetheart, you have to stop this," Mommy said. "You're making yourself overly excited. Come, we'll go to Tumbling Tykes. You can jump on the trampoline and drive the toy police car and get your energy out. Remember how you directed traffic last time? And you can walk on the balance beam from one end to the other without holding on. Won't that be more fun than sitting here talking to people who aren't with you?"

Mommy's cell phone rang, the special duck quacking she had for Grandma Miriam. Violet saw her mother's mouth drop open so big that she could have fit four Oreos inside it. The duck quacked six times and then was silent. "You missed Grandma's call," Violet said. "You have to call her."

"I'll call her later," Mommy said.

"But I want to talk to her right now, and she wants to talk to me. Please, Mommy.

"All right," Mommy said with a huff. She went in the next room and got the phone, but she didn't come back with it. Instead, Violet heard her saying to Grandma Miriam, "What are you doing to your granddaughter? Thanks to you, she can't play with her best friend anymore."

Violet ran into her parent's bedroom. "I want to talk to Grandma Miriam on the phone by myself," she demanded.

"All right, Mom," Mommy said, "I'll let you speak to Violet, but you'd better talk her out of this nonsense," and handed Violet the phone.

"Grandma, Grandma," Violet said, "I want to play with Lisa Green, but her mother won't let me. Lisa is in a whole different class now and her mother picks her up from school and brings her back so I sit with Darshan, but he doesn't like Barbies or Polly Pockets. I want to play with Lisa Green."

"I know this might not be a comfort to you right now," Grandma Miriam said, "but I see that when you and Lisa Green are in middle school, you'll be best friends again. She will ride her bike over to your house and you'll do everything together."

"I want to play with Lisa Green today," Violet cried.

"I wish I were right there with you now," Grandma Miriam said. "I'd rub my hands together very hard and then I'd run them over your aura, flicking away the sadness, like my bubbie used to do for me."

"When are you coming, Grandma?"

"Grandpa Rory and I will come as soon as we can," Grandma Miriam said.

"Listen very hard," Violet said, "so you'll be able to hear

me calling you without the phone because I hardly ever get a chance to use the phone."

Violet heard her mother sigh and saw her throw up her hands.

CARA PUNCHED THE THERAPIST'S ADDRESS INTO HER GPS. It was in one of the development houses in Roland Green. This therapist had been specially recommended by Violet's pediatrician. "I took my own son to her when he didn't stop bedwetting at eight," the pediatrician had confided. Cara had phoned Jessica to explain Violet's problem and the woman was reassuring.

"You're going to have a very good time with Jessica," Cara said over her shoulder to Violet, who was strapped into her car seat in the back. "She's not a teacher, but she likes to talk to children."

"Why doesn't she talk to her own child?" Violet asked resentfully. She had wanted to stay home and play with the magic set that Grandma Miriam had sent her.

"I'm sure she does," Cara said. "She just wants to get to know you too."

"When I'm grown up," Violet said, "I'm not going to make any child drive far in a car to see anyone unless it is her very own grandma."

Cara already felt guilty that she was doing this when Dan was set against it. She hoped this therapist would win Violet over, and most of all help Violet know the things she should say to people and the things she shouldn't. Violet had to realize that what she said about Lisa Green's father was the reason she couldn't play with Lisa anymore. She was sick at the thought that Violet might follow in Aunt Chaia's footsteps.

When they got to the therapist's, Cara saw three kitschy garden gnomes on the front lawn. One had toppled onto the walk. Violet bent down and patted the gnome's head.

"Mommy, we have to help him," she said.

Cara was so moved by her daughter's compassion that she felt even more committed to helping her curb the behaviors that were making others so angry with her. Why should her daughter be looked at as a troublemaker when she was so sweet? Why should her daughter become at risk for mental illness? Cara set the gnome upright again. They continued to the front door and rang the bell. "Listen, the doorbell is playing 'This Old Man,'" she said.

"No it's not, Mommy. It's playing the Barney song. 'I love you/You love me/We're a happy family,'" Violet sang.

Cara hoped this would be true again. Every day something awful happened to Violet as a result of her blabbering whatever was in her head. Just last week, Violet's kindergarten teacher, Mrs. Oliver, had called to say that Violet had asked what a tummy tuck was and then reported to the class that Joey Brandon's mother was getting one that very day. Mrs. Brandon had called from the hospital, furious, to tell Mrs. Oliver that her tummy tuck was nobody else's business. She certainly hadn't told Joey, so the Brandons wanted to know if Violet's parents were in the medical field and had somehow violated her privacy. There was no other way that she could understand how Violet could have known such a thing. *Violet could get us into a lawsuit someday, reporting all these things, whether they are true or not,* Cara thought. *And worse, her Violet could end up...*oh, she didn't even want to think it again.

The front door opened. The therapist, framed in the storm door, had shaggy brown straight hair and big startled brown eyes.

"You must be the one and only Violet Sachs," the therapist said gaily. "I'm Dr. Gray Wolf. You can call me Jessica." She bent so her face was on Violet's level. Violet backed away. Jessica rose. "Come right on in," she urged and opened the door widely, as if Violet had shown great eagerness to venture inside.

The hallway had a bench painted with totems and prancing deer and teepees in brilliant colors. Violet stopped and stared at it.

"This bench has American Indian designs," Cara said.

"Like Darshan?" Violet said.

Jessica smiled. "No, Darshan sounds as if he's from India. American Indians lived in this country before we did, like my husband's ancestors. He's a member of the Chippewa tribe."

Cara had thought that Gray was Jessica's maiden name and Wolf her married name.

"Does your husband have a totem pole?" Violet asked.

"No, he doesn't. But maybe you and I could make one about you and your family," Jessica said.

"Yes, I want to," Violet said, and went off, hand-in-hand, with Jessica.

Jessica really knows how to handle children, Cara

thought as she sat on the painted bench and happily wrote out a check.

Forty-five minutes later, Violet came out of the office with a big smile and a drawing of a totem pole that had seven heads.

"That's our family," Violet said, "and all the elders. Jessica said that anybody but me are elders. On the top is the most eld, Grandpa George."

"It's a wonderful totem," Jessica said. "I learned a lot from it. And now, Violet, I'd like to talk to your mother for a little while. I have lots of toys in that basket in the corner, if you'd like to play with them."

As soon as Violet had started going through the basket, Cara accompanied Jessica into her office. The yellow room was filled with dolls and puppets and games and art supplies. Jessica sat down on a couch and gestured to the chair across from her, the only other adult-sized one in the room.

"What do you think?" Cara asked, twisting the strap of her shoulder bag.

"Violet is a brilliant child, Mrs. Sachs." Jessica said. "I could listen to her forever."

"I'm afraid she'll get badly hurt if she continues telling people's secrets," Cara said. "My mother is a psychic and she encourages Violet to think she's one, too."

"Yes, Violet was telling me about the letters that pass between them. She told me how she writes the answer to a question in your mother's letters before she opens them."

"What do you mean?" Cara asked.

"For example, your mother wrote Violet to ask if she'd

seen the DVD of *The Wizard of Oz* and before Violet even opened the letter, she wrote back, 'I like *The Wizard of Oz.*'"

Cara clicked her tongue against the roof of her mouth. "I feel betrayed. I thought my mother was just sending her stickers and Violet was sending her thank-you notes. Do you see what's going on? My mother is training Violet to be psychic no matter how much harm it brings to her. My great Aunt Chaia, who was also psychic, was in a mental hospital most of her life. It's like a big ego trip for my mother. She's making my daughter *her* daughter, no matter how much jeopardy she's putting Violet in."

"Jeopardy?" Jessica said. "Your mother is teaching Violet so much. Why Violet told me that you say she's a big storyteller when she knows something that she wasn't told. But her grandmother told her that Mark Twain—and Violet knew he was one of the most famous American storytellers—used to send and receive letters like that between himself and his friends. He'd write to them with questions and on the very same day, he'd receive a letter from them with the answers to the questions he'd asked. He called it 'letter crossing.' Who even knew Mark Twain was psychic? Isn't that fascinating?"

"No, it's enraging. My mother knows I'm against her instigating Violet to become a psychic, but she does it anyway. I feel trapped. I love my mother, but I can't trust her with my child. I don't want Violet to be psychic."

"We give birth to our children," Jessica said, "but we cannot control who they are fundamentally. I'd stake my reputation on the fact that Violet isn't in any danger psychologically. If I do find that Violet has this gift, I can't tell you that

I'm going to stamp it out of her. I've gone on vision quests with my husband and other Native Americans. We fasted and went through the wintery forest until our minds opened to what we could not have seen before—our animal spirit guides. Mine is a hawk with a lion's mane. Maybe your daughter has this ability without putting herself in extreme circumstances."

Violet's pediatrician didn't tell me that this psychologist she was recommending had starved and frozen herself to get visions, Cara thought, or I would never have brought Violet here. What was Dr. Cohen thinking?

"It's such a wonderful talent," Jessica went on. "Others need to learn to be tolerant of Violet. And I'd like to help you change your reaction to Violet's sensibility. If she's comfortable at home, she'll do fine anywhere, no matter what anyone else thinks about her."

Cara felt accused. She wished she had listened to Dan and not brought Violet here at all. Jessica was giving her an assessing look.

"You must think I'm awful for not supporting what you see as my daughter's gift," Cara said. "But you don't seem to understand what the cost is to her. I'm just trying to protect her from pain. Isn't that part of a mother's job?"

Jessica just kept looking at her in a kindly, therapist way.

"Aren't you going to say something?" Cara asked.

"This is a place where you can hear your own thoughts without judgment or criticism or fear. What are you thinking?" Jessica asked.

Cara looked down at her hands. "This is the exact opposite direction that I wanted to take."

"It's not what you wanted," Jessica said, "but it's what you need. You have to learn to separate your issues with your mother from your issues with Violet in order to be able to decide what direction to take. You need to stop projecting your mother and your great aunt's experiences on Violet and respect who your daughter is."

Cara began to think of how she'd shouted at Violet after what had happened with Lisa Green. Shouting at her child, something she'd promised herself never to do. She thought of herself yanking the phone from Violet when she was talking to Miriam. She thought about having gotten rid of her landline so that Violet couldn't call Miriam on her own. Was that in Violet's best interest? Could this cause as much trouble as sharing Aunt Chaia's DNA? "I'm thinking that maybe I've been too hard on Violet," Cara admitted.

"It's only natural," Jessica said. "You want the best for her. From what I heard from Violet, the children don't seem to be upset by what she says. It's their parents who go ballistic. Whatever children say, the adults are accountable for keeping their heads."

It was true, Cara thought. Yesterday Lisa Green had slipped Violet one of her Silly Bands. She'd play with Violet in a heartbeat if it wasn't for her mother.

Jessica opened her appointment book. "Same time next week?"

Cara felt such relief when she agreed. Here was someone who could guide her with Violet, someone she could trust like you were supposed to be able to trust your mother.

The door opened and Violet came in, holding a tiny worry

doll, her own face scrunched with worry. "Do you have a boy named Izzy?" she asked Jessica.

"Why yes," Jessica said, laughing. "It's his nickname, short for Istaqa, which means Coyote Man."

"You hit Izzy," Violet said. "And you pushed him, too."

Cara heard the catch in Jessica's breath. "I never hit him."

"Yes," Violet insisted, "with a package of frozen fish. 'Ouchie, ouch,' he said and made a hat with his hands so you couldn't do it again."

Jessica stared a moment, her mouth open. Then she put on her glasses and studied her appointment book. "What was I thinking? I won't have time next week after all. I just realized that I can't possibly take on a new client at this time."

It took Cara a moment to let in what had happened. "Oh, well," she said, "at least you've had a glimpse of what I've been talking about. It's not fun having your secrets exposed, is it? But of course, you're the one who really knows how to respect a child's sensibility."

Jessica's face was vermillion.

"Can I have this little, little doll?" Violet asked Jessica with her sweetest smile.

"Put it down, honey," Cara said. "It's a worry doll. Other children have told their worries to it. We don't want to take their worries home with us."

"I want it," Violet said. "I want this doll and this doll wants to go home with me."

"This toy is here for all the children to play with," Jessica said, "but I'll make an exception for you. You can have the doll." She opened the door, looking eager to get Violet out.

Cara thought about the two-hundred-dollar consultation fee, only sixty dollars of which was reimbursed by the insurance company. "Come, Violet. You can bring the doll with you."

In the car, Violet said, "we could get an elf for our garden like Jessica's. We could buy marionettes of mommies and daddies and children. I won't twist up the strings."

"I'm sure we can find toys like that for our house," Cara said, her foot heavy on the gas pedal. How glad she was to get away!

"I'm going to call this doll Mimi and tell her all my worries," Violet said.

That's the girl in the story I named after my mother, Cara remembered, the girl who told everyone's secrets.

"Mimi," Violet told the doll, "I am worried that Grandma Miriam misses me too much like I miss her. I don't get to see Grandma Miriam hardly ever."

"You just saw Grandma Miriam three weeks ago," Cara said

Without answering her, Violet went right on talking softly to her worry doll. "I'm worried because Grandma Miriam misses me so much like I miss her. I worry that Grandma Miriam is sad. I'm worried because Grandma Miriam is going to have big troubles soon and she doesn't even have a worry doll to tell them to."

"Grandma Miriam is fine," Cara said. "You're a child. You're not supposed to be worried about grownups."

"Mimi," Cara heard Violet whisper, "I'll talk to you when we're alone."

Cara's stomach clenched. What if Violet wasn't just making up stories? By the way Jessica had reacted, Cara was sure she had bopped her son with a package of frozen fish. So if Violet was telling the truth, then Miriam was about to have big troubles. Was she sick? Dying?

XV

EVEN THOUGH KAYLEE HAD MADE A FOUR-MONTH commitment to work at the ashram, the minimum that you could, the guru gave her special permission to come home after six weeks when she told him she had to go to the lawyer to sign the papers and get her mother's inheritance. She'd taken the Metro North home all by herself and talked to everyone she met about the ashram, as if she was advertising for it. That was what the guru said everyone should do, and she got an accountant and a dentist interested in going up for a stay. She couldn't wait to tell the guru. She couldn't wait to walk out of her cabin and be in nature again. As she squashed her sweaters into her duffle bag, she admired her hands—calloused and dry now, working hands. And her whole body was different: strong, and she could bend this way and that.

Tom was in the shower, the water pipes groaning. She packed up more sweaters and socks and three pair of boots. It was so cold up there, but there weren't bus fumes and honking horns. Kneeling at the dresser, she thought about all the money that was in the bank now in her own account. The first she'd ever had. Tom had told her she could do whatever she wanted with it. It was hers, not his. "You can talk to that psychic every day if you want," he'd said. But since Miriam had told her to go to the ashram, Kaylee hadn't needed to call her and had been too busy to even phone her to tell her that.

The bathroom door opened and Tom came out in a cloud of steam with just a towel around his waist. Black hair brushed from the hollow of his chest. His knees faced each other. He had a grin on his face. "All those weekends I drove to the assram, knowing I couldn't sleep with my wife, and now I got you all to myself."

He came toward her, held his hand out to her. She took it and rose from the floor. He dropped his towel and drew her to him.

"I can't," she said.

"You can't what?"

"I can't have sex with you."

"You've got your monthly or something?" he asked.

She could lie to him. She could say yes. "No, I took a vow of celibacy at the ashram. It's part of the path to spiritual enlightenment."

Tom just stared at her. Then he picked up his towel and wrapped it around himself again. He started to laugh and then he started to cry. "That guru is robbing you from me," he said. "He's taking your mind from me, your affections from me, and even your body from me." He got into bed, covered himself, and turned to the wall.

Kaylee felt bruised on the inside. How could she hurt Tom like this? How could she? She got into bed beside him, but she couldn't bring herself to touch him. If she did, she felt as if everything she'd worked toward would spill out of her. She'd end up telling Tom what had happened and he would never understand. The guru had invited her to his own cabin for a private dinner a week after Tom left. They had sat on a Persian carpet at a low table. Besides the bowls of ashram food, he had wine, strong wine. "Drink, drink," he'd insisted. "It will help you lose the small self you have known, the self you have called 'Kaylee.' Your new name at the ashram will be Kaylee-ay. Your fears will drop away like leaves in autumn and you will be reborn." He filled her cup three times. He confided that his name had been Angelo and that he used to be Catholic like she was, and how free he had been since he had let it all go. He told her that her chakras needed opening to release her ki force and he did it with his own body. A heat rose through her just from the memory of the guru's hands on her, his face in her hair, his strong body against hers, her pulse ticking in places she never knew it could. If she told Tom any of this, he would see it as just sex instead of enlightenment and get even more hurt than he already was. Miriam had told her that her sex life would get better, but Miriam hadn't known that it would be a chakra opening.

"Is your chakra opened yet?" the guru had asked her, looking down into her eyes, his loose hair a tent around her head.

"Yes, yes," she cried out, just as Miriam had when Kaylee asked her, "Will my sex life get better?"

Tom was still facing the wall. He might look dopey at the ashram, but people loved him in Brooklyn. Even she sort of loved him in Brooklyn, but not in the way she loved the guru. She was glad Tom couldn't stand the ashram. Otherwise she'd have to be plain old Kaylee instead of Kaylee-ay. But if she had a magic wish it would be to be at the ashram while Tom was somewhere nearby in a place where he was comfortable.

The next morning, she left on her own, taking the Metro North back to the ashram, but this time she didn't talk to anyone else. She only thought of Tom saying to her, "Kaylee, you are my family and I'm your family, not that guru, not those weirdos floating in and out of that place. Me and you."

When she got back to the ashram, she saw a glossy brochure right on her pillow about a condo development that was being built near the ashram. It wasn't a real photo, but something they do with computers to make it real-looking. There was even a real-looking deer nibbling on real-looking grass. She read the bullet points. The condo was going to be feng shuied, all the buildings in a circle for harmony. There would be big sliding glass doors and tall, wide windows, and three acres of grounds with hiking trails, a sort of ashram away from the ashram. There was an insert announcing a free dinner in a restaurant right in town where they would show you the blueprints and a film, and you'd meet the architect, and other people who were interested in buying, people who might be your future neighbors. "Transportation arranged," it said. She had her mother's money now. She could use it to buy a condo so that she and Tom would have a home nearby when he came up on the weekends. And when he retired, he could live there full-time. Maybe she would even have sex with him sometimes to make him happy. She wouldn't have to tell the guru. After all, following the Ayurvedic diet and chanting was a way to stay on the spiritual path, wasn't it?

"Lee-ay," she said, "did you get one of these brochures too?"

Lee-ay looked at it and shrugged, her gray braid lifting on her shoulder. "I don't think so. But I wouldn't need it. I'm living at the ashram for the rest of this lifetime and more if I can arrange it," she said with a dreamy look in her eyes.

Kaylee remembered what the guru had said. *There are no accidents. Nothing happens by chance. It's all part of a plan.* Was this condo part of hers? She clutched the brochure to her heart. She would go to that dinner. If she liked the condo, she'd buy it without even having to ask anyone. The wood stove had gone low. One of the women was feeding it wood, but Kaylee felt so warm that she probably wouldn't need those sweaters she'd brought. *Angelo,* she thought. It was like knowing the biggest secret ever.

XVI

As Miriam waited on line at Poultry Mart, she doodled on her shopping list. The borders of her list filled with tiny eyes. Eyes, she'd been thinking about them all day. She covered her left eye and began reading the sign on the wall behind the counter: Sante Fe chicken, bbq chicken, chicken pot pie, grilled chicken cutlets, spicy baked floppy chicken..." Her mouth watered but her vision was clear. The same with her right eye.

She phoned Rory. "Did you ever get to the ophthalmologist?" she asked.

"Last week. I'm A-okay. First time in years Dr. Adida didn't have to strengthen my prescription." It was his lunch hour. He was chewing. "Please don't start in on the dentist and the perio guy," he said. "And don't call Cara to ask about her eyes or Dan's or Violet's. She won't be as patient as I am about it."

"Patient! Ugh, Rory, that's so patronizing. What? You have to count to ten every time you think of me?"

"It's moments like these when I get Cara's point," he said. "You didn't even say hello before you started in about your psychic hunch about my eyes. I just got off the phone with Cara. We had a good conversation about whether she should try to deal with an American factory, even though it will hike the price of her hats. And we talked about Violet.

"Rory, you know she hasn't called me for two weeks. I don't suppose you said, 'How about giving your mother a call?'"

"I can't get in between the two of you," Rory said.

She was broiling. "Chicken!" she yelled at him, and the man behind the counter said, "What kind?"

She ordered the drumsticks that Cara used to love as a child. She thought about when Cara was a teenager, the long, late-night talks they had had while Rory slept, the lunches they had eaten at Bruce's Bakery while Rory worked at Mirror. Now it was his time with Cara, she thought, but she couldn't help feeling cheated.

Outside, the window of Vision Associates caught her attention. All those glasses in the window without eyes. She itched to draw pupils in them. It was eerie, this whole eye-thing that was bugging her all day, as if she didn't have enough to worry about.

KAYLEE, HER NOSE ALMOST AGAINST THE BATHROOM mirror, could see that her eyes were definitely getting smaller. Her braid was ratty and her skin was like paste. She startled when she saw Tom's reflection behind her. Everything had happened so fast that when she woke up in the morning, she still expected to be in her bunk at the ashram, even though she had been home two weeks. She had slept in her yoga suit since and barely had the energy to brush her teeth.

"Stop looking at yourself already," Tom said.

"Tom, don't you see how my eyes are getting smaller and

my eyelashes have disappeared? God is erasing me feature by feature because I lost my mother's inheritance."

"Come on," he said. "Your baby browns are as big and beautiful as the day I first looked into them and you rubbed all your eyelashes out from all that crying. So you lost your mother's insurance money. Money is just paper. You can wipe your ass with it."

"You're mad at me for buying that condo," she said. "I just know it."

"You're so innocent, Kaylee, like a rube. You wouldn't know a scam from a clam. Who else wouldn't know that you put a down payment on something, not give over the whole amount at once?"

Her pasty face burned.

"All I'm mad at," Tom said, "is that you didn't tell me before you invested with those crooks. You should've told me first, is all I'm saying."

"But I knew if I did, you'd talk me out of it."

"And that would have been the right thing to do," Tom said, "because then you'd still have the money and you wouldn't be depressed."

She put her hand over his mouth in the mirror, like she was shutting him up.

"It wasn't your fault, Kaylee. It was the guru's for teaching you to think like that. You get a brochure from a land developer on your pillow at that ashram and you think, hey, this means God arranged it for my highest good. Meanwhile, I bet the guru was in on this. You went and told him that you got your mother's money, didn't you?"

Kaylee couldn't answer him. Her throat knotted from the memory of going to the guru's cabin that night to tell him that she'd bought the condo, and seeing him hurry into his robe while Lee-ay was still was naked on his futon.

"You made me take a vow of celibacy," she'd yelled at him, "promising myself to you for purification and no other while you diddle with other women?" The realization that she had been diddled with had made her burst into tears.

"Listen," the guru said to her, "my role here includes many responsibilities."

Kaylee smacked his face hard and ran out of there. When she was in her bunk, her knees to her chin, her arms wrapped tightly around them, she thought, *That was what I was going to do to Tom. I was going to keep allowing the guru to open my chakras without caring how much it would hurt Tom. Chakra opening! The guru fucked me! Fuck, fuck, fuck.* Coals of shame fell on her. She didn't think she could ever feel worse, but the next day, when she called the condo developers to cancel the deal because she didn't want to be anywhere near the guru anymore and she had twenty-four hours to change her mind, she found out their phone had been disconnected. She panicked. She didn't know what to do. How could she tell Tom what she'd done when she was trying to prove that she could stand on her own? She called the bank and asked them to stop her check.

"It's already been cashed," the man at the bank told her.

She had gotten on a train and dragged herself back to Brooklyn. Tom had called the lawyer. The lawyer had said that he would see what he could do, but those crooks probably had different names now and were in a different state, maybe even out of the country.

"Kaylee," Tom said now, "come out with me. We'll go buy *The Post* and get a cup of coffee."

She shook her head. "I can't go out. If I go out, people will be saying that they're sorry about Mother and then I'll feel worse for losing Mom's inheritance. She scrimped all those years to give me her money and look what I went and did."

"You're supposed to be the one who is so spiritual, so non-material, and here you are, kicking your own butt because you lost $250,000."

Kaylee pivoted around and faced him. "You do care about the money, Tom, otherwise you wouldn't have said the exact amount I lost."

"Jesus," he said. "There's nothing I can say or do right for you anymore." He looked like someone had let the air out of him.

"I'm sorry, Tom. I'm just a mess now. I'll get better. You just go pick up *The Post* without me."

"I'm afraid to leave you like this," he said. "I won't."

"I'll be all right. You have to go back to work Monday anyway. You can't take any more time off. I'll wait at the window. You'll see me waving to you. And when you get back, you'll see me there. You have to let me be alone. I have to sort things out in my mind."

He put his hands on her shoulders. "I love you to death, Kaylee. You know that. No matter what you done."

She wondered if he knew what she'd done with the guru. It made it harder to look him in the eyes. "Go on. I want to read my horoscope. Go get the paper." She went past him to the front closet, got out his down jacket, and held it out for him to put his arms in the sleeves.

"Okay," he said. "Okay."

She waited a few minutes and then went to the window. It was a week before Christmas. Most of the neighbors had colored lights blinking in their windows. The sky was bright as if it was lit up, too. Looking up at her, Tom shaded his eyes. She waved to him, waved hard and smiled big so he wouldn't worry. She watched him walk away, getting smaller, and then he turned down the avenue and she couldn't see him anymore.

part three

XVII

Miriam, slumped over her office desk, hadn't slept since Friday and today was Monday. She couldn't make herself catnap. She was even too jumpy to meditate. This was a warning. Her obsession with eyes had finally passed, but something was terribly wrong, that she was sure of. The last time she'd felt like this was when Rory had had to have an emergency appendectomy.

She closed her eyes, visualized Rory standing before her. She imagined her mind becoming an x-ray machine. There were no new black spots on Rory, just the ones from his old knee injury and the place where his appendix used to be. But she got no relief. She was as sick to her stomach as she'd been three years ago, when Dan's plane to Michigan bucked in the sky from a flight disturbance. Was Dan going to have some kind of accident? Was Cara in danger? Violet? she thought with a wrench.

Her phone rang, startling her. Kaylee's number was on her Caller ID. She hadn't heard from her in at least two months, maybe more.

"Hello, Kaylee. It's been awhile, hasn't it?" She flipped through the calendar in her mind. "Two and a half months, to be exact." Then she sensed a tidal wave of darkness smacking against her. She'd call Cara right after she got off the phone to see if everything was okay.

"This isn't Kaylee. It's Tom Fiorelli, her husband."

Miriam, startled again, could see his large nose, big brown eyes, and his dark pompadour. "Are you calling for your own reading?"

"No way. I'm calling to tell you that Kaylee is dead and it's all your fault," and he slammed down the phone.

Miriam's brain did a whirligig. Her heart shot up to her throat. She had thought someone in her family was in danger. She tried to see what had happened to Kaylee, but she was so distraught that she could barely see the white wall in front of her.

Miriam sat there, so cold and still that she felt as if she knew what death of the body meant. She slapped herself all over to get the blood going.

"Kaylee, Kaylee, please come to me. I want to tell you how sorry I am." But she heard nothing, saw no one. She put on a white noise CD to help her focus, a rippling brook. She pictured Kaylee as she might be as a spirit, all light and swimming in air. And suddenly she saw an open window, and her chest tightened. Had Kaylee jumped?

Miriam got up and paced her office. She had told Kaylee to go to that ashram against Mrs. O'Brien's spirit's wishes. Miriam wanted to confess to someone. She thought of her rabbi, a sharp-minded man with piercing eyes. If she told him, she could imagine him next Yom Kippur, the Day of Atonement, looking directly at her when he spoke of the sin of arrogance, because that's what it really was, wasn't it? Having the nerve to tell other people what they should be doing with their lives without taking the counsel of the spirits. She needed a darkened booth with a window where you didn't have to face your confessor, where he wouldn't even have to know your name. What she needed to do was find a priest to talk to.

A quick whiff of lavender and a shimmer in the air and there was Bubbie, standing close to Miriam's desk, her hands on her hips, a hankie tucked into her sleeve.

"*Nu?*" she said. "Just once you don't make a hit and already you're looking to sign up with the other team?"

"Oh, Bubbie, I know it would have been disrespectful to you to go to a priest, maybe disrespectful to the priest, too, but I was too ashamed to tell you what I did."

"And you think your Bubbie wouldn't know already?" she said, her round silver-framed glasses slipping down her tiny nose.

"Bubbie, did you ever cause anyone's death?"

Bubbie gave a long look to her right where the past lay and feelings began to agitate her face like a tic "You don't cause nothing," Bubbie said forcefully. "Each year it is written who shall live and who shall die and on what day and what time. No matter where you hide, death will find you at the exact moment it's supposed to."

"But Bubbie, you didn't really answer me," Miriam said, as the scent of Bubbie's lavender talc diminished along with Bubbie.

When Miriam started down the stairs, her mother's spirit was waiting for her on the landing. She had on a tall, black-feathered gendarme hat, the only one of her hats that Miriam hated.

"Of course you didn't see that harm was going to come to that poor girl," her mother said. "You didn't see it because it was a chance to fight her mother, and what do you like better than fighting mothers?"

"Mom, please, I feel horrible enough already."

"Maybe not," her mother said. "If you did, you'd stop playing mind games with Violet. Just remember your poor Aunt Chaia and that will keep you in check."

As soon as she said that her mother checked out.

Miriam lowered herself onto the stairs, her head in her hands. She'd pushed her great aunt, Chaia, so far out of her mind that she didn't even visit her grave anymore, didn't even light a memorial candle for her on the anniversary of her death. It was unbearable to think of beautiful Aunt Chaia who had shouted people's secrets at them in the street and became so hated that she couldn't go outside anymore. But Chaia couldn't stop. "Yoo hoo, yes you, Mr. Zalinsky, you pawned your wife's engagement ring and claimed it was stolen." "You, the woman with the big belly. That's not your husband's baby in there." "And you, Mr. Kilpatrick, you take a yardstick to your son now, but he'll take a shillelagh to you as soon as he's big enough." She couldn't go out in the street anymore because people threw stones at her and once the contents of a chamber pot.

Bubbie, who had been afraid to leave Chaia alone in the apartment, had gone downstairs for just a few minutes to pick out new eyeglasses from the pushcart vender. When she came back, she found Chaia trying to hang herself with a curtain pull. Bubbie had no choice. Chaia was only fifteen then, a girl who had never even been kissed by a boy, had never gone to a party yet, but Bubbie had to commit her to that state hospital where she lived for sixty years. Miriam respected the sacredness of life, but she couldn't help thinking sometimes that maybe Aunt Chaia would have been better off if Bubbie had tried on a few more pairs of spectacles.

Miriam's hands were wet with her tears. How could she have been so pushy about Violet being psychic when she knew where it could lead? She had learned her lesson. She wanted to call Cara and tell her right away, but if she mentioned Aunt Chaia to her now, she might just agitate her, and Cara was already prickly enough these days. If there was a lemonade to be squeezed from this horror, it was that now it was clear to Miriam what a pain in the behind she'd been to Cara since Violet was born. No wonder she'd been shut out of her daughter's life and Violet's. She would stop encouraging Violet to be psychic. She had to. Miriam knew that she was causing stress in Cara's marriage as well.

Within the hour she was in her Honda on the Jackie Robinson Parkway, headed for Tom's apartment. She had tried to call him, but as soon as he'd heard her voice, he'd hung up on her. Some nerve she had going to his place anyway, she thought, but she felt propelled, as if someone was pushing her to. Even with the heat on high, she was still cold.

Nothing could have prepared her for what she saw when she pulled up to the curb. The sidewalk was broken and cordoned off, and she knew that she had been right, that Kaylee had jumped to her death. In her mind, Miriam could hear the thud. She almost drove away, but the thought of Tom, whom she'd made a widower, wouldn't allow her to. She got out and stopped at the cordoned-off blocks of cement, the place where Kaylee had died. It was holy ground.

"I'm so sorry, Kaylee," Miriam said. Her wrists wobbled and she almost dropped the Pyrex dish of lasagna she'd brought Tom that was supposed to be for Rory's dinner.

She checked the buzzers. Fiorelli was 6C. Kaylee had fallen six stories. Miriam's heart took a plunge. A delivery boy came in and put down his carton to hold the door open for her. She hesitated, but thanked him and went in.

The bare lobby was so familiar to her. Kaylee had once asked her if she knew who was stealing the furniture, but there were too many people to name a single culprit. Moving men had hoisted the lobby couch and chairs into their truck, along with the furniture of a tenant who was leaving. Had it been at the tenant's request or had the movers just helped themselves? And there had been a woman in a fur coat visiting one of the older women who had left with a table lamp.

When she got off the elevator, she found Tom's apartment and rang the bell. She saw his eye in the peephole. He blinked once, then opened the door without asking who it was.

She handed him the lasagna. "I'm Miriam."

He was unshaven and had on a rumpled plaid flannel shirt and black jeans. His dark eyes were swimming with anger and grief.

"What the hell are you doing here?" he said, his voice like a growl.

He could kill me, she thought with Rory's dinner still in her trembling hands. "Even if you're not hungry, take this. I'm sure people will be stopping by."

"No, they won't. It was so shocking to the whole building when Kaylee jumped. The neighbors are too elderly to take this stress. Old lady McEnroe came in and I had to give her smelling salts because she almost fainted thinking about what happened." Then he glared at Miriam.

Miriam was so upset that she thought she would need smelling salts too. She leaned into Tom's doorway, set the lasagna down on a little table in his foyer, and turned to go.

"Wait," he said. "Do you want to see the window she jumped from?"

Miriam didn't. "Yes," she said.

The apartment was gray-blue, with old furniture inherited from Tom and Kaylee's families. If she had a moment, she could probably have told which pieces were O'Briens' and which Fiorellis'. Miriam followed him to a doorway and looked inside. There was a big bed with an angel carved on the dark oak headboard and a beat-up easy chair. The window was small. Kaylee must have had to hunch to get her leg over the sill, and then the other. Miriam clapped her hand over her mouth so she wouldn't scream.

"Good that you're seeing it," Tom said. "I want you to have it in your head every day for the rest of your life like I will."

She nodded solemnly. He had let her come in to punish her and she deserved it.

He walked to the living room and plunked himself down

on the gray couch, the seat cushions worn and bowed. Still wearing her coat, she sat in a gold corduroy tufted chair with a tall, pointy back and wooden arms. A Fiorelli chair, she thought. Tom crossed his arms over his chest and stared at her. Miriam chewed her lip in silence.

"You were like a second mother to Kaylee. She went to the guru because you told her to. That was the death of her. Kaylee trusted strangers and fakes like you instead of her own family. If you're psychic like you claim to be, you should have known what she was going to do. You should have called 911."

Like a spike in her chest, Miriam remembered having seen a gravestone when she told Kaylee to go to the ashram, but she'd thought it had meant that Kaylee's spirit would die if she stayed home, not that Kaylee herself would die if she went. Miriam had thought that Kaylee was doing well, that she had found her own inner resources. She'd glimpsed her sitting in a half-lotus posture with lots of other people, her face serene and a smile curling her lips. Now Miriam was a woman with her tongue cut out.

"That guru there taught her she could have many lives," Tom said, "so why should she care about this one? She could blow it and become the Queen of Sheba or some movie star." He was quiet again. Then his hands balled into fists. Miriam would have run for the door, but she didn't think her legs could carry her.

"I should drive to that ashram and wring the guru's neck and watch to see if he becomes a cockroach in his next life like he should have been in this one." Tom narrowed his eyes at Miriam with his top lip drawn back from his teeth, as if she were a cockroach he could step on. "The guru took my wife from me. He knew just when she got her mother's money and he hooked her up with phony land developers who stole it all and disappeared."

The windfall her father said she'd come into, Miriam thought.

Tom shifted on the couch. "After she lost that money, she stopped going to the ashram. Good, I thought. We'll be together again. Jesus, who knew what was going to happen?"

Miriam pictured the cordoned-off sidewalk and shivered.

"Kaylee was so depressed when she came home from the ashram that she thought her eyes were getting smaller."

Miriam stiffened. She had been fixated on eyes, but never knew she was picking up messages about Kaylee.

"I took more time off to be with her," Tom said. "I was scared to leave her alone. On Friday, when I came back from getting the paper, there was a big crowd outside, all looking down. Brooklyn is full of nosey parkers just waiting for something like this to happen. I forced my way through them and saw Kaylee lying all crumpled and bleeding on the sidewalk. The curtains were blowing out like they were saying goodbye to her."

Miriam could feel the buttons in the tufted chair like nails in her spine. *I caused this.* No matter how much Tom would blast her, she had to listen. He needed to talk and she needed to hear every detail.

His face was twitching as he struggled again to get his composure. "It took four cops to tear me off her."

Miriam's skin was too tight, as if she would burst out of it. Was that how Kaylee had felt before she jumped? Miriam had to stay quiet. Who else did Tom have to talk to?

"On February 20, thirteen years ago, Kaylee and me got married at St. Teresa's over on Flatbush. Tomorrow, at nine, her funeral will be there. I always bought her roses. This year I'll have to bring them to her grave." He broke into big heaving sobs.

Miriam felt helpless. "Please, may I come to the funeral?"

"How dare you ask me that?" he snapped. "Father DiCosmo says you should never go to a psychic, that it's a sin." He dropped his head into his hands. "God, I hope Kaylee's soul is at peace. After her mother died, she went and gave up the Church. She thought all her praying for that money made her mother die quicker. That must have been why this happened." He lowered his hand to his lap and glared at Miriam again. "You so-called psychics fleece people to think you can talk to the dead. Don't you think I'd love to hear something from Kaylee?"

Miriam was shocked. Tom, who didn't believe in psychics, was hinting for her to contact Kaylee. "I could try," she said quietly.

"Oh, sure, sure, like you can do it," he said, but he was leaning forward, expectant.

She closed her eyes. A vision of Kaylee now would be better than lasagna, she thought, but she didn't see anything, not a glimmer or a flicker.

"It's too soon," Miriam said. "Her spirit isn't settled yet."

His eyes flashed again. His jaw set. "You people have excuses for everything, don't you?"

"Tom, may I come to Kaylee's funeral?" she asked again. "I want to come out of respect for her and for you."

"You came here uninvited," he said, "so it looks like I can't stop you." He sprang up from the couch and opened the front door. The lasagna was still on the foyer table.

"Keep the dish," Miriam said.

That night Miriam cried into Rory's graying chest hairs. "I caused Kaylee's suicide," she told him. "Her husband, Tom, is furious with me."

"I hope he doesn't sue," Rory said.

"Rory! I expected support from you."

"I'd better have our lawyer go over your corporation insurance to see if this Tom could make a case."

"I hate you," Miriam said.

Rory rolled over and went to sleep like a man with an easy conscience.

AT THE DOOR OF THE CHURCH, TOM, TO HER SURPRISE, looked almost glad to see her. Miriam could see why. Nobody else was there.

He must have noticed her bewilderment. "I couldn't ask the neighbors," he murmured. "They'd be whispering about her suicide, and Father DiCosmo is doing his best to make it look like Kaylee stuck it out until the natural end of her life. Suicide is against the rules of the Church, you know. I wouldn't ask the guys from work, I don't want them here. I didn't want them to look at her when she was alive, so why would I want them to look at her now that she's dead? Nobody would come from the ashram. They don't believe in death."

As they went into the church, Miriam began to perspire and had to resist patting water on her face from the baptismal font. She began to sneeze. There were red anniversary roses all around Kaylee's casket and lining both sides of the aisle. Miriam was fine with outdoor plants, but once florists got hold of them, it was trouble. She kept sneezing. She was worried she'd spoil Kaylee's funeral, but by the time she got to the first row, she mercifully settled down to watery eyes and a runny nose.

During the mass, Miriam tried to keep her gaze soft as she searched for Kaylee's spirit. Kaylee, she said silently, if you're here, I want you to know that I was only trying to get you out of the apartment, give you new interests. I had no idea that you would be hurt in any way. Please believe me. She prayed for Kaylee to appear to her, and still she saw no sign of her spirit. I must be putting too much pressure on myself, she thought, and tried to relax, but all her nerves were sizzling like a fork stuck in a toaster

When the priest sprinkled holy water on Kaylee's casket, Tom passed Miriam a remembrance card. It was brain-boggling. Was it Kaylee photo-shopped to look like the Madonna? Miriam almost expected the card to speak to her with Kaylee's childlike voice. She turned it over.

"In loving memory of my wife, Kaylee O'Brien Fiorelli, from her loving husband, Thomas Frances Fiorelli," then the date of her birthday and her death. Kaylee was thirty-two years old now, only thirty-two, Cara's age. So much would still have been possible.

"It's beautiful, Tom. I will keep it always."

"You're coming to the burial, right?"

She was glad she'd come to the funeral. He'd really needed her there. But she hadn't considered going to the cemetery. She almost said, "My husband is waiting for me at home" when she realized how cruel that would be. No one would be waiting home for Tom.

"All right," she said. He wanted her to go in the limo with him, but she insisted on taking her own car. When she turned on the ignition, she sat there a moment. "Kaylee, please show yourself to me. I need to know that you know how sorry I am."

At the cemetery, while Kaylee's coffin was being lowered into the grave, Miriam saw Tom wobble as if he'd fall in too. She grabbed his arm and he leaned on her, sobbing. As the priest said more prayers, it began to rain, a cold rain. No one had an umbrella. Miriam had bought white roses for Kaylee from a vendor who had been selling them at the gate. She had planned to throw them in one by one, but with Tom so unsteady and the rain falling harder, she tossed in the whole bouquet with the plastic cone on as well.

There was no sign of Kaylee's spirit. She prayed that Tom would be able to endure his loss. She prayed that Kaylee's spirit would be at rest. If it gave Kaylee comfort to be with her mother again, let her mother find her. If Kaylee wanted to be with her father, let him know the way to her. And if there was any time left over, let Kaylee forgive me, Miriam added.

There was a long line to leave the cemetery. The flower vendor was still there, trying to sell his roses in the rain. The exhaust from the cars in front of Miriam rose up like a cloud. Her breath fogged the window. She put on her low beams. In the eerie shine before her, she saw a small fat woman with a gray bouffant that didn't flatten even in the rain, a spirit in a black dress with a black net circle pinned to the top of her hair. It was Mrs. O'Brien. Miriam would know Kaylee's mother anywhere.

"I told you to tell Kaylee not to go to the ashram, but you went against me. You lied to her, lied!"

Then the horn of the car behind Miriam honked again and Mrs. O'Brien was gone. When Kaylee and her mother were reunited, Miriam could imagine Mrs. O'Brien revving up Kaylee's animosity. "That Miriam was your undoing," she'd say. *Kaylee will never forgive me,* Miriam thought. And she didn't feel as if she deserved to be forgiven.

When Miriam got home, she was glad Rory wasn't there. She couldn't let him comfort her while poor Tom was in his apartment all by himself and with the rain still falling on Kaylee's grave and her spirit who knew where.

Over the next week, Miriam only answered the readings that she'd already booked and didn't call back any of the prospective clients. All she could think of was, *What if I do them harm?* When Amy Miller called to ask about whether or not her son would succeed in law school, Miriam got an image of the scales of justice over his head. Still, she worried if his parents paid for him to go to law school, he might not pass the bar exam and kill himself over it. "This is a family decision," Miriam had said, and returned Amy's money.

She had also returned the money to a man who had wanted to retire to Las Vegas and wasn't sure if he could sell his house on Long Island. She gave a common sense answer instead of a psychic one. "Always sell before you buy," she advised, and returned his money because she didn't trust herself anymore.

The same thing happened when a woman called who wanted to have a psychic reunion with her dead father. If she couldn't see Kaylee's spirit, whom she desperately needed to, Miriam lost faith that she'd ever be able to see the spirits of strangers' loved ones. She gave her back her money too.

After two weeks of this, there was no money left for advertising and no clients. With all her free time, she missed Violet more and more. She thought of the Mark Twain letter Violet had sent and how disappointed she must have been to not get back the answer she wanted, that Grandma Miriam was coming to stay, not just for a weekend.

When Rory came home, she said, "I have such a desire to spend time with Violet. I think that's the only thing that will heal me."

"Mim, don't push yourself on them. It will only be trouble."

It was cold but she went out for a fast walk. The sidewalk had ice patches here and there, but she couldn't look at the sidewalk without thinking of Kaylee's jump. As soon as she got back, she phoned Cara. "Hi, what's doing?" she said with as much casualness as she could muster.

"Is something wrong, Mom?"

Who's the psychic here? Miriam thought. "No, I'm fine," she said, the phone cord tightened around her finger. "It's just nice to hear your voice."

Before long, Cara said that she had to go. Conversation was empty, Miriam thought, when you couldn't tell the truth.

XVIII

IT WAS MID-JANUARY BUT WEIRDLY WARM OUT, SO
Cara took Violet to Federal Hill Park. Violet was safe in
the playground so Cara, on a bench with a cashmere scarf
wrapped around her neck, gazed out over the water. Her
mother had always encouraged her to meditate, but concen-
trating on her breathing or chanting "om" only made her
antsy. Looking out over the water was the closest she could
come to meditation. Glinting in the winter sun, the water
looked as if a leprechaun had flung his pot of gold coins
across it. Cara waited for peace to come, but she felt as raw
as she had this morning when she'd woken up at five a.m. to
make sure she saw Dan before he left for the lab. He'd been
so secretive lately. Skulking was how she'd describe it. He'd
drive home, sort the mail, then take off again. She felt like
checking his personal computer to make sure...make sure of
what? She swallowed hard. Dan, her darling Dan. As soon as
he'd stirred, she'd tapped him on his chest. "Let me in, Dan."

"Wha?" he'd said, blinking at her.

"Please, tell me what's happening between us. Please, don't
make me go around with all this worry and fear. I can handle
whatever it is," she said, although she was sure that if he told
her he was in love with someone else, she would burst apart.

He'd pulled her close. "Listen, last time I found a project, I told everyone about it and disappointed myself and everyone else."

"I wasn't disappointed in you," Cara said. "I was just disappointed *for* you. I knew what it meant to you. Loving someone means that you care about how they feel." Her eyes welled with tears. "Don't you care that I'm unhappy? Don't you care that Violet has no play dates anymore? That she doesn't get invited to birthday parties? The other mothers are doing their best to avoid me too."

"We have to help her accept herself first, "Dan said.

"Oh, and how are you helping her do that? By never being here?"

He'd scowled at her. "You give me no credit," he said.

"Hey, I don't deserve that," she countered, but he was already out of bed and starting his day. If only she had a normal mother, she could call her and tell her what was going on to unburden her heart. But her mother would believe she had all the answers, as though she knew Dan and Cara's life better than Cara did, she thought. And once her mother began with her psychic prying, there was no drawing the curtain. She turned to watch Violet, who was all by herself on the swings...but wait...she wasn't by herself anymore. She was swinging next to a little Asian girl whose face was round and her hair was cut short like a bowl. Cara couldn't hear what they were saying, but bursts of giggles went between them.

"May I sit?" a woman asked.

She was Asian with the same round face as the little girl.

The woman had on a gray down jacket that had the simple lines of the ones made in China, but not for export.

"I'd be glad for the company," Cara said, and she meant it. She had brooded enough. Besides, she had planned to build her new social life in Maryland around the parents of Violet's friends, and since Violet had none, that left Cara out as well. "I'm Cara Sachs. Is that your daughter playing with my Violet?"

Cara glanced back at them. They were bent over their swings, taking running starts to go higher. Two little jean-clad behinds with their heads hanging down, but still turned towards each other.

"Yes, that is Pacey and I am Fang-Hua. If you like, call me Fanny."

"Do you prefer Fanny?"

"No, but it is easier for American-born people to say."

"Fang-Hua is a lovely name," Cara said. Cara had been looking for knitting factories in China recently. From a business contact she'd made in Ningbo City, she knew Fang-Hua meant fragrant flower, but she didn't want to show off.

Fang-Hua smiled. She had just one dimple. "I am surprised Pacey plays with your girl."

Cara bristled. Did everyone in the surrounding area already know about Violet's threat to their reputations?

"Pacey never speaks English," Fang-hua said. "I read book that told me to talk Chinese at home and the child will learn English from other children outside, but not Pacey."

Cara let out her breath. It was Pacey her mother thought had a problem, not Violet.

"When I sent Pacey to pre-K," Fang-Hua said, "she came home so sad. 'All they say is bah, bah, bah,' she told me. So I put her in special school to learn English. All day the teacher picked up a pencil and told the class, 'Say pencil.' Pacey hated that. Soon as she knew some English she came home to shout at her father and me, 'Get me out of that school!'"

Cara was tempted to laugh, but Fang-Hua was so upset that she controlled herself. She didn't want to trivialize Pacey's mother's concerns the way Dan did hers. *If anyone should know how that felt, I should,* Cara thought.

"Pacey knows English," her mother said. "I teach her and I get a tutor. Academics is very important to Pacey's father and me. I teach Pacey maps and my husband is an engineer so he teaches math, even negative numbers and the binary system. I teach her the metric system and American system measures. I bought a model that shows all the bones and the liver and the heart so Pacey can learn the parts of body. In China I studied botany, so I teach her flowers and trees."

Cara felt as if her scarf had tightened around her neck. Should she and Dan be teaching all this to Violet? "Violet's only in kindergarten," Cara explained.

"So is Pacey," said Fang-Hua.

Cara had noticed how many after-school learning centers were springing up all over Baltimore. Should she enroll Violet in one?

"Pacey's teacher said Pacey has too much academics," Fang-Hua said. "Her teacher said she needs social skills. But most of children from her country do not like to speak Chinese at school. 'Shut up,' they tell her. 'Go away.' They want to be like the American kids. It is not right, but I wish Pacey wanted that too. Then she would not have so many problems as now."

Cara couldn't get over how much Pacey's situation mirrored Violet's. Pacey's refusal to speak English, the exasperation it caused her mother, and the isolation it created was the same pickle that she had with Violet blabbering people's secrets. "I understand," Cara said, but was afraid that if she opened up about Violet, Fang-Hua would hustle Pacey out of the playground and they would all never see each other again.

"Your mother lives in America?" Fang-Hua asked.

"Yes, in a suburb of New York."

"Oh, you are so lucky. You see your mother so often. Mine is in China. She cannot watch Pacey grow up."

"Yes, that must be hard on both you and your mother," Cara said. She couldn't help but wonder whether, if her own mother moved to China, would she have less influence on Violet?

In a moment Violet and Pacey were barreling toward them, Violet, with Cara's long legs, well ahead of Pacey. "She wants apple juice," Violet said.

"Ah," Fang-hua said, clapping her hands, "good girl, Pacey, you speak English to new friend."

"Pacey didn't tell me," Violet said, pointing to her temple. "I saw it in here. A box of apple juice. I don't like apple juice so much anymore, so I knew it was in Pacey's head."

"Pacey loves it," Fang-hua said. She reached into the backpack that she'd set in her lap and gave Pacey a box, pushing the tiny straw through the tiny hole for her. "You both tricked me," Fang-hua said. "I like good humor."

Violet's face got serious. "What color is your mother's car?" Violet asked Pacey.

Pacey stopped sipping her juice and answered her in Chinese.

"It's blue," Violet said. "Blue, dark blue."

"So, this is the answer to the riddle," Fang-Hua said. "Violet can speak Chinese."

Cara's jaw dropped. She covered her open mouth with her scarf. She wanted to cover her whole face with it. "Violet, we have to go now."

Violet stayed put. "Pacey, when is your birthday?"

Again Pacey answered in Chinese. Cara couldn't get over that Violet had met her match in stubbornness.

"Mommy, when is Valentine's Day?" Violet asked.

"February fourteenth," Cara said, her voice coming out as if her throat were the pinched top of a balloon from which air was escaping.

"Yes, that is Pacey's birthday," Fang-hua said, taking eyeglasses out of her bag and putting them on to see Violet more clearly. "How can you tell that?"

Violet pointed at her temple again. "I saw a Valentine heart with lace around it."

Every slat of the bench seemed to dig deeply into Cara's behind. "Violet, we have to go to soccer now."

"I will give you my number," Fang-Hua said to Cara. "Please call. I would like that so very much."

"Yes, wonderful, I will. Cara knew she'd never call. This

would be terrible for both Violet and Pacey. Pacey wouldn't have to force herself to speak English and Violet would be trying to read her mind, which was just what she had to learn not to do.

Cara hurried Violet off to the car.

"Silly Mommy, you made a mistake," Violet said. "Today isn't soccer. Today is Wednesday. Soccer is Thursday."

"Yes, I'm silly all right," Cara said. She thought how horrible it was that her daughter had been trying to help Pacey by getting her the apple juice, but since it involved Violet's reading the girl's mind, Cara didn't feel proud of it.

When she got home, she did what she had stopped herself from doing that morning. She turned on Dan's computer, then typed in genome23, his password. He'd told her that at a time when he hadn't kept secrets from her. She was both relieved and frightened when it worked, relieved that he hadn't changed it because he was doing something wrong and frightened at what she was doing. She saw nothing unusual in his emails. Several letters from his parents with the subject line, "Find a new research topic yet?" and a dozen or so "Re: Find a new research topic yet?" Then she saw one about a credit card account she didn't recognize. There were so many scams on the internet. But Dan had kept it in his "New" mail instead of deleting it.

She opened it. It was a monthly statement from Amex, but it wasn't their personal card and he didn't use one for business, since he worked at the university. She rolled down the itemized purchases: Linda's Getting to Know You, $150; Keep Your Secrets with Celeste," $100; Monique's Parlor of Intimacy, $200." Cara shut the screen. She did a 180-degree turn in Dan's swivel chair, gripping the arms as if she were in danger of being ejected. Was Dan going to massage parlors? No, he couldn't be. Where was he right now? She was about to phone him when Violet came in holding the worry doll that she'd taken from the psychologist's office. Cara wanted to ask if she could borrow it.

"Know what, Mommy?"

"What?" Cara said, trying to sound upbeat even though she was shaking inside.

"You promise you won't get mad at me?"

"Just tell me," Cara said with agitation. Then Cara saw the light go out of Violet's eyes. *No matter what I'm going through,* Cara thought, *it's not right to puncture Violet's joy.* She untensed her hands from the arms of the chair. "Just tell me," she said more softly.

"I saw Daddy," she said, pointing to her temple. "I saw him in a room with a lot of kinds of curtains, even one hanging from the ceiling. He was with a lady and he told her to open her mouth for him. Isn't that silly?" she added, laughing nervously.

Cara's hands flew to her face. Her own mouth dropped open. Something was terribly wrong and even Violet knew it.

AT 1:30 A.M., CARA WAS COOKING, BUT NOT AT THE stove. She was in bed, steaming herself up against Dan. Her laptop was balanced on her bent knees when he walked into the bedroom. She looked up at him. His eyes were sliding around the room as if he couldn't meet her gaze.

"Hi, honey," he said, unbuttoning his shirt. "What are you working on?"

"I'm googling Divorce Mediation."

"For a friend?"

"No, for me," she said, raising her voice. "I know what you're up to."

"For God's sake," he said, "don't let Violet hear you. Don't use her as collateral in whatever case you've built up against me or I don't think I'll ever forgive you."

"Forgive *me*? Are you crazy? After what you did? Taking out a secret charge card and going to other women to do who knows what with them?"

"You," he said, stabbing the air with his finger, "you hacked into my emails?"

"Don't point your finger at me. You told me what your password was when we had no secrets from each other, when I trusted you and you trusted me."

"Before you get on a high horse, you'd better hear me out," Dan said, standing at the foot of the bed, his arms folded across his chest. "I was trying to do something for myself and my family at the same time. After Ingebord beat me to the punch for the research I had been doing, I had to find a new topic. It hit me that if I could find a gene for the psychic trait, I would not only be helping myself, I'd be helping Violet. And I'd be helping you leave her alone and stop trying to prune her like a bonsai. You're making her nervous by trying to stop her. I mean, you're so careful with Violet, you only feed her organic foods and filtered water, but you're willing to paint her nails with a polish made of acetone, alcohol, and lacquer to try to get her to stop biting them. I threw that poison out. I want Violet to grow up free to express herself in any way she wants to, without us shooting her down when she's a kid."

"So you went to call girls to help you with that?" Cara spat out.

Dan flushed, but Cara thought he looked more amused than guilty. "Call girls? Is that what you think?" he said. "I went to psychics. None of them were my type, I might add. The closest to anything physical between us was when Star Bright told me that if I peed in a cup and gave her an extra five hundred bucks she could take the curse off my family."

"Really." Cara wasn't ready to abandon her rage. "Well your own daughter reported to me that you were telling these women to open their mouths for you."

"If I wasn't so ripped," Dan said, "I'd be laughing my head off. I've gone to scores of psychics to test their psi abilities with the closest to a scientific method as anyone has come up with yet for this, those Zener cards that were designed way back in the 1930s. Once I determined that the women were psychic, I asked them to open their mouths so I could take a swab for a DNA test to see if I could isolate a gene for psychic ability. I didn't want to go to your mother and ask her to open her mouth so I could collect the DNA inside her cheek. Then she'd have to tell you, and I wanted to keep it a secret until I'd reached some conclusion."

It took a moment for what Dan said to sink in, and then she felt a hot spurt of venom pouring through her veins. "You had no right to do something that would encourage Violet when it's costing her her social life and me such aggravation," she yelled. "You had no right to absent yourself from the family like that. And since when are you financing your own research?"

Dan did his nervous throat-clearing. Still not looking at her directly, he said, "I don't have the department's approval on this yet. In fact, I didn't even ask them. They would have laughed at me, sent me packing to Duke University parapsychology department, which, needless to say, they don't have the highest regard for."

Cara lowered her voice and folded her arms across her chest. "Maybe they are right."

Dan sat down on his side of the bed. "Can't you see that as Violet's father I should have some say in how she's being raised? If we have respect for who she is, which includes being psychic, then she'll have respect for herself. She's too little to worry about how she'll make a living. When I was her age, my parents were already grilling me about what I would become, and whatever I said, they shot it down. 'Firemen, cops, and cowboys make zilch,' my father would say. And my mother would chime in, 'You don't get wealthy or famous in those jobs.' From Day One I felt their pressure to be a groundbreaker, an *ubermentsch*. Please, let Violet just be. Even if she has some rough bumps along the way, at least she'll be her own person someday."

"Nobody's asking Violet to be a superwoman," Cara said. "Don't get your story confused with hers. Anyway, you don't really see what she's going through. Whenever Violet's around you, she's sheltered from what's happening in the rest of her life. I'm there on the front lines. I see her hurt, her shock at being rejected. I'm the one who has to explain to her why she isn't getting invited to play dates, why everyone else got an invitation to someone's birthday party and she didn't."

"I was picked on as a kid," Dan said, "because I was an egghead. Looking back, it was good for me. By the time I was eleven, I was doing fifty pushups a day and shadow boxing. When I flew from Ithaca to Michigan to visit my parents, I ran into one of the guys who used to torture me, a bruiser even in elementary school. He was a cab dispatcher with a lard belly and spindly arms. I could have decked him in a blink."

"You keep going back to you," Cara said. "Are you that self-centered?" Even as she said this, she thought of how she kept going back to her own childhood, the wedge her mother's gift had made between them. "Violet's situation isn't the same as yours," Cara went on. "Parents want their kids to hang around the brightest kids. Teachers are their allies. But Violet's blabbering people's secrets is setting everyone against her. If I gave her karate lessons, it wouldn't help her at all."

"But if we celebrate her gift, it could turn things around," he said. "Other people would begin to celebrate it too."

She couldn't believe that he had taken his shirt off as if they were just going to be in bed together and everything was la-di-dah. "You're pressing this argument like you should have done when Ingebord took credit for research you paved the way for," she said. "If you had argued with the panel back then, they might have given you at least a footnote." She watched as he curled over as if he'd been punched in the gut.

"I never would have believed that you could say that to me," he said. "It's just what my parents would say, what they've in fact already said. You have always been so proud of me, and then I have one setback and you think I'm mud."

He was eyeing her with his top lip drawn back in disgust. She could imagine that he was seeing her dark, tumbling hair become a precision beauty parlor cut, her green eyes the gray/blue piercing eyes of his mother. She couldn't bear him looking at her like that.

"You're not sleeping in this room tonight," she said.

"I wasn't intending to."

As he walked to the guestroom, she felt he was crossing a bridge whose toll was their marriage. She wondered whether, if he wasn't living here with her and didn't see Violet everyday, would he forget his daughter altogether? For a moment she felt her old pull toward him, a stirring inside her. She was about to call him back, but the wallop of what he'd done, all those secrets, practically lying by omission, rushed back at her, and she let him go.

XIX

"MRS. MCENROE," KAYLEE CALLED OUT LOUDLY TO her elderly neighbor, who was dragging her shopping cart up Ditmars Avenue, but Mrs. McEnroe didn't turn her head or stop. Tom probably forgot to put new batteries in her hearing aid, Kaylee thought. Even with her bad knees, Mrs. McEnroe managed to walk at a fast clip because she was always afraid of getting her purse snatched.

When Kaylee went after her, she was weirded out that she didn't feel any of the cracks in the sidewalk or even her own feet on the pavement. "Mrs. McEnroe," she hollered into her neighbor's ear, "I'll remind Tom to change your batteries," but Mrs. McEnroe kept going without a nod.

Kaylee was not only surprised at Mrs. McEnroe, but surprised at herself for wanting to talk to anyone at all. After she'd lost her mother's inheritance, she hadn't wanted to talk to anyone. Now suddenly she felt hungry for someone to talk to; desperate, actually.

"Hello," she called out to Mr. Hashani, who owned the candy store where she had bought her lottery tickets. Whenever his wife came to the store to help out, he would leave to go to the hookah shop and smoke flavored tobacco and who knew what else? with the other men. Whether in his store or outside, he had always had a big, gold-toothed smile for Kaylee, but he just went on his way. Kaylee was really offended. She promised herself she'd never go to his store for lottery tickets again.

She gave a stranger a try, someone who looked safe to her—a woman at a bus stop with no makeup on and her wheat-colored hair pulled back in a bun.

"Excuse me," Kaylee said. "Do you happen to know where the post office is?"

Without answering, the woman took *Watch Tower* pamphlets from her tote bag and began to distribute them to the four other people at the bus stop, but she didn't give one to Kaylee. Kaylee couldn't get over being dissed by her. Had even a week gone by without a Jehovah's Witness ringing her doorbell to press pamphlets on her and tell her how to become a true believer? She couldn't imagine one missing an opportunity like this.

A Dunkin' Donuts was on the corner. There was always a line at the counter. She'd definitely find someone to talk to there. She was so eager to get there that she jay-walked. A cab bore down on her without honking.

"Moron!" she yelled, jumping out of the way. She was sure she hadn't gotten away in time, but nothing had happened to her. She was able to cross the street without even a limp. *Weird*.

She had been right. There was a long line at the counter and getting longer because of the woman wearing a coat that looked like something you'd see in *Glamour* who was going off that she had earned a free cup of coffee with her discount card when she hadn't.

"Wouldn't you know it?" Kaylee said to the cop in front of her. "There's always someone like that. You should arrest her." She expected at least that he would laugh, but he acted as if she wasn't there.

Tom would say, "Why are you worried about what other people think of you? If they don't like you, ef'em, that's all." But whatever was going on now felt bigger than people not liking her. It felt huge, cosmic. She was so glad to finally be next. The clerk would have to answer her. That was his job.

"A medium decaf, black," she said, but the clerk waited on the person behind her instead.

Now she knew something was up for sure. She was about to argue that she was next, but then she realized that she didn't have a purse with her and no money in her pockets either. She didn't even have pockets.

"Does anybody hear me?" she shouted at the top of her lungs. Nobody flinched. Nobody looked her way.

God, this was like one of her nightmares where she walked through the streets naked, sobbing. "I have no money, no cell phone," she'd tell each passerby. "I've lost my identity. Help me, help me. I've got to get home." She'd wake up sweat-soaked on her mattress, her blanket kicked off and her fitted sheet loosed from its corners. But now she wasn't naked. She was wearing a light blue silky long dress with an empire waistline that she was sure she'd never bought or never even had in her closet. If Tom had bought it for her, she would have made him return it. This dress made her feel like Tinker Bell. And everybody else was wearing coats. How come she had no coat on and didn't feel cold? What was happening to her? She had to get home.

Just thinking *home* brought her to the front of her building. How did she get there? Had she blacked out? But if she had, she wouldn't have been able to walk the seven blocks. Was she dreaming? She pinched herself, but didn't feel it. How could something so crazy be happening while ordinary things were all around her, like these men repaving the sidewalk in front of her building? Kaylee didn't bother to say anything to them. She already knew they wouldn't hear her. But she stared at those squares of wet concrete and began to feel a chill inside her that she was sure had nothing to do with the weather. She doubled over, her fists at her chest. Then she remembered the falling, the air pressing against her belly, her face, her thighs. Was it at the fifth floor or was it later that her arms shot down in front of her, palms open, fingers splayed, as if she had planned to break her fall, as if she'd changed her mind at the last minute? And then the impact. The blackness, the blackness and the sounds of people screaming, and then nothing, nothing. There had been a whoosh, a rushing up from her body, a peeling out from deep inside it, her body lying, unmoving, on the sidewalk, but some part of her... her consciousness? had been looking down at herself, at her blood spreading like a dark river. She had been wearing her yoga tunic and it had begun turning deep red. Her arms, which she'd held straight out, had twisted and turned like gnarled branches.

Her arms were regular arms again and this dress, she remembered, was what she had worn while lying in her coffin. Maybe the undertaker had chosen it. At her funeral, even though she could no longer breathe and her eyelids had been pulled shut, she had been so scared of having the lid closed on her coffin that she didn't see anyone or hear her own eulogy. It was just like her wedding, when she was so scared of having to go on a honeymoon with Tom, whom she'd only kissed and held hands with under her mother's scrutiny, that she never even heard the music playing and no one was more surprised than she when the pictures came back and she saw Aunt Shinead doing the jig and Uncle Finn sneaking a scotch.

I'm dead, she thought. *Dead.* Jumping out the window had seemed like her only choice after she came home from the ashram without her mother's money. Now she hated this existence, if you'd call it that. She must have been crazy to jump from the window. Why couldn't she have changed her life without killing herself, like all those people on Oprah? Even without her mother's money, she could have done some-thing. Where had suicide gotten her? She was still back in Brooklyn and she felt more alone than ever. She could never go back to the ashram after the guru had betrayed her and helped those developers rob her. In anguish, she tore at her dress, but it didn't rip. She was so mad she could kill herself. *Lesson not learned,* she thought. Minutes? Weeks? Months? How long had she been dead? She had no idea. *Dead.* The word cut through her mind like a sharp rock. She actually raised her arm to protect herself, as if more rocks were going to come down on her. She put her arm down. If a rock fell on her, she probably wouldn't feel that either.

Here she was, not part of this life anymore, but not part of any other either. She was so angry at what she'd done that she could...what? kill herself? And she hadn't just done this to herself. She thought of Tom all alone, coming home from work, calling out, "Kaylee, so how's your day?" and remembering all over again how he had found her the last time he saw her. She thought about going upstairs to see how he was doing, poor Tom who had always meant well, but she was afraid. His skinny arms were surprisingly strong. Just her luck, he'd be the only one who could see her. He'd grab hold of her and never let her go. Then they would be dead together all over again.

The cement guys had finished the job. They cordoned off the wet cement blocks and packed up their equipment in their truck. After the truck wheezed away, Kaylee stepped right into the wet cement. Even with all that had happened since she somehow rose from the grave, she was still freaked out that she didn't leave footprints.

She couldn't stay here anymore below the window she'd jumped from. It was like smashing to the ground all over again. She could see her fall, over and over, like a movie on continuous loop. She could see herself twisted and bleeding. Even though her heart couldn't be working anymore, she still felt pounding in her chest. Who knew you could still feel terror when you were dead? She had to go somewhere to figure out what to do. Like a mind snapshot, she saw the church where her coffin had lain. It wasn't the closest one, but without having to take a train or a bus, without having to walk at all, she found herself inside St. Teresa's. This was the only good thing about being dead that she could see, this instant travel.

Inside, she hesitated at the font. After her mother's

funeral, the only time she'd gone to church again was for her own funeral. Did it count when you were already embalmed? She had given up Catholicism for the guru, like she'd given up Tom. She dipped her fingers in the holy water. They came out dry. Still, she made the sign of the cross and continued down the aisle. There were a few people kneeling in the pews, their heads resting on their folded hands. Even if she weren't dead, they probably wouldn't have seen her.

When she sat down, she put her palms together and began to recite the Hail Mary prayer like she used to with her mother. "Hail Mary, full of grace. The Lord is with thee." She choked up. She couldn't think of her mother without thinking of losing the money her mother had left her. Her mother had squirreled away all of Kaylee's father's insurance money and wouldn't even go to a movie unless Tom took her in order to pay the premium on the highest life insurance policy she could get on herself.

"Mom, I'm so sorry," Kaylee cried. "Are you still mad at me for losing the money you left me? I didn't mean it. Is this why I'm in limbo, because of that money? I can't wander the earth forever. I can't be here all alone. Don't you see there's no place I belong? There must be somewhere that people can hear me and see me, where I can talk to someone. Please, tell me what I have to do to get there." She listened hard. "Please, please," she cried. Still, there was no answer.

A band of panic tightened in her throat. She pictured what had been drummed into her about heaven, a pearly gate with St. Peter waiting there. When she opened her eyes, she was still in the pew. She pictured her mother: her mother's brown eyes, white bouffant hairdo, and the two rouge spots on her plump cheeks, but that didn't take her anywhere either. She looked up at Jesus on the cross, his crown of thorns, his pained eyes, the wooden veins standing up on his wooden forehead, and felt that he understood her sorrow. Was there really a heaven? Who knew? But there had to be somewhere that spirits lived together, talked to each other. She had to find out how to get to that place, the intersection between the worlds where she could step across and be with other souls. Would they accept her after what she'd done? She felt the same popping out of her skin that she had when she'd told herself that she couldn't take life anymore. All her life and all her death she'd gotten nowhere.

A man in the row behind her sneezed loudly. "God bless you," she said over her shoulder; he didn't respond.

Hopelessness poured its lead into her. She crossed herself, got up, and left the church. *What to do? Where to go?* By the way her dress was flying behind her, she could tell she was walking into the wind, a wind she couldn't feel. A short, stocky guy came toward her with a pit bull straining on a leash. When she was alive, how scared she used to be of pit bulls!

"Bite me," she said with a snarl, but the dog lifted its leg against a tree instead.

She began to laugh and cry at the same time. Her throat felt wrenched.

She kept going, heading nowhere, like the homeless people. At least she didn't have to pick through the trash like that poor ragged woman leaning into a garbage pail.

Kaylee came to a storefront with a beaded curtain. The sign on the window said, "Palm or Tarot Reading, $10." No way; she remembered all too well the place she'd gone to where Lena had told her that she'd have miscarriages in her future.

Miriam had been her psychic all along. She had only seen Miriam's picture in the newspaper where Miriam advertised, but she remembered it well: her curly red hair and blue eyes and that smile making you trust her even if you shouldn't. *Miriam, Miriam, Miriam,* she thought, keeping that picture in her mind, not letting anything else in.

XX

As Miriam paced her living room, each overhead beam she passed under felt like a prison bar. It was late afternoon, but she was still in her bathrobe, a striped one. The floorboards creaked with each step. Rory had come down in the middle of the night to find her here, pacing.

"Honey, come up to bed," he'd said, squinting at her. He hadn't stopped to put on his glasses.

"I can't. I have to stay in motion to breathe."

"That's for sharks," Rory said. "If you lie down, at least you'll rest your body."

"But my mind won't rest, Rory."

"Maybe you can call the doctor, get some Xanax."

Miriam was afraid if she had Xanax she'd take them all at once. "I'll drink Valerian tea," she said.

"If all my customers were like you," he said, "Mirror would be out of business." He went back upstairs. "Hope you join me soon," he called over his shoulder.

What Miriam hadn't told him was that she had already drunk nearly a quart of Valerian tea and it had had no effect. *Don't think about her anymore,* she warned herself. She didn't even want to think the name of the person she didn't want to think about for fear of thinking about her. Miriam had gotten bursitis in her knees from kneeling to ask that person's forgiveness. Jews weren't used all that kneeling. She had tried every which way to contact Kaylee again, to explain why she had sent her to that ashram. Oh, she'd gone and said her name and now she'd let the floodgates of guilt loose inside her, drowning her.

Since Kaylee's funeral, Miriam had meditated forty-five minutes, three times a day. She'd studied the Kaylee look-alike Madonna on the remembrance card from Kaylee's funeral, even talking to it.

"Kaylee, forgive me," she'd begged, but no matter how fervent her prayers, they seemed to be as thin as the cardboard that the portrait was printed on. Mrs. O'Brien's accusation rang loudly in Miriam's ears. "You lied, you lied."

"Kaylee," Miriam said to the stucco ceiling, "even though for some reason I can't see your spirit, I can't hear it, not in Brooklyn, not at your grave, not in Great Neck, please know that I'll carry you in my mind and heart for the rest of my life." Miriam knew this was true. She felt black and blacker.

She stopped pacing beneath the fourth beam. "Bubbie, Bubbie dear, would you please intercede for me?"

She didn't see Bubbie, but she smelled lavender. "*Neshomelah*," she heard, "night and day I hear you call for this Kaylee. I call for her too. But some spirits still got wax in their ears from the undertakers. You can't force things. Stop making yourself *meshuggeh*."

"You're right," Miriam said, but panic was still a bronco kicking against her ribs. She went up to bed, not expecting sleep, just to be near Rory's snoring. He was asleep on his stomach, his hands tucked beneath the pillow. She burrowed close to him and closed her eyes. She dreamed that she was watching Kaylee jump out of her bedroom window. Miriam's body jerked and her arms flayed as if she were falling herself. "*No, no*," she screamed.

Rory opened his bleary eyes. "Maybe you'd better not try to sleep," he mumbled. "I have to be up in an hour." He yawned a jaw-clicking yawn and went right back to sleep.

She got out of bed, went downstairs, and began to pace again. She had to take some kind of action to enable herself to tell Kaylee what her motivation was, how she'd just been trying to help her. She couldn't just wander her house in her bathrobe anymore, like a homeless person inside her own home. Every conversation she had ever had with Kaylee was so fresh in her mind, as if she'd just gotten off the phone with her. She remembered when she'd had trouble contacting Kaylee's father. Miriam had found a different medium for her to speak to, but Kaylee had refused. *If only she had gone to that woman instead, Kaylee might be alive today*: the thought like a dagger in Miriam's heart. And then, like the answer to a question she hadn't realized she was asking, she thought, *I can go to that medium myself. She'll be able to contact Kaylee for me and speak on my behalf.*

She went up to her office and flipped through the M's in her Rolodex: masons, mold removers, all the people she had meant to contact to fix up her house, but had never followed through on; the Matternicks, cousins of Rory whom she couldn't stand. Finally, she found the medium—Sabrina Zarcadoulus. Miriam dialed the number.

"Hullo," a woman said with a voice so low and flat that she sounded as if she were already dead.

Miriam got an image of a shadow over the medium's nose and around her eyes and cheeks. "It's your sinuses, isn't it," Miriam said.

"Who is this?" asked Sabrina, snorting back mucus.

"Oh, excuse me," Miriam said. "I was calling to make an appointment with you. You came highly recommended from a Florence Greenblatt who knows Kenny Kirsch and Marisca Fuertes. Do you work over the phone?"

"What kind of medium works over the phone?" Sabrina said in a thick Greek accent.

"I can't imagine," Miriam said. She was surprised to find herself behaving like one of those clients who would reveal nothing, the kind of client that Miriam herself couldn't stand, the sort who wanted to make sure she was getting her money's worth even though keeping things back could block the flow.

"I'm in Mineola," Sabrina said. "From your number I see you're in Great Neck. It wouldn't be much of a trip for you, and I have an opening at three." Sabrina pronounced "have" as "chav."

Miriam was delighted to have a reason to force herself out of the house. She agreed, and Sabrina gave her her address. "I'm apartment 5C," she said. "I'm not supposed to run a business from my apartment; it's against management rules. So if you see somebody in the hallway, don't go announcing you're my customer."

"I'm good at being discreet," Miriam said.

· · ·

THE HALLWAY CARPET WAS SPATTERED IN FRONT OF Sabrina's apartment, as if she'd broken a jar of tomato sauce while trying to unlock her door. When Miriam buzzed, she saw a dark eyeball eyeballing her through the peephole.

"It's Miriam Kaminsky," Miriam called, and the door opened onto a heavyset woman with straggly dark hair, maybe sixty or so like herself. Sabrina was wearing an orange muu muu that made Miriam, in her long cape, flowered skirt, and white peasant blouse, look like a fashionista. Everyone's face was asymmetrical, but because of how Sabrina applied her makeup, hers was as mismatched as the face of one of Picasso's women. A lot of mediums are eccentric, Miriam reminded herself. After all, how many glam tips or even social skills could you absorb while listening to the dead all day?

Miriam stepped inside. The apartment was darkened with heavy drapes and mahogany furniture and smelled of scented oils that she was sure were aggravating Sabrina's sinuses. But it wasn't her place to offer advice when she had come to seek it.

"I have always worked at my dining room table," Sabrina said. When they sat down, she added, "I hope I remembered to tell you to bring cash."

"No, no you didn't," Miriam said. She looked through her bag. "I only have eighty dollars with me. If there's an ATM nearby I could get you the extra twenty."

"I take it," Sabrina said, and Miriam handed it over. As Sabrina counted it, Miriam noticed the silver ring on Sabrina's finger with a blue glass eye setting. Miriam knew it was supposed to ward off the evil eye, but it looked pretty evil on its own.

Sabrina took hold of a glass bowl centerpiece on the table, emptied it of fake fruit, and turned it upside down. *She's going to use it as a crystal ball,* Miriam realized. If she weren't so glum she would have laughed out loud. But then Sabrina waved her hands over it like Bubbie had over the *shabbes* candles on Friday nights, which quieted Miriam inside.

With one of her lopsided eyebrows raised, Sabrina looked at Miriam suspiciously. "I see the High Priestess in my bowl. Why didn't you tell me you are in the same business as me?"

Miriam had never met a crystal ball reader who envisioned tarot cards in her crystal ball. As embarrassed as she felt, she was glad Sabrina had just proved herself a real psychic. Miriam began to sputter excuses, but Sabrina went back to her bowl.

"You were born with the caul and you have a daughter who was, too," Sabrina said.

"A granddaughter," Miriam corrected her. Miriam was antsy to get to Kaylee, but she knew that a psychic had to meander along to get anything at all, so she tried to be patient.

"There's trouble between you, your daughter, and her daughter," Sabrina said. "And trouble between your daughter and the baby's father."

She's the real deal, Miriam thought. "My daughter's husband," Miriam told her. "I knew there was trouble from their bride and groom statue. I could sense it."

"So, if you know it all, what did you come to me for?" Sabrina asked testily.

Miriam couldn't wait another moment. "I came about a young woman named Kaylee."

"Is she a relative?"

"No, a client."

Sabrina's forehead crisscrossed with lines. "I see slit wrists," she said.

Miriam didn't bother to tell Sabrina that she was wrong. Dead was dead and suicide was suicide. Technicalities only mattered in court.

Looking in her bowl, Sabrina shook her head. "Kaylee blames you."

"I know," Miriam said, tears springing to her eyes, though she hadn't known. The only thing that she'd been sure of was that she blamed herself and deserved to. "Could you contact her and explain that I didn't mean to lie to her, but I couldn't go along with what her mother's spirit was telling me, so I said she should go to the ashram even though her mother wanted her to stay home and do nothing like always?"

Sabrina smacked her palm on the table. Miriam could swear that the glass eye in Sabrina's ring blinked.

"You mean you didn't say exactly, word by word, what her mother's spirit said?" Sabrina demanded. "Don't you know what kind of punishment you've heaped on your head? You might as well have spit in the gods' mouths. You can prophecy all you want now, but no one will believe you anymore."

Sabrina was giving her the tongue-lashing Miriam thought she had coming. "I don't care," Miriam said, her voice breaking. "I don't want to prophecy anymore. It's too big a responsibility. It could and it did cost someone her life."

Sabrina gave a Cheshire Cat smile, as if she'd just eliminated her competition.

Despite this, Miriam tried to appeal to her. "Couldn't you contact Kaylee and tell her that I didn't mean it?"

Sabrina grew serious, turned her chair toward Miriam, and reached for Miriam's face, held it firmly in her hands, and looked into her eyes. "Your eyes, such blue, they could chase away the *matiasma,* and instead, by trying to contact this spirit who is angry with you, you draw the evil eye toward you."

Miriam began to sob. "Is there any way of taking the curse off?" She felt so vulnerable, as if the stars and planets had her locked into some destiny that she wanted no part of.

"You can't let Kaylee's spirit get hold of you," Sabrina said, loosening her grip on Miriam's face. "She's an immature spirit, like an adolescent, and as a result, capable of anything."

Miriam remembered Cara's tantrums when she was a teenager. "I hate my life," Cara used to scream when she didn't get her way, and Miriam had been so frightened; now she grew afraid again. "My whole reason for coming here was for you to be an intermediary between me and Kaylee, so you could make things better between us."

Sabrina shook her head gravely. "The only way I can help you in this matter is to teach you how to shield yourself against her vibrations so she can't haunt you or harm you in any way."

Here it comes, Miriam thought. *She's going to ask for God knows how much money from me because she's hit my rawest nerves*. Miriam had a client who was a school-teacher, a good citizen, a smart cookie, but she had forked over $5,000 to a psychic who claimed she could make a sterling silver amulet for her to get her boyfriend to come back to her. The woman was so frantic and despondent that she paid the money, and when she came back for the amulet the storefront was empty.

"I would charge a $1,000 dollars for this if it were anybody else," Sabrina said, "but for you, professional courtesy. I will help you for no extra charge. I will help you because we are alike with our gifts."

Miriam was touched. She knew that this wasn't Sabrina's usual way. Miriam saw, in her mind, big cans of cash hidden in the back of Sabrina's closet, all those tax-free dollars.

"You are right in what you think," Sabrina said. "I live simple here, but I am saving my money to buy a big house on the island of Kythria, and someday I will go back to Greece and live good. And now, here is what you do to keep this vengeful spirit from you."

Miriam sat on the edge of her seat, waiting for an amazing ritual to begin. For a woman who was convinced that her widower husband's former wife was haunting her, Bubbie had pulled down the darkening shades in her parlor and begun to chant the Kaddish, the prayer for the dead, as a loud growl. The alley cats began to screech. People were shouting out their windows and throwing shoes, but still Bubbie chanted. Miriam had been a little girl, sitting on a footstool, so scared that she'd put her hands over her ears. But she saw a flickering near the curio cabinet, just a moment, and then it was gone.

"Tillie won't bother you no more," Bubbie told the woman, and the woman walked away with her back straight, her arms swinging, as if she were already free.

"Whenever you think this spirit might be around you," Sabrina said, her voice so low that Miriam could barely hear her, "just say in your mind, 'Click, click, click' and keep blinking hard, like you got a cinder in your eye."

"Click, click, click and blinking?" Miriam repeated. "That's all?"

Sabrina nodded. "It will block her so you won't be able to see her or hear her."

Useless, Miriam thought, her heart dropping.

"You don't believe me," Sabrina said. "It sounds too easy. But it works."

Sabrina had been so on target that Miriam reconsidered, and then it almost seemed logical. Whenever Miriam wanted to get rid of a vision, she blinked hard. And the clicking? Well, she'd read in the science section of the *Times* that a hearing aid that makes a regular click can help block the person from hearing his own tinnitus, those horrible ringing noises from nowhere, the snaps, crackles, and pops. Maybe clicking could stop a spirit from talking to you. It sounded crazy, but it was her only hope. "I'm going to try it," Miriam said.

"Try means nothing," Sabrina admonished her. "You must do it."

Miriam startled. "You said that so strongly. Is that because Kaylee is around me now?"

Sabrina didn't answer.

Miriam began to blink hard. "Click, click, click," she said.

"Good," said Sabrina.

Miriam felt like hugging Sabrina, but she didn't seem the type who would want a hug.

Back outside again, Miriam thought the plain old town of Mineola looked like Oz, everything extra bright and shimmering. And then she thought of how, just because Kaylee might not be able to haunt her, she still had had a hand in Kaylee's death. She might be safe from Kaylee, but not from her own guilt.

"Mim?" Rory said when she came home. "The other pharmacist was in, so I left early to see how you are. I've been worried."

She gave him the hug that hadn't been spent on Sabrina and followed him into the kitchen, where he lifted the crock pot lid to smell the simmering split pea soup.

"How's everything at Mirror?" she asked.

"Instead of people worrying about the flu," Rory said, "this season they're hopped up about bedbugs. They keep asking me if I have any way of getting rid of them or warding them off. I tell them, 'That's a job for an exterminator, not a pharmacist.' Everyone was telling me about infiltrations with such panic that at first I thought they were talking about terrorists."

"Bedbugs are so hard to get rid of," Miriam said, making her voice louder. Rory needed a hearing aid and had been putting off going for one. "One of my clients had to hire a bedbug-sniffing dog. I hear bedbugs smell like cilantro to the dogs."

Rory covered the lid of the crock pot. "Let's not talk about them."

Over dinner, she said, "I really want to see Violet."

"Remember, that's not up to you or to Violet," Rory said. "It's up to Cara."

Miriam sighed. "If only we lived nearer, I wouldn't have to impose. I could just be with Violet for an hour or so, and I could show Cara that I wasn't trying to turn Violet into a psychic. I wouldn't be a threat. I could be a regular grandma and make Violet cocoa and read her bedtime stories."

"But we do live far and you have to accept that, Mim, as hard as it is."

"Maybe I don't."

"What do you mean?" Rory said, but Miriam didn't answer. She was too busy making a plan. She started by going online to look up the bedbug registry for any infestations at hotels in Baltimore. If she were staying at a hotel in Baltimore and Cara did let her come over and she brought bedbugs with her, that would be a lousy end to any possibility of reconnection. The Marriot, she learned, was one of the few that hadn't had any infestations.

Rory came up behind her and bent to look at the screen. "No, you're not really going to go to Baltimore without an invitation, are you?"

She swiveled her chair around to face him and stood to level the foot of height that separated them. "I'm free to go to Baltimore," she said. "Anyone is."

"You're going to make trouble," he said. "I just know you will."

"Hmmph. That's some goodbye." She wondered whether she'd go Amtrak or fly.

· · ·

No matter what the bedbug registry said, as soon as Miriam got into her hotel room, she pulled back the bedspread and turned on all the lights to see if anything skittered. She couldn't believe she'd come all the way from Great Neck to Fells Point with Rory telling her what a mistake it was and without asking Cara first. If Miriam was right and there was trouble in Cara's marriage, Violet would need her and Miriam needed to be needed. Besides, she couldn't stay by herself all day, not working and tormenting herself.

She checked the drawers too. No skittering there either, but she kept her clothes in a ziplock bag anyway. She hated to leave Rory alone in Great Neck, even though he could easily fend for himself. But thinking of Rory alone made her think of Tom all alone forever in Brooklyn, and Kaylee's suicide hit her again like a meteor. Miriam blinked and clicked.

She had to call Cara and tell her she was here. But when she took out her cell, she just stared at the screen. Then she smelled Old Spice and Lucky Strikes.

"Dad?"

"Over here," he said.

She looked to her right, where his voice seemed to emanate from. At first she didn't see anything unusual; then the globe light hanging from the wall on a chain began to get dimmer. She watched as the brightness came back into the globe, shaping itself into her father's face. The light may have been too bright for him as well, because on his tortoise-framed glasses he wore a pair of sunglass clip-ons. He would have looked prepared for anything, but he had forgotten to put his bottom teeth in.

"Daddy," she said happily. "I was so lonely in this hotel room until you came."

"Only in America are people afraid of their own children," he said, and then, as if someone had switched off the light, he was gone.

Miriam garnered her courage and made the call. "Hi, Cara," she said. "I have a surprise for you."

"I don't think I can take anymore surprises right now," Cara said.

Miriam, emboldened by her father, blurted out, "The surprise is that I rented a hotel room in Baltimore so that, for this week, I can come by to see Violet casually, the way Darcy's mother can see her grandchild who lives up the block from her. Or I can babysit if you need me, or we can go out to lunch together without me being underfoot all the time in your house."

She could hear that little "tuh" sound that Cara made when she was flabbergasted or disgusted. Which emotion had prompted it now? Miriam began to back-peddle. "If it's inconvenient, I can just take the Metro to Washington D.C. and go to the museums."

"Mom, Mom I do need you," Cara said, her voice breaking. "I didn't even know how much until you told me you were right here."

"I'm so glad that I'm wanted, Cara. It's been too long since I've felt that way. And honey, don't worry about me filling Violet's head with psychic nonsense as if I was giving her an advance on the greatest inheritance I could give her. I'm cured of that. Something awful happened to me—or really to someone else as a result of me working as a psychic."

"What happened?"

"Please don't ask me. It's all too raw now and probably will always be. But I can assure you that if there is any lesson in..." Miriam got a clutch in her throat and had to swallow hard. "I can promise you," she went on so quietly that she wasn't sure Cara could hear, "I can promise you that I'm never going to mention anything about spirits or telepathy or Ouijia boards or pendulums or anything else you've heard of or even never heard of."

"I would laugh if I wasn't so miserable, Mom. If you need someone to talk things over with and don't want to tell me, I know a therapist who believes in psychics. Her name is Jessica Gray Wolf, and if you don't mind a therapist who hit her son over the head with a package of frozen fish, she's for you."

That was it. Miriam started to laugh and Cara did too, laughter that turned quickly to hysterical tears. "I'm so miserable," Miriam said, sniffing.

"So am I," Cara said. Between sobs, Cara hiccupped. "Check out of the hotel and come right over. I'd offer to pick you up, but I'm such a mess that my hands are shaking."

Miriam pretended that she didn't know why. "What happened?"

"Dan and I had another big fight and I told him not to come home tonight."

Miriam wondered if staying with them would be the best idea. She couldn't imagine ever having been able to settle anything with Rory while her mother was present. "Just apologize," her mother would have said, "because no doubt you're wrong." She hoped she'd done the right thing by coming, especially since Rory was so against this visit.

"Mom?" Cara said.

There were so many things on the tip of Miriam's tongue, but they all sounded too much like her own mother's advice, such as *Why didn't you ask me before you decided to do that?* "I'm so, so sorry to hear that," Miriam finally said. "But no matter what you told him, Dan might come home to try to patch things up, and then I'll be there as a hindrance. It would feel as if we were in league together against him."

"He deserves a league against him, Mom. Just come and I'll tell you all about it. I didn't want him here because I was afraid that one of us would have a fit and Violet would find out that there's trouble between us. Dan doesn't want that either. His parents never had screaming fights like you and Dad did. He'd be horrified."

Miriam couldn't remember screaming fights between her and Rory, just seething ones like the one they were in now. But this wasn't the time to argue with her distraught daughter.

"Dan called to say that we should give ourselves a week to cool off," Cara continued. "The only thing I want to cool off is my feelings toward him. I want to not love him anymore." She began sobbing again.

These weren't the circumstances under which Miriam had wanted to be reunited with Cara. But she thought that if she talked to Cara alone, she might be able to do some good here. After all, she had failed as a psychic, causing a terrible death, but she had managed to stay married to Rory for thirty-eight years, most of it happy, however Cara saw it.

"I'm coming," Miriam said.

In the Arrow Cab with her suitcase bumping in the trunk, Miriam got the vision of a bouquet of long-stemmed black roses, a wedding anniversary for someone she knew, someone dead. She didn't know who, but then she remembered that Tom had told her that on February 20th, he and Kaylee would have been married thirteen years. The cab was well-heated, but she was so chilled that she put up her collar.

As soon as the cab pulled up to Cara's house, Cara rushed to the car, a white down coat pulled together over pink pajamas and it was only six p.m. Her nose was chafed and her eyes were bloodshot. Cara thrust a twenty-dollar bill at the cabbie. "Keep the change," she said. The meter, Miriam noticed, said nine dollars.

When the driver popped the trunk, Cara didn't wait for him to get out of the cab. She lifted Miriam's suitcase and pulled it up the pathway so fast on its wheelies that Miriam had to trot along beside her to keep up.

Inside the house, Cara threw herself into Miriam's arms. "I'm so glad you're here. I didn't know how I was going to keep it together in front of Violet. Good thing she's already used to hardly having Dan home. It won't be such a stretch for her. I didn't tell her you were coming. You can surprise her. We'll talk later."

"Grandma?" Violet called down from the banister. "I heard Grandma." She came running downstairs wearing a purple shirt that had a glittery LOVE on the front and a black velvet skirt with net trim and sunglasses. "Grandma,

Grandma, Grandma," she sang out, doing a little jig that made her long hair bounce.

Troubles flapped off Miriam like birds scared from a tree. "You look like a genuine movie star," she said.

When Miriam bent to kiss her, Violet whispered in her ear, "Don't tell Mommy, but I knew you were coming, Grandma. My mind told me so."

Miriam's stomach flip-flopped as she experienced this further evidence of how she'd made a triangle between herself, her daughter, and her granddaughter. How could she have put Violet in the position of having to keep secrets from her own mother?

"It's a feeling-hurter to whisper to one person while another is present," Miriam explained to Violet.

Violet looked baffled. Miriam and Violet had always had their secrets together, had relished them. It was part of what made their time together so special. And then Violet broke into a dimpled smile, as if she thought that Miriam's new rules were part of some new psychic game between them. "Want to come to my room and see the card I made you, Grandma?"

"Sure," Miriam said, taking off her boots slowly. She was going to wean Violet from their psychic camaraderie. "Let's go."

"Hold onto the banister like Mommy says," Violet said, taking the steps primly in front of Miriam. Miriam couldn't help chuckling. She had been horrified when she'd seen Violet in her mind go down these steps while Cara wasn't looking. Violet had lain on her belly at the top of the steps and surfed down, feet-first, bumping the front of her body against every step. *She'll break her ribs,* Miriam had worried. She'd been tempted to call Cara and tell her what was going on, but then Cara would know that she had been using her psychic powers to look in on Violet and that would have caused more chaos.

"I'm holding on," Miriam said.

"When you read my card you will know for sure that I wasn't being a storyteller," Violet said, "that I really knew you were coming today." She handed it to Miriam.

A rainbow was on the front, a rainbow in the right color order. Because the paper was narrow, Violet had bent the arc so it looked like a rainbow igloo with deep purple on the inside. Did Violet know the trouble in her home? Miriam wondered.

"You don't look happy," Violet said. "Don't you like my card?"

"I love it. It's just that it makes me want to study it the way I do a work of art in a museum." She opened the card. Violet's handwriting was legible, even though the d's were backwards. She read out loud:

"Grandma is coming today. I love you, Grandma. Love, your Grand Violet."

"Daughter is too hard to spell," Violet explained.

"This is better," Miriam said. "You are my grand Violet."

They sat on Violet's bed, their backs against the welter of Barbie throw pillows.

"This bed pulls out into two beds," Violet said. "Could you sleep in my room tonight?"

Miriam thought about how wonderful that would feel,

listening to Violet's snort breathing at night, seeing her little face in the glow of the nightlight. "If it's okay with your mom," she said.

"It's so lucky you're here," Violet said. "Tomorrow is Lisa Green's birthday."

"I'll be here at least a week," Miriam said, "so you should go to every party and play date you want to. I can amuse myself."

Violet's bottom lip curled down. "I wasn't invited to Lisa Green's birthday party. And not to Lisa Gray's and not to Elizabeth Martin's either. I was only invited to Darshan's birthday, and that's because his mother said that in India there's a fortuneteller in every family, so she's used to me."

Miriam's heart dropped. "It's hard being psychic," she said. "I've decided not to do it anymore. It makes people not like you and can cause harm."

"But you have to do it. If it's in your mind, you just have to. Besides, Grandma, we have so much fun with our psychic games."

"There's lots of other things we can do. We could play a game I used to play with your mother. I make a squiggle on a page and you draw something out of it. Then you make a squiggle and I make something out of it. Watch."

Violet's desk was piled with papers. Miriam got one and a box of crayons and drew a squiggle. Violet stared at it a moment and made a worm out of it, a worm with long eyelashes. The worms made Miriam think of Kaylee again. She blinked hard and thought three clicks. Miriam made a blue squiggle that was practically already a bird.

"This is fun, Grandma."

We're going to stay on the straight and narrow, Miriam thought, as she made another loop-de-loo squiggle.

Violet took the paper from her and drew a red bug with bent legs.

"It's a bug, all right," Miriam said, smiling.

"It's a bedbug, Grandma. You were worried about them, right? Before you came here, I knew you were worried about bedbugs, so I looked them up in my bug book."

Miriam began to scratch her arms, her legs, not from bedbug bites, but from nerves. She had promised Cara, and herself, not to go near the subject of being psychic, but was that was impossible with Violet, whose mind was like a psychic popcorn machine bursting kernels of visions. She would try. She would definitely try. She had to. She loved her gift, at least she used to, but Kaylee's death had changed all that. Now, when she thought of Violet being psychic, she shuddered.

XXI

MIRIAM, MIRIAM, MIRIAM, KAYLEE SAID FERVENTLY with closed eyes, all the while keeping the picture of Miriam from her ad in her mind. Miriam had contacted Kaylee's mother before, when she told her that her mother said it was okay to go to the ashram, so Miriam could do it again. The energy of that promise gave her a feeling of flying. When Kaylee cracked open an eye, she found herself outside a Tudor house on a hill. *This must be Miriam's house,* she thought, with a quicksilver feeling inside. She walked up the slate path. It horrified her, the thought of having to ring the doorbell. Even though she was dead, she was still shy. She had no idea how those Girl Scouts did it. Still, she pressed the bell. It didn't ring, but somehow she was inside the arched wooden door anyway, standing right in Miriam's living room. It was stucco with rough exposed beams on the ceiling and there was a stone fireplace. But where was Miriam? She probably had an office in her house.

Kaylee went up the spiral staircase, passed the stained glass window at the landing, and moved from bedroom to bedroom. Miriam wasn't there, but there were photos, lots of them, on the walls and on the dressers. There was a wedding picture of Miriam and her husband, he in top hat and tails.

And there was a wedding picture of a young woman with her husband. The woman, tall like Miriam's husband, was probably Miriam's daughter. And everywhere there were pictures of a little girl with long dark curls and blue eyes, Miriam's eyes. There were two sets of bronze baby shoes. The name Cara was inscribed on the base of one with her birth date, and the other set, with a birth date only six years ago, had "Violet" written on it. Cara must be Miriam's daughter and Violet her granddaughter. Somehow, Kaylee had never thought Miriam had any life outside of being a psychic. She had only come alive to Kaylee on the phone during their readings.

Kaylee went downstairs to the kitchen. The wallpaper was printed with bunches of fruit and there were wooden shutters and a round oak table with three chairs: Mama Bear, Papa Bear, and Baby Bear, Kaylee thought. She had read *The Three Bears* to herself when she learned how to read. With her father always about to die and her mother preparing for widowhood, then becoming a widow, nursery tales were considered too frivolous.

Kaylee thought that Miriam probably would sit in the chair nearest the window, but she couldn't picture her eating. The dining room was just as empty, but off the back door, she found another staircase. She was as excited as if she'd just won a game show. She went up the steps and opened the door onto a white room shimmering with crystals. A big white desk held a white phone, the phone that Miriam must have talked to her on. She half-expected that if she picked up the receiver she would hear Miriam's voice, but when she reached for the phone, the receiver didn't lift in her hand. Then she noticed a card on the desk printed with a Madonna's face that looked just like her own. The remembrance card from her funeral! Tom had slipped one into her casket. It was in her pocket now. It was the only thing from life...no, really from death, that she'd been able to hold onto. And to find one here on Miriam's desk! It meant that Miriam had held her in her mind, maybe even in her heart. Miriam would not only be able to see her, she'd be happy to see her. "Miriam, Miriam, Miriam," Kaylee called out with her eyes closed.

When she opened them, even though she should have known how it worked by now, she was startled to find herself outside, standing before a red brick row house with tall windows and a white door. Miriam must be inside this house! She jumped up and down like a kid. She pictured Miriam's face again. Before she knew it, Kaylee was in a brightly lit, large kitchen that had copper pots hanging from ceiling hooks, the kind of kitchen you would see in magazines. And there was the little girl from all those photos, Violet, twirling spaghetti around her plate. The woman with the green eyes was Cara, and sitting across from her was Miriam in the flesh. It was hard not to just shout out "Miriam!" but she had to go slowly because of Cara and Violet. Miriam must have used the same picture in her ad for the last ten years, Kaylee thought.

She listened as Miriam told Cara and Violet about a woman who had brought a live chicken into Grandpa Rory's pharmacy and asked him for ointment for the chicken's beak.

"That lady must have thought Grandpa Rory is a chicken pharmacist," Violet said, and they all laughed.

Then they each began telling jokes about chickens crossing the road to get to the other side.

Staying back, Kaylee thought about how she'd wished that there had been more people at her table for a meal instead of just her mother, with her mother's loud, breathy chewing, and burps. Then, after she married, Tom had sat at the table with his newspaper, reading parts aloud to her, his mouth full of sausage. Once they went Ayurvedic, the brown rice and beans didn't look any better. There was rarely any laughter.

Bolstering her courage, Kaylee sat down in the empty chair right next to Miriam. There was a knocking inside her chest as if her heart were still beating. She wondered if Cara and Violet were so used to Miriam seeing the dead that they wouldn't freak if Miriam turned to her and said, "Kaylee? Is it you?"

"Mom, you're blinking so hard, like a twitch," Cara said. "Is something wrong with your eyes?"

"Just a little dryness," Miriam said.

"You'd better get your eyes checked by a real doctor," Cara said, "and not just use one of your home remedies."

It was Kaylee's chance. "Psst," she said, like one of those guys on a corner selling fake Rolexes, "Miriam, it's me, Kaylee. Please, I have to talk to you."

Miriam didn't answer, but Kaylee was sure that she wanted to because Miriam stretched her lips and her tongue kept touching the back of her top teeth. Maybe she wants me to lip read, Kaylee thought, and got up and went around behind Violet's chair so she was facing Miriam. It looked like

Miriam was saying, "Click, click, click." Was it some kind of code? What was going on here? Kaylee felt like screaming, but she calmed herself the way the guru had taught her to.

"*Om mani padme hum,*" she chanted. "The Supreme Reality is the Lotus of the Jewel of Oneness."

She'd have to wait and talk to Miriam when she was alone and free to respond. Yes, that was it. *Miriam is trying to pretend that she doesn't see me,* Kaylee thought, *for Cara's and Violet's sake.*

"These tofu meatballs taste like the real thing," Miriam said.

Violet just kept twirling and twirling her spaghetti. "Grandma," she said, "tell me a story about you and your bubbie when you were a little girl."

"I'll tell you the story of how Grandpa Rory and I met," Miriam said as quickly as one of those nut-under-the-shell guys. Cara was watching Miriam, and Miriam, Kaylee saw, was on guard.

"I see you when you were young, Grandma," Violet said. "Your hair was way out sideways and you were wearing a fur coat with icicles on it. It was snowing and you slipped and said, 'ow, ow,' and then Grandpa Rory picked you up in his arms. He wasn't bald then. He had big curly hair and it was brown."

Squirming, Miriam glanced nervously at Cara. "Violet, I must have told you that story already."

Violet looked at her mother uneasily too. "Yeah, you must have," she agreed and poked at the fake meatballs on her plate.

There was a lot more going on here than Kaylee had first noticed, some tension between Violet, her mother, and her grandmother. And Kaylee wondered where Violet's father was, the big blond guy she'd seen in all those photos.

"When is Daddy coming home?" Violet asked.

"Very, very late," Cara said. "You'll see him in the morning."

Violet put down her fork. "Then I'll go to bed right away so I can see him sooner."

Kaylee sized the whole thing up. Violet's father was either dead or not living with them anymore and nobody had come out and told Violet. No one knew better than Kaylee how hard it was living in a family where no one told the truth. Her mother had claimed that her father was still in the hospital months after he had died. She had never gone to his funeral. The first one she'd been to was her own, and that didn't count.

"Three more bites of dinner and you can leave the table," Cara told Violet.

With a fetching sigh, Violet lifted the fork twirled with spaghetti above her mouth, cocked her head back, and sucked some strands from the fork. "One," she said. "Two," a few more strands, "three. Finished."

"But you only ate the spaghetti," said Cara.

"Cara, it's whole wheat spaghetti. It's got protein in it," Miriam said.

Cara shrugged. "Okay, I'm outnumbered."

"I'll clean up," Miriam offered. "You can go up with Violet."

Oh, I'll be alone with Miriam any minute, Kaylee thought with excitement, but Violet insisted that Miriam put her to bed and Cara...darn...she said it would be a good idea. "*Om mani padme hum,*" Kaylee chanted. She followed Miriam and Violet up the steps, Miriam favoring one leg, Violet bouncing on each step. As soon as Violet got upstairs, right at the landing, she stripped off her clothes, laughing as she threw them here and there. Her skin was so creamy, so new to the world. Kaylee could never remember herself that free, not even with the guru.

"Kaylee-ay, let me see you," the guru had said, turning on the lamp in his cabin. She'd thrown her arm across her breasts and made her hand a fig leaf over her privates. He'd taken her hands away, but then she couldn't look at him. He'd laughed, and she'd been sure it was with delight at her modesty. She was so different from the other women at the ashram who threw themselves at him. But now, since she'd seen him with Lee-ay and Tom had told her that the guru had probably been in with the phony land developers, she thought he might have just been laughing at how easy it would be to take her money. She used to love thinking of the guru, but now she tried to push away the ruined memory.

Miriam, her back to Kaylee, was kneeling on the bathroom floor, filling the bath with water. Violet went around her, one leg over the tub, and then she was inside, her body losing its edges in the water. Miriam squirted liquid soap onto a washcloth and handed it to Violet. Although she had never been allowed in the sandbox or in mud, Kaylee remembered her own mother scrubbing her down in the tub as if she were filthy. It hurt to watch the tenderness between them, like looking at snow in sunshine.

"Grandma, your eyes are still twitchy," Violet said.

"I'll have to see an eye doctor when I get back," Miriam told her.

This was taking forever, Kaylee thought. Her whole body felt twitchy. She couldn't wait to be alone with Miriam. She couldn't wait to find out how to connect with other spirits instead of walking the earth invisible. "*Om mani padme hum.*"

Violet was finally out of the bathtub. Miriam wrapped her in a pink towel. *Soon,* Kaylee thought. But then Miriam sprayed conditioner on Violet's hair and combed it through, then dried it with a blow dryer section by section. *This is more like eternity than eternity,* Kaylee thought.

Miriam and Violet left the bathroom and went through a door that had "Violet" written in pink wooden cookie letters on it. She could have followed them in, but she just couldn't stand watching them together anymore because of the delay it was causing and the contrast of how she'd been treated when she was Violet's age. Instead, she listened at the door.

"I can put my p.j.'s on myself, Grandma," Violet said, "but I didn't tell you because I know you like to."

Miriam laughed. "Is there anything else you can do yourself that you feel like you have to let me do?"

Kaylee remembered how her own mother never let her do anything herself, no matter how much Kaylee had begged her. Her mother had even squeezed the toothpaste out on Kaylee's toothbrush. "When you do it, you waste it," her mother had said.

"I can read myself my own stories," Violet said. "I can even read them to you, Grandma, but I'm tired. I'm so tired that I want to sleep by myself tonight, because if you sleep here with me, I might not sleep. I'll talk to you all night."

Kaylee heard Violet's overblown yawn that she was sure was faked.

"I'm a little tired too," Miriam said. "We'll have lots of time together tomorrow. "I'll see you in the morning. Sweet dreams, sleep tight."

"Don't let the bedbugs bite," Violet chimed in.

"I used to think that was funny until the bedbugs infiltrated New York City," Miriam said.

The doorknob turned. Kaylee stepped back into a corner of the hallway where she and Miriam could be together without anyone hearing them.

"Miriam, it's Kaylee. I desperately need a reading. I need to find out my future."

Miriam, blinking and clicking, didn't say one word to her. She didn't even make eye contact, Miriam who was her one hope, who Kaylee had been sure would help her. Miriam could see the dead. *Why can't she see me?* Kaylee thought. *I have to make her notice me.* She tried to reach for Miriam's arm, but her hand passed right through her. "Oh, God," Kaylee cried. Miriam just kept going down the steps. *Not even Miriam can see me or hear me.* Maybe Miriam could only see spirits of people who hadn't committed suicide. Kaylee felt lonelier than ever. How would she ever get off this earth, where she would be invisible to everyone for eternity?

Oh, Miriam was coming back up the stairs. *She is going*

to talk to me after all. "Miriam," she said, as Miriam reached the landing.

Instead of looking at her, Miriam was touching her earlobe and examining the carpet, running her bare foot over it. "Maybe I left my earring at the hotel," Miriam said. "Well, it was just costume jewelry anyway. Things come and go, especially earrings."

"Miriam," Kaylee shouted as loud as she could. "Miriam, I need you. Please, I can't stay lost like this forever," but Miriam just walked back down the steps, checking each for the earring as she descended.

Kaylee doubled over and fell to her knees. There was no blissful forgetting in suicide. Everything that she'd done, everything that had been done to her, was clearer now than ever. She was doomed to wander on earth forever, part of nothing, cared about by no one, and remembering all the awful things that had happened "Help me," she sobbed. "Somebody help me."

Violet's door opened and Violet peeked out in Kaylee's direction. *Does she see me?* Kaylee wondered. *No, she's probably looking right through me at a spot on the wall,* but Violet tiptoed right over to her.

"Shh," Violet said, putting a finger to her lips.

Kaylee just stared at her. "You, you can hear me? You can see me?"

"I saw you in the kitchen," Violet whispered, "but I pretended not to or Mommy would get mad at me and Grandma for teaching me to see you, even though Grandma won't play any of our special games anymore, but just regular grandma games like Grandma Hillary plays with me." She stuck her face closer to Kaylee, looking at her carefully. "Are you a bubblegummer?"

Kaylee forgot her misery and started to laugh.

"I mean," Violet said, looking up at the ceiling, "a doppelganger."

"What's that?"

"If you don't know, then you aren't one. I thought you were because you're wearing a long dress like Grandma Miriam does."

"You really can see me? You really can hear me?"

"You silly," Violet said, smiling a dimpled smile.

This child can see me and hear me. Kaylee felt as if she were in heaven. This was heaven, to be able to be recognized. What a wonderful girl this was, Kaylee thought, to be able to see someone who is dead, especially since her grandmother, whose job it was to be a medium, had looked right through her.

"How old are you?" Violet asked.

"Seventeen," Kaylee said. If she had to stop at a certain age, it might as well be before she married Tom and before she got talked out of going to college.

"I was five on my last birthday," Violet said. "Grandma Hillary says I have to practice my 'th's' because I say them like *f*. Grandma Hillary says that birfday is an 'Aunt Ethel word.' But I don't have any Aunt Ethel."

"Neither do I," Kaylee said. "I had an Aunt Cora, an Aunt Nora, and an Aunt Dora."

Violet did a quirky laugh, exhaling a gust of air, flapping her lips. "Where do you live?"

"Nowhere anymore," Kaylee said.

"Aw," Violet said, "that's so sad. Do you want to sleep in my room?"

Kaylee burst into tears. "I would love to, Violet."

"I can't pull out the extra bed all by myself," Violet said.

"That's all right. I can sleep on the floor or anywhere in your room. It doesn't matter. I don't even need to sleep anymore."

"Are you a fairy?" Violet asked. There were fairies printed on her pajamas.

"Yes," Kaylee said. It would be too awful to tell this lovely child that she really was a woman who had jumped out her window to her death and left a grieving husband behind whom she never should have married in the first place.

"You won't be lonely in my room," Violet said. "I have lots of Flower Fairies from Toys R Us."

Kaylee felt a tiny spark that left as quickly as a blown-out candle. What if Miriam could see her and hear her, but had ignored her because she didn't want her around? Or what if Miriam got wind of her being here and somehow banished her from the house? Kaylee needed time to convince Violet to speak to Miriam on her behalf. *But Miriam couldn't just chase me out when her granddaughter has welcomed me in,* she thought.

"My name is Kaylee. I want to speak to your grand-mother. Would you be able to tell her that I'm here? It's really important to me." She saw Violet chewing her lip. "Please," Kaylee said.

"I will because I like you," Violet said, averting her eyes.

"I like you too. But I bet everyone does."

Violet shook her head slowly. "Not Lisa Green or Max or Lisa Gray or…"

Kaylee cut in. "I didn't have friends when I was your age either. We're alike in that way."

"But you're a fairy. You can stick onto anyone like Post-its."

"Violet?" her mother called upstairs. "Are you still up?"

"No, Mommy," Violet called.

They hurried into Violet's room and closed the door.

"It's like a garden in here," Kaylee said, "like you live indoors but outdoors all at once, with all these flowers on your walls." She thought of her own childhood room with its white walls. "I love it in here," she said. "You sleep and I'll watch over you."

Violet got into bed and pulled her pink comforter up to her chin. "You won't go away in the morning, will you?"

"Will you still want me here?" Kaylee asked.

"Yeah. You can stay with me always, like Tinker Bell."

Kaylee just couldn't get over that she had found such a beautiful place to bide her time. Then old regrets started bouncing in her head. "I was going to buy a house, a dream house," Kaylee told Violet. *Did fairies have real houses?* "It was a fairy house," she added. It might as well have been, the way it disappeared, along with the land developers and her mother's inheritance. "It was near other houses, but not attached like yours; more like a circle of houses with spaces in between. If I ever get a house like that again, I'm going to make my room just like yours."

"Grandpa George said he's going to make me a little house for my flower fairies," Violet said, "but I think it would be too small for you."

"Your room is just right for me," Kaylee said.

Violet blew her a kiss. Kaylee, who couldn't feel anything from the outer world, felt the kiss on her cheek, like warm honey. *Violet trusts me,* Kaylee thought. *At the right time, she will definitely speak to Miriam on my behalf. Miriam will contact my mother and get her to forgive me so I can move forward.* Kaylee sat down in Violet's little foam chair. "Lavender's blue, dilly, dilly, lavender's green," she sang. Uncle Finn had sung that lullaby to Kaylee so long ago. She couldn't remember the rest of the words, so she just kept singing that one line. It did the trick. She watched Violet drop off to sleep, her thumb near her open mouth on the pillow. Kaylee didn't feel in any rush to go anywhere else for now. She could wait for the perfect time for Violet to be her spokes-child.

XXII

"Hurray, you're still here," Violet said when she woke up the next morning and saw Kaylee in the rocking chair, her long hair like dark vines on the white wicker.

Kaylee laughed. "Good morning, Violet."

Violet booty-bumped three times in bed, then jumped off and went straight to Kaylee, standing on her toes to give her a kiss.

"No, don't touch me," Kaylee said. "Fairies can't be touched or their lights could go out. Only your plastic fairies can be touched."

Violet felt a little bit like when Lisa Green's mother wouldn't let her play with Lisa anymore, but she knew there were rules. Daddy had read her the real *Peter Pan*, so she knew that fairies couldn't fly in the rain and they could only hold one feeling at a time. She blew Kaylee a kiss like she had the night before, and Kaylee pretended to catch it in the air and put it on her cheek.

"Violet, I need you to tell your grandmother that I'm here and I have to talk to her. Will you do that for me?"

Violet rubbed her big toe in the carpet. She didn't want to tell. She was afraid that Grandma Miriam would chase Kaylee away. Just like Mommy, Grandma Miriam now didn't want Violet to see anybody that nobody else could. But Kaylee's eyes looked like Mrs. Cooper's cocker spaniel's eyes when he scrabbled at the window, wanting to go out.

"Okay," she said. She was so nervous that her legs felt wobbly. She took her doll with her to have something to hold on to and went off to the guestroom. She stood at the side of Grandma Miriam's bed, staring at her so she'd get up. Grandma Miriam slept with her arms out and bent and one knee bent against her other leg. She looked like the Hangman in the tarot cards that Violet wasn't supposed to look at anymore. Soon Grandma Miriam's eyelids started bouncing and then her eyes opened.

"Hah, it's my darling. I thought I dreamed you."

Violet kissed Grandma Miriam on her nose. It was good to be able to kiss someone you loved. "Grandma, what did you dream? Was it anything that is going to happen to me or someone I know? Did you get any signs?"

"So, how did you sleep?" Grandma Miriam quickly asked.

Violet knew Grandma was just trying to make her think of something else and not think of things that Mommy wouldn't want her to think about.

"I slept very well," Violet said. "And so did my doll, Kaylee." She said Kaylee's name for a hint.

Grandma Miriam bolted up in bed. "What did you call her?"

Through her flannel nightgown, Violet could see Grandma Miriam's boobies shaking. Her whole body was shaking. Her face looked as though she'd seen a scary movie. Grandma was going to be very upset if she knew that a fairy was right now in Violet's room.

"Katy," Violet said. "Give Katy a kiss."

Grandma Miriam let out a big, big sigh and threw her arms around the doll. "I've never been so glad to kiss a Katy in my life," she said.

"I'll get dressed all by myself, Grandma. And you get dressed too. We can have breakfast together before I go to school."

"Good idea," Grandma said. "We'll have a dressing race. See who can finish first?"

"I better run," Violet said, but after she left the guest-room, she walked slowly. If she told Kaylee that she hadn't asked Grandma Miriam to talk to her, Kaylee would ask her to again and again.

"Well?" Kaylee said as soon Violet came in and shut the door.

"I tried very hard," Violet said, starting to cry.

"Oh, Violet, I'm so sorry. It's all right. Your grandmother will see me and talk to me when she's supposed to, I guess."

Violet stopped crying and hurried into her clothes.

FOUR DAYS LATER, IN THE PLAY KITCHEN OF VIOLET'S kindergarten, that annoying Max was using the measuring cup, so Violet had to be patient and not grab it from him like she had yesterday or Mrs. Oliver would tell her that wasn't nice. Max was taking his "sweet old time," as Grandma Miriam called it, pouring and pouring his make-believe milk into the bowl. She tapped her foot and Max stuck out his tongue.

She tried to think of bad words to call him. Poopy Head, Pee Pee Poop. She couldn't decide which was worse. Then she repeated what she heard in her head. "Tell Max that his father is gong to be added-it by the I.R.S." But she didn't tell Max, because she wasn't supposed to repeat things that she heard in her head or everyone went bobble, blah, bobble, and she got into trouble.

"Now I'm adding eggs," Max said, cracking and cracking them when anyone could see that they really weren't there at all.

Violet knew what was real and what was not. Like she knew that right now Kaylee was out in the schoolyard on the monkey bars, at the very tippy top, her blue fairy dress blowing up around her.

"My own fairy is in the playground," Violet told Max. "Do you see her?"

Holding tight to the measuring cup, Max looked out the window. "Yah, there's nobody out there. You always tell lies."

"Poopy Head," she mouthed at him, and like a big baby, Max ran and told Mrs. Oliver.

Mrs. Oliver had broken her eyeglasses that morning and had a little safety pin in the corner of the frames. When she bent down to talk to Violet, Violet couldn't help looking at it. The safety pin was so tiny.

"You know when you call a classmate a name it hurts his feelings," Mrs. Oliver said.

The frames were plaid, red and pink plaid, and the pin was a shiny brown.

"Do you understand, Violet, or do you need a time out?"

Violet saw how sad Mrs. Oliver's eyes were. She knew that Mrs. Oliver would hate to send her to the corner for time out. "Sorry Max," Violet said with her fingers crossed behind her back.

He stuck his tongue out at her and Mrs. Oliver didn't even see him.

Violet went to the window and pressed her nose against the pane. Kaylee waved her to come outside.

I can't, Violet thought as loudly as she could, but Kaylee waved her to come anyway. She wished she could. She missed Lisa Green. The other children already had their best friends and stayed with them most of the day, except for when Mrs. Oliver picked partners. Violet backed up to the door.

"Violet, where are you going?" Mrs. Oliver asked.

"Nowhere," Violet said. And she was stuck in the classroom when she wanted to be outside with Kaylee.

"Lavender blue, I'm right behind you," Violet heard, and she spun around and there was Kaylee right in kindergarten.

"Oh, my," Violet said. She looked around. Nobody else seemed to know there was a fairy in the class, not even Mrs. Oliver.

"Did you sign in at the Visitor's Desk?" Violet asked.

"Fairies don't have to," Kaylee said. Kaylee scrunched herself up and ducked into the playhouse. Lisa Gray was in there with Molly. Lisa Gray and Molly always hogged up the playhouse and if anyone else came in they said, "You can't come in. It's too crowded." Now Molly and Lisa Gray came out.

"It's too crowded in there," Molly complained.

Violet, giggling, went into the playhouse, where Kaylee was sitting on the floor. Her shoulders were round so she wouldn't bump her head.

"You're like Mary's little lamb," Violet said. "You followed me to school one day."

"But I didn't get you into trouble like Mary's lamb. I would never get you into trouble."

"Like Max does," Violet said, and Kaylee nodded as if she had been right there instead of outside on the monkey bars.

"It's not much fun at your house without you," Kaylee said. "All day long your mother is on the computer trying to make her business grow and your grandmother is on the phone, telling clients that she's trying to make her business shrink."

"Business, business, business," Violet said with the squawky voice of her toy parrot.

"I missed you," Kaylee said.

Violet forgot she wasn't supposed to touch a fairy and moved her head to rest it on Kaylee's shoulder, but her head went right down, like there was nothing there. Violet let out a yelp of surprise.

"Violet?" Mrs. Oliver said, sticking her head in the window of the playhouse.

"I was just pretending that I had a puppy and I stepped on the puppy's paw," Violet said, "but just by mistake."

"Come out," Mrs. Oliver said. "We're having story time now."

When they were all sitting in the circle, Kaylee sat just behind Violet. Mrs. Oliver read to them about a frog that went a-courting.

"I know a story of a fairy who nobody could see or hear except one little girl," Kaylee said.

"Is the fairy's name Kaylee and the little girl's Violet?" Violet asked over her shoulder.

Mrs. Oliver stopped reading. "Only one person tells a story at a time," she said.

"No one else could see or hear the fairy besides the little girl," Kaylee said. "The little girl had to speak for the fairy to the people who couldn't hear her or see her."

"I can do that for you," Violet said. She could feel a party in her heart at the thought of helping.

"Violet, please stop talking and face front," Mrs. Oliver said.

Violet forced herself to look straight ahead. Mrs. Oliver was singing, "Mmm hmmm, mmmm hmmm," in her froggy voice.

"At first," Kaylee went on, "the fairy just stayed with the little girl so that she could speak for her to the little girl's grandmother."

"Do you have your own grandmother?" Violet asked.

Mrs. Oliver looked crossly at Violet again.

"Someday I'll tell you more about myself," Kaylee said. "It's all hard to explain. But for now, just let me finish this story, will you?"

Violet nodded.

"After getting to know the little girl," Kaylee said, "the fairy never felt happier than when she was with her."

"Violet, what a lovely smile on your face," Mrs. Oliver said. "I never saw a child so pleased that Miss Mousey married Mr. Frog."

Violet almost laughed out loud at how much she and

Kaylee were mixing up Mrs. Oliver. *Kaylee, come to school with me tomorrow and even tomorrow after that and after that,* Violet said in her mind. This was the most fun she'd had in school since Lisa Green's mother took Lisa out of the class and put her into one all the way down the hall.

Max stuck his tongue out at her again, but Violet didn't get a bit mad. He didn't have his very own fairy and she did.

LATER, AT THE SAND TABLE, KAYLEE WAS HAVING second thoughts as she smushed around with Violet. She had hoped that Violet would somehow get through to Miriam so that Miriam could contact Kaylee's mother and find out how to get to the spirit world. But being with Violet was even better for Kaylee than having her own child. At Violet's side, the prediction Uncle Finn had told Miriam was becoming true. "Cushla Machree," he'd said, "you're going to be playing someday like a child ought." Even though she couldn't feel the sand and she couldn't add to the mound that Violet was now patting, her heart knew what it was like.

"Don't tell anyone about me, Violet," she whispered, even though she knew no one else could hear her.

"Not even Grandma Miriam?"

"Not even Grandma Miriam. If you tell anyone, I might have to disappear and never come back again. That's how it is with fairies."

When Kaylee saw the look of alarm on Violet's face, she loved her even more. Kaylee could see what she'd come to mean to Violet by Violet's trembling lips, the sudden paleness of her cheeks, her wide eyes.

"I promise I won't ever tell," Violet said.

Kaylee smiled at her. "Good then. I will never leave you. I don't even want to. Not a bit."

MIRIAM WAS DELIGHTED WHEN HER CELL PHONE RANG and it was Rory. "Hi, honey," she said. Then whispering, "I have to admit that it's a bit boring being in Cara's house while she works and Violet is at school."

"You should come home," Rory said. "I'm not one of those guys who expects his wife to cook him a meal when he gets in from work. I can pick up a hero at Subway just as easy as the next fellow. But you'll cause trouble if you stay in Baltimore too long, hotel or no hotel."

"Rory, stop it! I'm not causing trouble. I'm not even at a hotel. Cara begged me to come. She really needs me since Dan..." Her voice trailed off. If she told him that Dan had moved out he'd blame her for that. "Since Dan is working so hard," she added quickly.

"Then you're going to cause trouble with pumping Violet full of psychic know-how. Maybe Violet will get sick of it, too."

Miriam flinched as if he'd actually thrown a punch at her. "Well, at least if I stay here, you won't get sick of me," she said, and snapped her phone shut. She waited for an apology, but he didn't call back.

Lonely here and lonely in Great Neck, Miriam thought. She was tempted to psychically peek into Violet's day at school, but in her effort to become a regular grandma, she stopped herself. She'd ask Violet about her day instead. She knew how disappointing she was to Violet now that she wouldn't play "what am I thinking" games with her, but she couldn't go on encouraging her to be psychic.

An hour later, Miriam's heart quickened when Violet's bus wheezed to a halt and put out its stop sign. Violet got off, carrying her backpack and holding rolled-up drawing paper in her mittened hand.

Miriam waved hard, eager for the moment Violet would see her, but Violet's head was looking up and to the side, and she was talking to someone who didn't seem to be there. Out of habit, Miriam felt her eyes blinking hard and heard herself click-clicking. *Nerves,* she thought. Then Violet motioned to someone, as if waving someone away, and finally smiled at Miriam.

"Grandma, do you want to see my drawing?" Violet asked, already holding it out.

Miriam unfurled it and knew right away who was who. She could recognize herself with her curls and long skirt; Rory, the tallest, with his bald head and the earpieces of his glasses going straight up in the air; Dan with his blond hair flattened on top and the cleft in his chin; Cara in her jeans and red high-tops; and Violet with her long brown hair. Next to Violet, there were a few tentative lines with dark scribbles over them.

"That's all of us," Miriam said, "but who did you cross out?"

Violet's mouth made a little "o." Snatching the drawing from Miriam, she said, "It was just a mistake, Grandma."

Miriam didn't want to go from revered psychic grandma

to dope. She closed her eyes and asked herself what Violet had scribbled out. "You started drawing a fairy here," she said. "A fairy in a blue dress."

Instead of being delighted as she would have in the past, Violet stamped her foot. "Grandma, I want you to just see what I tell you to see."

Miriam felt pained. Rory had been right. She was causing trouble here. Violet was getting sick of her.

"Violet, speak nicely to Grandma," Cara said. In her reading glasses and old Guns N' Roses t-shirt, Cara looked like an MTV librarian.

"Sorry, Grandma," Violet said.

After Violet went up to her room, Cara chuckled. "This is the first laugh I've had since Dan moved out," she said softly. "Now I know I won't have to watch over you, Mom. Violet is starting to get like me when I was a kid. She'll stop you from intruding all by herself."

Even though Miriam didn't want to do psychic work anymore, she was hurt to be seen as an intruder. She thought of Kaylee again, how she still might have been alive if only... Miriam began clicking and blinking just to get the thought of Kaylee away from her. She went back to the guestroom and closed the door. She was desperate to talk to Bubbie, but she wasn't about to invoke spirits into Cara's house. How could she seal herself off from Violet's thoughts? Violet had a right to privacy. Twiddling her curls with her fingers, she remembered sitting in Bubbie's parlor, listening to Bubbie do a reading for Mrs. Zaren, the tea-leaf reader from the other side of town in their old neighborhood.

"I'm in bed, schloffing and snoring away, and suddenly I have a dream that my Yossie is making love to that chippy waitress from Shloime's Deli," Mrs. Zaren said, her brown frizzy wig slipping down her narrow forehead. You could see the hair stitched to the mesh cap at the part. "I open my eyes and I see what Yossie is thinking, like a whole show, the stage right over his head. He's got that chippy on his lap and don't ask what he's doing with his hands."

"Shh," Bubbie had said, "Miriam is here."

But Mrs. Zarin couldn't contain herself. "So I wake Yossie up to tell him, and what does he say? 'A man, he can dream, can't he?'"

"What you need to do, Zarin," Bubbie had advised, "is to think of that *sheitel* you wear on your head as the way to keep your mind out of Yossie's." Later, she'd told Miriam that Mrs. Zarin's cheap *sheitel* was what kept Yossie's mind away from Mrs. Zarin, so why shouldn't it work the other way?

Now Miriam imagined herself wearing a sheitel like Mrs. Zarin's. She pictured it so strongly that her scalp felt itchy, but she didn't scratch it. She thought of Violet in her room. All she saw now was a closed door. She listened. There was only muffled sound. She would keep the imaginary wig on, even sleep in it. She didn't want Violet to have to reject her. She didn't want to have to live five hours away in order to be loved.

XXIII

It felt strange to be so distant from Dan and yet have him sitting beside her in at the principal's office at Violet's school, Cara thought. But she was relieved he was here. She wanted him to get it, really get it, that Violet had a genuine problem that needed addressing. She wanted him on her side.

"I'm so glad you both could come," Mrs. Vincent said to them. Usually she wore a skirt and blouse, but now she had on a blue suit, as if she were armored for what she had to tell them. Her hairline was solid auburn. Her scalp, at the part, was the same color. She must have freshly dyed her hair for the occasion.

"As I told your wife on the phone," she said to Dan, "we've been so worried about Violet and her imaginary companion. We'd like your permission to have her evaluated."

Cara twisted the strap of her pocketbook in her lap and gave Dan an I-told-you-so look. If he had paid any attention to what she had been trying to tell him instead of being so fascinated with Violet being psychic that he had to delve into it scientifically, they might not be sitting here right now.

"What exactly is wrong?" Dan asked. "Many children

have imaginary playmates. Why is Violet's case so ominous that you want her evaluated?'

"Violet is a brilliant child," Mrs. Vincent began, which gave Cara the creeps since that was how Jessica, the psychologist, had begun. "And not only is she intellectually gifted, but she's kind and sensitive as well. Before she got overly involved with this imaginary companion of hers, whenever a child began to cry, she would tell her teacher why the child was crying, even if the child hadn't told her. Violet would do everything she could to help. She gave away her Hello Kitty change purse to a girl who had lost her own. And she gave her cookies to a boy whose mother doesn't believe in sweets. Of course, we had to stop her from violating a parent's dietary preferences, but the impulse for generosity and connection was there. Sadly, even with Violet's terrific qualities, some parents were upset about things that she was saying, things that could defame them, that she couldn't possibly have known about in a regular way."

"So," Dan said, the heel of his palms together, two fingers up like a teepee tent, "what you're telling me is that my daughter is being evaluated because some child's parent, and I'm not mentioning names, has a problem with the way in which my daughter's mind works?'

He was so uppity, so contrary, that Cara couldn't take it. "Will you listen to what Mrs. Vincent has to say?" she insisted.

"I know how hard it is to take it all in secondhand," Mrs. Vincent said, her hand cupping a snow globe paperweight. "But I'd like you to come with me and observe Violet from the doorway of her classroom."

Cara had a lot riding on this. She needed Dan to understand that there was really something going on with Violet, something he couldn't argue away. "If Violet sees us, won't it change her interactions? she asked.

"Believe me, when they're playing, they don't notice anything or anyone. Plus, we won't open the door all the way. We'll just peek." Mrs. Vincent rose from her chair.

Cara and Dan rose too. As they followed her down the hallway, Dan muttered, "Spying on our on child as if she were a criminal."

If he lived at home, you'd have seen it for yourself, Cara thought.

The doorway to Violet's classroom had been left ajar with a wooden wedge as a doorstopper. Cara spotted Violet right away. She was at the sand table, pouring sand from a scoop into a sieve. Cara didn't want to think of herself as shallow, but she couldn't help noticing how gorgeous Violet was. *She could be a top children's model if I weren't against putting her through that,* Cara thought. And then Violet began talking out loud, though there was no one else near her, just as she had been doing at home. What was she saying? Cara leaned forward. How she wished she could read lips. Violet was chattering away, not talking to herself, but to someone Cara couldn't see, and she even held out the sand scoop to give her imaginary companion a turn. It had been easy to find Violet because all the other children were in bunches, some at the play kitchen, others building towers with blocks, and one boy wrecking them. Violet's friend, Darshan, approached her, but Violet was so entrenched in her conversation with no one that he probably thought it would have been rude to break in and went off to join another boy at the painting easels. One girl was by herself, talking, Cara noticed, but she was cooing to a turtle in a tank. Violet was talking into the air. Cara bolstered herself with a hand on the doorjamb.

"Is Violet like this all day?" Dan asked, the cocksureness gone from his voice.

"Mrs. Oliver tries to distract her," Mrs. Vincent said. "She devotes individual time to her, brings in special materials, learning games, sequins, anything that she thinks will catch Violet's fancy. But within moments, Violet is demonstrating what to do with the materials to whomever she thinks she's talking to. There's a little bathroom in the corner of the class, and Mrs. Oliver even heard Violet talking in there, telling someone that she should wash her hands."

Cara felt ill, chilled and sweaty as if she had the flu. Violet had been chattering away at home too, but it hadn't been as glaring there. She hadn't known that Violet was behaving like that elsewhere. Violet and her invisible sidekick! Her psychic mother hadn't been fazed by it, but nothing seemed "off" to her mother, who had been on speaking terms with poltergeists until the recent tragedy that she still couldn't bring herself to speak of. *Why did I stop trying to help Violet be normal just because the first psychologist I took her to had bonked her own kid with frozen fish? There are tons of psychologists and psychiatrists. I should have tried someone else.*

And then, as if her imaginary friend had pointed them out, Cara glanced at them. She didn't run to them. She didn't call out, "Mommy, Daddy." She didn't even wave. She just looked at them blankly and went right back to talking to whomever.

"You saw that, didn't you?" Cara said to Dan, her voice trembling. "I think it could be considered alienation of affection, couldn't it?"

"If you'll allow me," Mrs. Vincent said, "we can go back to my office and I'll give you the papers to sign so I can set up the observation. Early intervention will make all the difference." Mrs. Vincent prattled on about how even autistic children had come out of their shells, begun speaking, but none of this comforted Cara as she watched Violet laughing hysterically—but about what? With whom?

When the meeting was over, Dan walked Cara to her Navigator and opened the door for her. He had on his gray wool coat with his collar up against the wind. "May I come in and sit with you for a bit?" he asked.

She was so overwrought that she could only nod. When he went around and got in beside her, they were quiet, looking ahead as if they were both driving. She turned on the engine to put on the heat.

"Violet has been distant to me too," he said. "Always looking somewhere else other than at me, even when I'm talking to her." He pulled at his face. "I thought it was personal, that she was punishing me because I wasn't living at home anymore."

Cara didn't even know where Dan was staying these days. He just came in early and had breakfast with Violet while she and Miriam stayed back to give them their time together. Maybe Dan had moved in with one of his psychics, she thought bitterly.

"Well, Mr. Psychic Researcher," she snapped, "you were the one who didn't want Violet to see a psychologist, and now that it has gone public it will it be on her school record forever. Now are you going to give up your study for a psychic gene?"

Without a word, Dan swung his door open and stepped out. She wanted to call, "Wait! Stop!" But Dan had drawn a thick line between them. She had never expected that he would actually stay away as long as he had—a whole week and a day, though who was counting? When she'd told him to leave, he hadn't even tried to come back. Was she any happier without him? Was it easier to cook dinner, knowing for sure that he wouldn't be there to eat it instead of guessing? Was it easier to wake up in the morning, knowing Dan hadn't been in her bed all night instead of worrying about how early he was leaving for work? And the nights she wasn't without him, were they any better? Every night she tried to snuggle up to him and woke, shocked, remembering that he didn't live there anymore. She didn't think she was any happier, and Violet surely wasn't. "Dan!" she called, but he was already in his yellow Saab, looking behind him to pull out of the lot. She took out her cell phone, then put it back in her bag. She was still angry with him. She felt it in her gut. If he came back, it had to be because there was peace between them; otherwise it would all just start over again.

She remembered the time that she and Dan had been driving to Great Neck when they got caught in a blizzard. Cara was driving because Dan had injured his right shoulder lifting free weights. "Slow, go slow," he'd said. "I can hardly see," she told him. "I'll be your eyes," he said. "Don't worry. Okay, we're going to have to stop at the light. Don't come to a full stop. Let the tires inch along." She'd been terrified, but with his guidance they were able to get safely to a gas station, where the attendant let them wait out the brunt of the storm. What was happening with Violet was another kind of storm, one she couldn't see the end to. She wanted that Dan back, the Dan she'd trusted, relied on, but he wasn't there anymore. At least she had her mother with her.

After he drove off she sat there, the heater blowing into her face. Before long Violet's kindergarten class filed out into the playground, all in snowsuits, mittens, and boots. Mrs. Oliver believed in fresh air and took them out for short stints in all kinds of weather. The kids had to hold hands on line as they filed out two by two. Violet was holding Lisa Gray's hand, but Violet was turned away from Lisa while she chattered excitedly with her imaginary friend. Cara began to tremble. She had thought that being called to school was going to make Violet's situation clear to Dan, but what it had done instead was make it terrifyingly clear to herself.

She had to get away. She jerked the car into gear. She was glad that she wasn't going home to an empty house, that her mother was there, waiting to hear all about what had happened. Who else could she tell? Would her mother already know?

When she got home, Cara's head felt as if an ice pick was jabbing her behind her eyes. She couldn't bring herself to lift her head to look at her mother, who was waiting in the foyer, so anxious herself that she kept clicking, blinking.

"Was it as bad as all that?" her mother said.

"Worse. Much worse."

"I put up a pot of tea."

Cara liked coffee, but she was so beaten down that none of her preferences seemed important because her biggest want, for Violet to be well, had just gone kaput before her eyes. She took off her coat and boots, but as she dragged herself to the kitchen, she still felt as if she had on all that heavy outwear.

"Mom, do you know what Aunt Chaia was like when she was a little girl?"

Her mother looked startled, then took a gulp of tea. "Chaia was my father's favorite sister," she said slowly. "She was everyone's favorite, so chubby back then, because anyone who had a sweet gave it to her, even the *muzhiks*, the peasants who hated Jews. My father could never talk about Chaia without tears." Cara saw the tears in her mother's eyes now. "She was a real mischief, that Chaia. In Berdichev there was an ink factory where spilled ink from broken bottles always ended up in puddles on the grass. No matter how much Bubbie hollered, Chaia would wander off to stamp in those puddles. She'd come home with blue feet and promise she wasn't anywhere near the factory." Her mother's laugh came out like a cough. "Oh, and I remember another one of my father's stories. Once, my grandfather couldn't find his eyeglasses anywhere. He searched the field, the barn. He asked the children and they all said they didn't see his them. Chaia said it especially loudly. Finally my grandfather found a chicken wearing the eyeglasses around his throat, the frames tied together by Chaia's ribbon. The lenses were badly scratched. After a *patsh* on the *tuches,* Chaia admitted that she had tried to make the chicken wear the glasses to protect his eyes because all the chickens pecked at each other when the feed was thrown at them. She was worried this chicken would get her eyes pecked out. Grandpa was so mad that he insisted Bubbie cook that chicken for shabbes dinner."

"Those things sound just like things Violet might do," Cara said, the ice pick of pain stabbing more ferociously. She leaned forward in her chair and looked her mother in the eyes. "What I want to know is, was Aunt Chaia as psychic as you and Violet?"

Her mother looked stricken. "Yes."

All Cara's good will toward her mother bled out like the tea in the teabag. "If you knew that and you saw how your aunt ended up, how could you have encouraged Violet to be psychic?"

Her mother sighed. "Being psychic didn't cause Aunt Chaia's breakdown. It must have been schizophrenia. In those days there weren't good medications or diagnoses or any suitable therapies."

"Mom, I'm scared. I'm so scared that Violet is headed in Aunt Chaia's direction. The genetic counselor I went to before I got pregnant with Violet said that as long as Aunt Chaia's condition was only on my side of the family, Dan and I probably had nothing to worry about. He said in many cases of mental illness, a lot depends on nurture."

"That's what I've been trying to tell you. Chaia was separated from her father for ten years."

Cara felt a wave of fear. "That might very well be part of Violet's story, too."

"When your family has to escape a country, the story is different," said Miriam. "Bubbie and her children had to hide in the forest, eat roots and berries, and be on the lookout for wolves and bears as well as Cossacks."

"I know," Cara said. "But you've seen how much Violet likes to keep to herself around here, how she spends so much time in her room and is always talking to someone. She actually prefers being alone now to being with me and even with you."

Her mother nodded. "I see that, and it hurts. It hurts so much. We couldn't wait to be together, and now I'm right here with her and she prefers an imaginary playmate."

"When Dan and I observed Violet in her classroom, we saw how completely she's withdrawing from everyone except whoever it is that she's dreamed up. They are going to have her evaluated and get her early intervention. It doesn't seem early enough to me. I want something done right now. My poor baby."

"Let me try to speak to her when she gets home," her mother said. "Maybe I can help. Violet might have thought I was pushing her away when I wouldn't play psychic games and that left room for her to create an imaginary companion to fill the void. I even put on Mrs. Zarin's sheitel to block myself from getting into Violet's head. Now I can't seem to get it off."

Cara didn't bother to ask her mother what she was talking about. They just sat there, gripping their teacups with both hands, as if anything in the world could happen, as if the cups could suddenly fly up to the ceiling and pour tea on their heads. And then they heard the bus and both of them rushed to the side door. Through the small decorative windows that framed the door, they watched Violet walking up the path, chatting away, animated, nodding, laughing.

"I've seen Violet like this before, but it seems worse now," Cara said.

"God help us," Miriam murmured as Cara opened the door.

"Hi, my precious," Cara said, kneeling and holding out her arms to Violet.

Violet gave her a perfunctory hug. As she slipped off her boots and jacket, Violet said, offhandedly, "Hi, Grandma," and then kept going toward her room.

"Violet," Miriam said, "Mom and I want to talk to you."

"Don't worry," she heard Violet whisper, "I won't tell."

Cara sat down on the couch next to Violet, but Miriam stood before her. Cara guessed that she saw the "sweetsy" method hadn't worked and was trying for authority instead.

"Violet, Mom and I are worried about you," Miriam said. "Your dad is too. And Mrs. Oliver and even Mrs. Vincent, the principal. We need to know who you're talking to all the time in order to help you. You see, Violet, whoever you think you're speaking to couldn't really be a friend because you're being taken out of your own life, taken from the people who love you, like Mom, Dad, Grandpa Rory, and me. And you're so wrapped up in this invisible friend that it's affecting your learning in school."

Violet stamped her foot. "Don't say that, Grandma. You don't know. I'm learning a lot of things like time travel and levit...levitation."

Cara felt as if a thunderbolt had hit her. The sweat on her skin burned. Her mother clutched her throat as if she was about to throw up.

"From who?" Miriam demanded.

Violet's face closed like a fist. "You'll get too upset if I tell you."

"You will tell me," Miriam said, blinking hard.

In the midst of everything Cara reminded herself to make an appointment for her mother with an eye doctor.

"You will tell me," her mother went on, "because you know how much we love for you, no matter what." Violet bunched her lips and shook her head hard. "Tell us," Miriam insisted.

"I won't."

Even in the vise grip of Cara's fear, she watched her mother touch the tip of her index fingers to the tip of her thumbs, forming circles, the same gestures she used while meditating. She knew her mother was trying to pull in whatever forces of help there were around her. Her mother's back was now straight, her chin forward. Dan wasn't with her to help, but her mother was a lioness for Violet, and for me, Cara thought. She felt as if she had never loved her mother more, the way her mother wouldn't give up, wouldn't give in, no matter how upset Violet seemed.

"Who are you talking to, Violet?" Miriam repeated.

Violet squirmed on the couch, looking to the side, then

back at her grandmother, and back again to her invisible friend. It was like seeing a child on a witness stand who was had been prompted to not tell the truth.

"I will protect you, Violet," Miriam said. "Tell me."

"I don't need protection," Violet said. "She will never hurt me."

"Who?" Miriam said.

Violet put her hands to her head as if it was all too much. She looked to her left, then looked back at her grandmother, to the left, back at her grandmother.

"Tell me," Miriam said, raising her voice.

"Kaylee," Violet finally blurted out. "Kaylee is my friend."

"Kaylee?" Miriam echoed, and Cara watched in horror as her mother, the lioness, went pale, put her hands to her chest, and collapsed with a clunk on the hardwood floor.

"I can't stay here overnight," Miriam told the ER doctor who was tightening the blood pressure cuff on her arm. She felt delirious and still woozy from her fall, but was desperate to get back to Cara's in order to protect Violet. "I can't imagine why my daughter thought she should call the ambulance just because I fainted."

The doctor's hair was the putty color of an Ace bandage. She could tell by the way his brow furrowed on his thirty-something forehead that her blood pressure had spiked.

"My blood pressure is actually fine," she assured him, taking deep breaths to calm down so she could prove it. "I'm just upset about finding myself in the hospital."

The doctor had a yeah, yeah look, as if he heard this

excuse each shift. "Your daughter was right to take your symptoms seriously, especially since she told the EMT that you'd been twitching and making clicking sounds with increasing frequency. You'll need to be seen by a neurologist as well as a cardiologist."

Miriam thought of how much time it would waste. She had to convince him that she was okay. "I definitely don't need a neurologist," she said. As she was thinking up a pitch to get her out of this, it hit her that while she'd been at Cara's, Kaylee must have been right in her space, up close. *I must have sensed her,* Miriam thought, *but instead of confronting her so I could protect Violet, I clicked and blinked like Sabrina told me to.* Miriam felt like the A-hole of the psychic world. I should have done battle with Kaylee, no matter what, instead of trying to block her. "I was clicking and blinking," she told the doctor, "because I was staying with my daughter for two weeks and I wanted to keep my body busy so I wouldn't be a busy body, if you know what I mean. But don't tell her," she added. How could he? Cara wasn't there. She'd had to stay home with Violet. Miriam's agitation felt like a washing machine gone wild, but she feigned a fetching smile, even though she was way too old to flirt.

Finally the doctor smiled back. "I wish you could teach that trick to my mother-in-law."

He tightened the blood pressure cuff again to give her a fresh try. If only she could tell him the truth, she'd feel so much better that her blood pressure would be normal again. But if she told him "A spirit who blames me for her losing her mother's inheritance might be trying to harm my granddaughter to spite me," he would probably call in a psychiatrist besides a neurologist and she'd end up in a locked ward and not get out for who knew how long. *I have to tune into what's happening between Kaylee and Violet,* she thought. She could feel her blood pressure mounting at the thought of Kaylee being anywhere near Violet. Just Kaylee having access to Violet made Miriam's blood pound. *Kaylee might try to kill Violet, maybe not outright, but draw her into a dangerous situation to get back at me,* Miriam thought. She was desperate to be alone to try to contact Kaylee. *Go already,* she silently begged the doctor. If he didn't leave, she'd appeal to his grandmother, who now was hovering over him, her dyed red hair like a zinnia, her black laced-up oxfords dangling inches above his head.

"My grandson, he graduated first in his class," his grandmother crowed, her palms together, her shoulders gliding as if she were a diva singing an aria. Then she gave Miriam a look of pity and said to her grandson, "*Gai, gai already.*"

"Well, Mrs. Kaminsky," the doctor said, "I'll get things rolling so you can be out of here as soon as possible."

As he disappeared through the gap between the green striped curtains pulled around her bed, Miriam took it as a sign that there was definitely hope she would be freed soon to help Violet. She nodded a thank-you to the doctor's grandmother, who faded away.

Once he was out of there, she took more deep breaths, but she had so much anxiety that the deep breaths were about as effective as the Dutch boy sticking his finger in the hole in the dam. At five, when she'd had double pneumonia, Bubbie had wrapped her in warm blankets, swaddling her like a baby, and held her close on her lap. She had felt Bubbie's heartbeat against her cheek. The memory quieted her. Soon, from her hospital bed in Johns Hopkins, her mind became ten Nanny-cams, searching each room of Cara's house simultaneously. Cara was in her bedroom, lying across her duvet with an ice pack on her forehead. Violet wasn't in her room, nor the kitchen, living room, her parents' room, the guestroom, bathrooms. Where was she? Miriam's blood began pounding again. And then she saw Violet in the den, setting her Polly Pockets at the tiny stations along the side of the tracks of Dan's electric train set that he'd bought himself after he and Cara had gotten married. He had always wanted one, but his parents had been afraid it would distract him from his studies. Violet was talking, but was it to Kaylee or her plastic miniature dolls? Miriam didn't see anyone else.

Suddenly the air next to Violet began to waver. It was Kaylee, Miriam knew it. She waited for Kaylee to take form.

The hospital curtain opened. Miriam didn't look. She couldn't risk a moment's distraction, but she sensed that a nurse had come in. She could hear the toilet plunger sound of thick rubber soles and smell face cream, Nivea, she thought.

"Mrs. Kaminsky, I'm going to give you an echocardio-gram," the nurse said.

Miriam didn't answer. Doubling her concentration, she continued to focus on Violet.

"Mrs. Kaminsky, are you all right?" the nurse asked. "Can you hear me?"

The swirling air in the den was beginning to shape itself into a woman's form. It would just be another moment.

The nurse began cuffing Miriam's wrist. "Can you hear me?" she shouted.

Her shouting pulled the plug on Miriam's Nanny-cams. The screens went blank. "I hear you," Miriam spat out furiously.

"Phew, you had me scared for a moment. Nobody likes being here, but we'll get you right as snow," she said soothingly.

Nothing would be right, Miriam thought, not like snow, not like rain, unless she could get out of here.

"Here we go," the nurse said, reaching behind Miriam's head to untie the hospital gown, then draw it down to bare her breasts and trunk. *Should I phone Sabrina?* Miriam wondered as the nurse swabbed her with alcohol. Would Sabrina just tell me to keep blinking and clicking now that it was clear that instead of bedbugs, Miriam had dragged an evil spirit into Cara's house and given her a personal introduction to Violet?

"You are a puzzle, a real puzzle," the nurse said. "When I came in, you were so still, barely breathing, and now you're so jumpy that I have no idea how I'm going to take this test."

Miriam could feel tears leaking from her eyes. "Do I get a phone call?" she asked as if she were doing time. And in a way, she was. She wasn't in charge of anything, not even her own body, let alone figuring out how to face down Kaylee.

"Of course you can make a phone call," the nurse said. "You can talk on the phone all you want. Just let me finish."

Miriam closed her eyes and stayed as still as she could. She had to cooperate so she could get out. If she just signed herself out the hospital without taking the tests, Cara would be beside herself. She'd probably drag her right back. Miriam tried to send a mental message to Cara. *Don't leave Violet alone.*

"That's a girl," the nurse, who was at least twenty years younger than Miriam, had the nerve to say.

The curtain opened again. "Oh, I'm so sorry," she heard, and that was that. Her concentration had been TNT-ed. She opened her eyes and saw her son-in-law standing there stupidly, his long arms dangling at his sides from having barged in to find his mother-in-law bare-breasted.

"Puh-leese," the nurse said indignantly. "Can't you wait until the patient is decent?"

After Dan stepped outside, Miriam felt that she would never be decent again. What decent grandmother would sic a crazed ghost on her granddaughter? She tried to focus on Violet, but Dan came into her mind, standing outside the curtain, slapping himself on the forehead. All she wanted to do was protect Violet. "Go home, Dan," she called through the curtain. "Tell Cara not to let Violet out of her sight, not even for a minute. And you need to guard both of them. I'll be fine. I'll be out of here in no time."

"Rory is coming," Dan called.

Oh, no, Miriam thought. *He'll be wagging his finger at me, blaming me for everything, and I have to be alone to help Violet.* She had no time to lose. She waited until the nurse left, wheeled the echocardiogram machine out with her, and began to focus on Violet again. Soon she saw her. Violet was still in the den with the electric trains and the swirling air that would turn into Kaylee's spirit if only people would stop bothering her, Miriam thought. In her vision she heard a ring tone to "When I fall in love it will be forever," the song that Dan had chosen to put on Cara's phone for his calls to her. It almost made Miriam burst into tears. In a few moments Cara was at Violet's side, talking about the trains with her. *Dan delivered my message,* Miriam thought. Cara wouldn't let Violet out of her sight and Dan would be joining her soon.

How stupid Miriam felt for having listened to that medium, Sabrina, who told her to click and blink to keep Kaylee's spirit away. She could have confronted Kaylee in her own home and never dragged her with her to haunt Violet. And then putting on that imaginary wig to block Violet's thoughts! Couldn't she have heard Violet's thoughts and kept her mouth shut about them? And how could she blame Sabrina when she herself had caused Kaylee's death?

"Kaylee," Miriam called out, "come, haunt me if you have to. Just leave my granddaughter alone. You hear me? You hear me, damn you?"

The air in Miriam's hospital room began to swirl. *Kaylee is coming to me,* Miriam thought. She wasn't frightened. Whatever happened, she'd save Violet, her dear Violet. But the air smelled of lavender, and in a moment Bubbie's worried face leaned over her, a lock of her white hair loose from her bun.

"*Neshomelah,* I been up there, running around like a chicken without a head, looking everywhere for this girl's mother so she can take her to the other side and leave Violet to her family."

"But Bubbie, her mother isn't a good influence on her."

"Och," Bubbie said, "whose mother ever is? Still, a mother is a mother."

"What can I do in the meanwhile?" Miriam asked. "I can't just do nothing. Violet is at risk for losing her mind. I have to drive Kaylee away from her."

"You can't give a ghost who committed suicide *a frosk in dem ponem,* a slap in the face," Bubbie said. "One way or another, the world already did that to them."

"Bubbie, why did I go to that Sabrina when I had you?"

"You could fill oceans with the tears of why," Bubbie said, and then she was gone.

Miriam couldn't worry about protecting Violet's privacy anymore. She had done it far too long. Now she had to be able to get into Violet's mind to protect her from Kaylee. She yanked off her imaginary wig. This time it yielded. She could actually feel the air on her scalp. She tried to focus on Violet, but by this time Miriam was so exhausted that her bones felt heavy. For a moment she worried that she'd come down with one of those awful incurable diseases people got from hospitals. But then she thought of all she'd been through that day, the anxiety over Violet, the ambulance with its siren and flashing lights, and sleep came over her as suddenly as if a spell had been cast on her.

In her dreams, she saw Cara and Dan, entwined in their bed. Even in sleep, she felt herself smile. Violet's crisis was bringing them back together. A curtain came down in her mind. She was a psychic, not a voyeur. Drifting, drifting on a luxury cruise of sleep, her mind eased into the port of Violet's room. Violet's bed was empty. Miriam bolted up and looked around her. *Where am I? Where is Violet?* She reached for the phone on the night table beside her hospital bed and dialed Cara. It was ringing, ringing, ringing. They couldn't still be having sex, she thought.

"Mom?"

"I don't think Violet is in her room," Miriam said breathlessly as her mind scanned every room. "I don't think she's anywhere in the house."

"What?"

"Go look," Miriam ordered.

As she waited, Miriam never knew that her heart could beat that fast. She could hear Cara and Dan calling out, "Violet, Violet," as they dashed about. They wouldn't be doing that if Violet were home. Hadn't she told Dan to tell Cara not to let Violet out of her sight?

"Call the police," Miriam said, so loudly that a patient who had been put in Miriam's room during the night began yelling, "Help, help!"

Cara was on the phone again. "Mom," she said, "Violet's gone."

part four

XXIV

MIRIAM HAD TO GET OUT OF HERE. SHE WENT TO THE closet, threw on her clothes. Cara had sent her off with a tiny pocketbook, something Cara would use when she went dancing at clubs before she had Violet. All that was in it was a comb, lipstick, and Cara had thought to tuck in Miriam's insurance card. But Miriam had a just-in-case twenty sewn into a secret pocket in each of her coats like Bubbie always did. She would get to Cara's. She'd given the hospital enough of her blood, enough of her time. Bubbie had said that you couldn't give a person who committed suicide a slap in the face, but Miriam wanted to tear at Kaylee's ghostly eyes, rip at her shroud. *Violet, I have to get to Violet,* Miriam thought. She sneaked out of the hospital with the same determination that Bubbie must have had when fleeing her sacked village in Russia and leading her little ones to safety. *I'm coming, Violet,* Miriam silently called. *Grandma's coming.*

IT WASN'T A REAL TAXI. IT WAS ONE OF THOSE CAR services, maybe just a regular car driven by someone who needed extra money, but she was so desperate that she got inside anyway.

"At night in Jamaica," the driver told her, "the dobies come out to haunt when the owl screeches." He had long dredlocks and a dangling earring with a bell on it that tinkled every time he took his eyes off the road to look back at Miriam.

"Why are you telling me this?" Miriam snapped at him. She felt as if he were Charon transporting her over the River Styx.

"You look like a woman who knows these things, a woman who wears green foam hospital shoes in winter."

Miriam realized that she'd left her boots in the hospital. Her hands shook as she loosened the stitches to her secret pocket in the lining of her coat. The twenty-dollar bill was crisp from the last dry cleaning. A few blocks from Cara's house, Miriam saw that Cara and Dan had wasted no time in alerting everyone. The night was filled with bobbing flash-lights and neighbors calling out, "Violet, Violet." The search party made it all the more real to Miriam that Violet was missing. She clamped her teeth together so hard that her jaw popped. When they turned onto Cara's block, Miriam saw a police car parked in front of it.

"Oh, mahn," the cab driver said, "if you need a place to hide, I can take you to one."

She gave him the twenty and got out of the cab. "If you see a little girl with a dobie, tell the police," she said and then ran up Cara's walk in her green foam slippers.

The front door was partly open. When she walked into the foyer, Miriam hung back at the sight of two policeman interviewing Cara in the living room. She didn't want to dis-tract Cara, have her go on about what the heck her mother was doing out of the hospital. And she needed to absorb the vibrations of the house to see if she could find out what had happened. She took deep breaths and closed her eyes.

"She's my only child," she heard Cara say, as if that would make the police work harder.

"Does the father live here?" one cop asked.

"My husband, Dan, is out looking for her right now."

It struck Miriam that if Dan hadn't been there, he would have been considered a suspect. Most missing children were snatched by estranged spouses. Miriam shivered. She couldn't let herself think of Violet as a missing child. She had to think of her as a found one.

"What was your little girl wearing?" the policeman asked.

"When I put her to bed, she was wearing her blue Ariel nightgown, but she might have put on her clothes. She'll be six soon. She can put on her own shoes and coat and even put her hair up in a ponytail." Cara started to cry. "She can do a second grade workbook."

"How did she get out?" one policeman asked.

"I don't know."

"Was one of the doors unlocked? A window?"

"God, I didn't think to look," Cara said, choking back tears.

Miriam shifted her eyes slightly to the right, where the near past was, and saw Violet pulling a pair of jeans up beneath her Ariel nightgown, going to the closet near the front door, tugging her jacket off the hanger, putting it on with her boots, and going out through the front door. She burst into the living room.

"Violet is wearing jeans, a lilac puffy jacket, and a pair of brown Uggs," she said.

Gasping, Cara jumped up from the couch. "Mom, you scared the hell out of me. Why aren't you still in the hospital?"

"If you were in the hospital, how do you know what the child was wearing when she left?" one policeman asked with a look that implied, *Where did you stash her?*

"I'm psychic," Miriam said, which made them look at her with even greater suspicion.

"Do you know how many false leads we get from people trying to make a name for themselves as a psychic?" a cop asked.

Miriam couldn't hold back her temper. "How dare you! I'm her grandmother."

"I'm going out to the car to call in the report," said the policeman who looked a bit older. "Grady, you check the house. The kid might be hiding somewhere or gotten shut inside something."

Miriam could see what was in his mind: opening the lid of a deep freezer and finding a frozen child. She would have lost her dinner right there had she eaten any.

"Violet wouldn't have put on her outer clothes to stay in the house," Miriam said, but the younger cop began his search anyway. Miriam closed her eyes again. She had seen Violet leave through the front door. But now she saw that Violet had crossed the street in the middle of the road. *Which way did she go?* Miriam asked herself. She had trouble with directions. Even with clients, she often said that she saw a big cavity in the right molar when it was actually the left or torn cartilage in the left knee when it was really the right one. How horrible to be a dyslexic psychic when your granddaughter's life might depend on you.

"Mom, I'm so scared," Cara said. She huddled into Miriam in a way that she hadn't since she was Violet's age.

Miriam wrapped her arms around her. She wanted to say, "Violet's all right. She's coming back." But how could she say that if she didn't know for sure? Did she have to know for sure? Wouldn't an ordinary mother tell her daughter that everything would be all right just to comfort her? "Everything will be all right," Miriam said, patting Cara on the back.

Cara backed up and looked her in the eyes. "Do you know that psychically or are you just saying that?" she asked sharply.

"I...I don't know," Miriam admitted, and Cara, looking betrayed, backed away, sealing herself off, her aura getting a thick wall.

The doorbell rang. "I'll get it," Miriam said, needing to escape Cara's coldness. She answered the door. "Rory, you're here." He had on the winter jacket he'd bought on sale that made one of his shoulders look way lower than the other.

"Mim, what are you doing here?" he asked, rolling his suitcase in to the hallway. "I flew in from La Guardia and went straight to the hospital. I got heart palpitations when I found out that you weren't there and they didn't know where you were. I was afraid they were going to have to admit me."

"Come in and sit down," Miriam said. She had to prepare him for more heart palpitations.

"Just tell me," he said, stepping inside. "Are you very sick, Mim? Was there nothing they could do for you?"

"Violet is missing."

"What? What did you say?"

"Violet wandered off during the night and everyone is looking for her."

"And you didn't call me, her grandfather?"

She started to explain that she had just found out herself, but Cara sang out "Daddy" and brushed past Miriam to fling herself into his arms. They stood, swaying together, him rocking Cara in his arms, and her just relaxing against him, getting the support she needed.

Miriam, watching them, once again felt the toll her psychic abilities took on her relationship with Cara. *Stop feeling sorry for yourself,* Miriam thought. She went up to Violet's room, slid open her closet door, and ran her fingers over the clothes that hung from double racks, top and bottom.

Grady stuck his head in the door. "I already checked the closets," he said. "She's not anywhere upstairs. I'll look around downstairs."

Miriam didn't answer him. She had to concentrate on getting vibrations that might tell her where Violet was. Violet's quilt was bunched on her bed. She had already been asleep or had pretended to be asleep. Miriam touched Violet's sheet, her pillowcase. She lay down in Violet's bed and settled her head on Violet's small pillow. The glow-in-the-dark decal stars were still shining on the ceiling. Had Kaylee woken Violet to tell her to leave suddenly or had they had this plan all set up beforehand? Had they been plotting this while Miriam was blinking and clicking? A shot of anger went through her. Kaylee had no right, no right at all, to lead

Violet away from her family. She would find Violet, she had to. And she'd banish Kaylee, whatever it took. She just had to have quiet. The answer would come if she could only stay quiet and be patient.

She heard Dan come in. She listened. "Cara, did you hear anything?" he asked breathlessly, and Miriam's heart sank. If he had to ask, then none of the search parties had found Violet either.

"My parents are being flown in on their friend's private jet," he said.

Miriam lay there, feeling defeated. How was she going to find Violet with Coxey and his Army bustling around? But she had no right to say who could come and who couldn't. It wasn't her house. *Bubbie, Mom, Dad,* she called out. *Help me. Help me find Violet.*

XXV

Violet peered around the graveyard. The moon looked liked it did in a storybook, big and round and low in the sky. The trees were too black in the night. Violet would have liked them purple. The hedges around the graves were black-looking too.

"Which is your stone?" she asked Kaylee.

"I was buried in Brooklyn," Kaylee said, "not near here. But I brought you to the closest graveyard so you could see what it's like."

"You were buried?" Violet asked. Her nose was beginning to run.

"Just my body was buried," Kaylee said, "but with a whoosh, my soul rose up." She flapped her hands in the air. "The soul is the real part of you. The soul is where all the memories of your life and the other lives you've lived before are stored."

"I didn't live before," Violet said. "And Lisa Green never did either."

"Everyone has," Kaylee said. "A soul passes through many times and comes right back again. It's just the body that doesn't last."

"Oh," Violet said. Some of the stones had angels on

them, and she could read the writing. "Virginia Lewis," she sounded out. "Be-beloved-ed wife and mother. 1904-1956." She backed away. "Somebody's mother is dead," she said, her puffy coat suddenly feeling like the thinnest sweater.

"Of course," Kaylee said. "My mother is dead. Mothers will always die someday. That's how the world works. It's just a fairy like me who won't ever die. Actually, Violet, I'm a spirit. I just told you I was a fairy so you wouldn't get scared."

"Mommy!" Violet shouted out. "I want to go back home to Mommy."

Kaylee bent down and looked into Violet's eyes. "Don't worry. I'm with you. You're safe. I wouldn't bring you anywhere that was dangerous. You know that. I am your special friend and I love you. I didn't mean to scare you, Violet. I only wanted you to understand about me, who I really am. While I wasn't telling you the truth, claiming to be a fairy, I couldn't feel as close to you as I do now."

Violet started to cry. "I want Mommy. I want to go home. I want to see Mommy and Grandma and Daddy."

"I wish I could give you a hug," Kaylee said. "Then you'd feel so much better."

Violet stamped her foot. "But you can't give me a hug. You can't even touch me. I had to cross all those streets without you holding my hand. Mommy would be very, very mad about that."

"But I kept you safe," Kaylee said. "I'll always keep you safe. I never had a child, but if I did, I'd want a little girl and I'd want her to be you."

"That's so sad that you never had your own little girl,"

Violet said. "Didn't a man ever want to put his penis into your vagina?'

Kaylee started to laugh. "You make everything that I ever went through worth it," she said.

Violet had thick mittens on, but she jammed her hands into her pockets. "Am I standing on people who are dead?"

"People get buried in thick wooden boxes with metal linings and thick cushioning inside," Kaylee explained. "They don't really need the cushions, but it makes the people who are sad for them feel better."

"Oh," Violet said. "I like my room much better than this place, don't you?"

"Yes," Kaylee said. "The happiest day of my life was when you saw me in your hallway and you could hear me and you invited me to sleep in your room with you."

"The happiest day of my life was when I saw that Grandma Miriam knew what I was thinking and I knew what she was thinking and we both knew what everyone else was thinking, too. We would tell each other and it would be a secret between just us. Now Grandma Miriam doesn't want to have secrets with me anymore, but you do."

"I'll always want to," Kaylee said.

"Let's go home," Violet said. "I want to go back to my room and see the stars on my ceiling. I want to get under my quilt and be warm."

"Sure," Kaylee said. "We'll be back before anyone knows you're gone."

Violet stayed right at Kaylee's side, as close as she could without touching her, because it still scared Violet when her hand went right through Kaylee. They walked along the pebbled road of the graveyard. There were little graves of children whose bodies didn't last. Violet kicked the road pebbles with the toes of her Uggs. Kaylee would have to go back to a place like this if she didn't have me, Violet thought, and kicked the pebbles harder.

When they were outside the gate, Violet said, "We'd better cross at the corner."

"You're right," Kaylee said, and they waited for the light to turn green.

Before stepping off the curb, Violet looked both ways like she was taught to do, even though she wasn't allowed to cross the street by herself yet. No car was coming. They started across the street. When they got to the other side, a car pulled up to the curb.

"Little girl," a man called out, "what are you doing out at night all by yourself?"

Violet was scared. "I'm not allowed to talk to strangers," she said and began to run.

"Wait, wait," he called out. "I don't want to leave a young child alone on a dark night."

Mommy had warned Violet about not going near strangers' cars. Mommy had told her that if a stranger tells you he wants you to help him find his puppy or that he needs directions or wants to help you in any way, get away from him. He could mean you terrible harm.

"Go away!" Violet shouted at the man. "I am not alone. I don't need you to protect me. Kaylee is protecting me," but the man kept driving along slowly, following them.

Violet was so scared that she felt pee running down her leg.

"You shouldn't tell anyone you're with me," Kaylee said. "They won't understand."

"I'm calling the police," the man said. "When they come, I'll leave. But not a moment before."

Violet wished he would call the police. She didn't want this man who couldn't see she was with Kaylee to follow her anymore.

"What a buttinksky," Kaylee said. "Violet, can you run any faster? We're almost home."

"I can't run any faster. My Uggs are too slow and my panties are wet."

Another car came by. A dark-skinned man called out, "There she is, the little girl with the dobie." He talked funny, like a sliding voice. "Your grandma with the green foam slippers is looking for you."

Just then Violet saw bobbing lights ahead and heard people calling out, "Violet, Violet."

She had been so eager to get away from the house without anyone seeing her. Now she called out loudly, "Here I am. I'm here."

One of the bobbing lights came running toward her. It was Daddy. "Daddy!" she called out. Her father picked her up and squished her against him.

"Why did you worry us all like that?" he said. "The police are looking for you. We've been frantic."

"Daddy, I peed in my pants," she whispered in his ear. "I didn't like the cemetery one bit."

"What were you doing in a cemetery?"

Violet didn't want to say another word about that spooky place where mothers and children died. She started to cry.

"It's all right, Violet," Daddy said, holding her tightly to him. "It's all right. You're safe."

Within moments, Mommy was there. "I'm so happy to have you back," Mommy said. "I love you so much. I don't mind if you know everyone's secrets. I don't mind if you know my secrets. I just want you to know that I love you, no matter what."

"I love you too, Mommy. I wanted to get back to you so much."

Mommy started to cry. In Daddy's arms, Violet suddenly felt how tired she was from going off in the middle of the night, from having to run home from the graveyard with two strange men following her. Resting her head on Daddy's shoulder, she yawned a long and loud yawn. Daddy carried her back toward the house. Everyone was asking her questions, but she was tired, so very tired that after her bath, Daddy and Mommy put her right to bed, without even brushing her teeth.

XXVI

MIRIAM PUSHED THE TRAY OF DOUGHNUTS TOWARD the two policemen. A neighbor whose husband had been in the search party had brought them over. "You'll get better service from the police with doughnuts," she'd said.

"Those were the two longest hours of our lives when Violet was missing," Miriam said.

"You folks are lucky," the policeman said. "Too many kids go missing and we never find them, or find them dead, or find them years later when they no longer know their original families. But in this case, two people called 911 to report that they saw your child. A cab driver said that a dobie had hold of her and that her grandmother wears green foam slippers." He rolled his eyes. "The other said that she told him she wasn't alone, that she was with someone named Kaylee. Do any of you know a Kaylee?"

Rory squinted at Miriam. "Wasn't Kaylee the name of the client whose funeral you went to?"

Miriam shot him a don't-make-anymore-trouble-than-there-already-is look.

Rory, still glancing suspiciously at Miriam, said, "We should all get some sleep. It's been quite a night."

"I'm going to sleep in the hallway right in front of Violet's door," Dan said. "I'm afraid to ever let her out of my sight again until all of this calms down."

"I'll sleep right there next to you," Cara said.

Rory cornered Miriam. "I knew you would make trouble," he said through his teeth. "You made trouble with your client and now you're making trouble for Violet. I'm so mad at you I could spit."

Miriam gave a weary sigh. "Can't you just be grateful that Violet is safe?"

"You're shifting everything," he said. "You've caused trouble in Cara and Dan's house and you've caused trouble in your own. I don't know how much longer I can put up with this."

"You make me feel like a bad luck charm," Miriam said.

"Well, we'll talk about this when we go home, and it'd better be soon or who knows what other trouble you'll cause?"

Miriam was about to tell him what he could do with himself when the doorbell rang. Cara and Dan came down in their pajamas to open it. George and Hillary were there with their suitcases.

"Mom, Dad, in all the rush," Dan said, "I forgot to call you to say that Violet is home now."

"So you're telling us we should turn right around and fly back?" said George.

"Where is Violet?" asked Hillary, a skip of panic in her voice. "I want to see her right now."

Miriam had never seen Hillary without makeup before. She looked like a regular angry person.

"She's asleep, Mom." Dan took their luggage. "You can have our bedroom tonight. Cara and I are going to sleep in the hallway outside Violet's door. We might sleep there every night after the scare we had."

Hillary pulled off her high-heeled boots. "What possessed a five-year-old to leave home in the middle of the night?'

Possession, Miriam thought, *that's what.* While Kaylee was alive, her mother completely controlled her and isolated her from everyone except Tom, who agreed that Kaylee was too childlike to venture off on her own. And now, Miriam thought, a drumbeat getting louder in her head, Kaylee was trying to completely take over Violet.

They all went into the living room. Each of them threw themselves onto the couches and chairs as if they were sacks of laundry in a chute. Miriam offered the doughnuts. Hillary forgot all about her dieting and actually took one.

"God," Hillary said, multicolor sprinkles in the corners of her lips, "I thought Violet's only problem was that she didn't pronounce her 'th's' well."

"You're supposed to be psychic," George said to Miriam. "How come you didn't know where Violet was?"

"I didn't see the cemetery, but I knew what she wearing when she left," Miriam said in her own defense. She got a sudden cramp in her left arm that made her wonder if this time she really was having a heart attack.

"Cemetery? She went to a cemetety?" Hillary said. "How could a child with two parents and a grandmother in residence wander off in the middle of the night to a grave-yard? If she had tried to get to a candy store, maybe I'd understand." Hillary shook her head. "What is it with her?"

"We'll find out soon enough," Dan said. "Violet has shown signs of being psychic and lately she's been obsessed with an imaginary friend. Cara and I have signed papers at her school to have her observed by a psychologist."

"I'll have you know," Hillary said, "that there isn't any mental illness on my side of the family or George's."

"Of course not," Cara spat out. "The two of you are too perfect for anything like that. I'm sure you never drove Dan to a state hospital to visit his great aunt who just happened to be psychic as well as mentally ill."

Miriam's intestines shriveled like slugs with salt dumped on them. She should never have taken Cara to see Aunt Chaia all those years ago, no matter what Cara had said. Hillary had turned up her nose-job nose when she'd first found out that Miriam was psychic. Since she'd learned that there was mental illness in the family too, Hillary's aversion toward Miriam had gathered weight. Now Hillary looked at her with her top lip pulled back over her teeth.

Rory sprang up from the love seat and tamped down the air with his hands. "Let's not go at each other," he said, but everyone kept talking over each other.

They were arguing nonsense, things that had nothing to do with what was actually happening, Miriam thought. "It's all my fault," she suddenly declared, wringing her hands. "Violet doesn't need a psychologist. She needs an exorcist. She's being haunted by my former client who committed suicide."

George's face splotched with red. "Have you lost your mind?" he sputtered. And at once they were all arguing again, Cara attacking George, Dan defending Cara, Rory telling Miriam, "See what you did?" then demanding some darn civility from everyone else, and Hillary telling Dan, "If you were a man, you'd tell your wife to respect your father."

Miriam's neck felt no stronger than a dandelion stem. She dropped her head into her hands and sat there wondering how she would ever get Kaylee to leave Violet alone. She wished she could set all of the furious people in the room on Kaylee. That would get her out.

Then she remembered Bubbie telling her, "You can't give a ghost who committed suicide *a frosk in dem ponem*. The world has already given them a slap in the face."

While everyone kept arguing, Miriam thought about how much Kaylee had suffered in her life, all her losses, and how much she'd wanted a child. Of course it would be hard for her to leave Violet. "Kaylee," Miriam murmured, "I understand."

All the relatives were still battling and accusing. "Stop!" Miriam ordered. They froze as if it was a game of statues. In the silence, Miriam detected a draft coming from the top of the stairs. "Kaylee is here in the house, and I want your help to make contact with her. We need to join hands in a circle."

"For a séance?" Dan asked.

"This is asinine," George said. "I'm not going to pander to this nonsense. There's no such thing as ghosts."

"Dad, at one time I would have agreed with you," Dan said, "but I've been doing research on psychics, and now that I've been working with them, I've come to think that anything is possible."

"You're working with psychics?" Hillary blanched. "We spent all that money sending you to the best schools and this is what you come up with?" The vein in her forehead was ticking.

"Yes, I'm working with psychics," Dan snapped at her. "And I don't care who knows it. Next week I'm going to be describing my project to the department chair. It's even more important to me now that Violet needs help."

"You'll be a laughing stock," Hillary said. "I can't stand it." She burst into tears.

Cara, Miriam knew, had agreed with Hillary that Dan shouldn't be working on finding a psychic gene, but now Cara wrapped her arm around Dan's shoulder. "Dan's research project is crucial, and I'm sure that one day everyone will agree."

"Not likely," George said with a snort.

Miriam felt as if Cara had put her arm around her shoulder as well. *Finally, a public declaration of support for her psychic mother,* Miriam thought. And with that, as if Cara had heard her, Cara turned and walked over to her. "What do you need us to do, Mom? We'll do whatever you say."

Miriam felt deeply touched that Cara believed in her even with all that had gone wrong.

"Count Hillary and me out," George said.

"Mom, Dad," said Dan, "you either cooperate or leave. You have nothing to lose by doing what Miriam asks, nothing at all. If it doesn't help, we'll just be back to where we were, which is in chaos."

Miriam glanced at Cara and saw her head jolt. Dan had stood up to her many times, but this was the first time he had put his parents in their places.

"What do you want us to do?" Hillary asked, her perfect speech hiccupy with tears.

"I just want you all to join hands in a circle," Miriam said. George made another remark, but Miriam was too focused to even hear it. Standing in the center of the Chinese silk carpet, Miriam called out, "Kaylee, please come to talk to me." She waited. She heard nothing, saw nothing. Then a blue light came down the steps, bouncing slowly like a beam from one of the flashlights of the neighbors who had been searching the night for Violet. The blue light got bigger, brighter, and then hovered at the foot of the steps. In a moment it was right in front of Miriam, and slowly, within the blue light, Miriam could make out Kaylee, just as she'd looked on the remembrance card.

"Kaylee, I'm so sorry," Miriam said. She remembered the shovelfuls of dirt falling on Kaylee's grave. She remembered the rain pouring down like the tears of the Universe for this young woman who had died by her own hand, which wouldn't have happened unless Miriam had had a hand in Kaylee's life. "I'm sorry," Miriam said, but the shovelfuls of earth kept falling.

She heard George whisper to Hillary, "You don't see anybody, do you?" But Miriam ignored him and kept her gaze on Kaylee. "If you're angry at me, don't take it out on Violet, please. She's innocent."

"I'd never take anything out on Violet," Kaylee said.

"Being with her has been the happiest time in my life. I'm going to stay with her forever."

Miriam felt as if a helicopter had landed in her ears. "But you're hurting her by staying with her," she argued. "Violet can't grow this way. If you stay with her, neither of you will be able to move forward."

Miriam saw what was in Kaylee's mind. Kaylee was remembering herself and Violet in the graveyard, Violet crying, terrified, wanting her mommy, and Kaylee unable to calm her. *She's going to be reasonable,* Miriam thought.

"You told me that one day a child may fall into my lap," Kaylee said, "and she has. I can't leave Violet. I won't."

Miriam gripped the hands she held harder. Dan's was sweaty, Cara's ice cold. "Bubbie, please help," Miriam called out. In a moment the air above Kaylee looked as if a ceiling fan was set on high, stirring it frantically. Miriam smelled lavender and another scent. Evening in Paris, her mother's cologne? Yes, Bubbie and Miriam's mother appeared, shoulder to shoulder, Bubbie's shoulder being much lower.

"Even though you got yourself into this mess as usual," Miriam's mother said, "you didn't think we'd abandon you, did you?"

Her mother truly was an angel now, Miriam thought. When she was alive, her mother's favorite motto had been "You made your bed, now lie in it."

"We found her," Bubbie said. "We found the girl's mother. She's not so easy to schlep along," she added, panting as if in the ethers she still needed breath.

Mrs. O'Brien was still wearing her widow's weeds. She

looked puffy and uneasy, bobbling in the air like a Macy's Day float. She was almost a comic figure, but when she opened her mouth, she roared, "Kaylee, you lost all my money, the money I practically starved myself for."

It was unlikely that Mrs. O'Brien had ever starved herself, Miriam thought, even on Lent.

"And I told you not to go to that ashram, that cesspool of germs and adultery," Mrs. O'Brien said.

"This is where you want me to go?" Kaylee said, looking straight at Miriam. "To my mother, to be bullied and shamed for the rest of eternity?"

Miriam didn't know what to do. She couldn't let Kaylee be smothered in her mother's bosom again, but she couldn't let her stay with Violet and ruin Violet's life.

"Oy, Dorothy," Bubbie said to Miriam's mother, "we should have brought the devil with us instead."

"Is anything happening?" Hillary asked.

Something was happening. The air was whipped up once again, and there was Aunt Chaia, still in her hospital gown. But she had begun to reverse death. She'd put on weight and her hair had grown back, gray and fuzzy instead of red and wavy, but back nonetheless.

"Mrs. O'Brien," Aunt Chaia shouted, "you think you're so good and so pious. I see you. I see you before your husband died. I see you with your skirt pulled up. I see you under that man in a bed with angels carved into the headboard. His name was Quinn and you didn't look so holy then."

Miriam almost laughed. Aunt Chaia was up to her old tricks again, shouting out people's secrets. But now Chaia was protected. No one could do anything to her anymore.

Mrs. O'Brien's mouth fell open. She put both her hands to her heart. "It was only once with Quinn," she said. "I was lonely. My husband was a sick man from the time I married him and I took good care of him every day."

"My God," Kaylee said.

"O'Brien, nobody's blaming you," Bubbie said. "People do all kinds of things when they are sad. Like your daughter going to the guru. She was living with a man who you should have married, not her."

"But I told her not to go to that guru!" Mrs. O'Brien said. "And your granddaughter, Miriam, lied to Kaylee right in front of me. She lied."

"I've got to go the bathroom," George said. "My prostate, you know."

"Miriam, you lied to me?" Kaylee said.

Miriam dropped her eyelids and nodded slowly. She had lost. Kaylee was going to want revenge against her for sending her off to that ashram, where she'd had so little life experience that she could be braided like challah dough, manipulated into having sex with the guru and giving up her mother's inheritance to buy a house that didn't even exist. She forced herself to look at Kaylee again. As if she could see a video inside a cartoon bubble coming from Kaylee's head, Miriam glimpsed Kaylee's memories of being with the guru. She saw the guru let his hair loose from its long ponytail, saw that gleaming hair cascade down his back like a dark river. At least Kaylee had known what great sex could be like, Miriam thought.

"At least," Kaylee echoed. "And Miriam, I was never mad at you. I know how hard you always tried to get me to do something with the life I had, and I just couldn't."

Kaylee never blamed me? Miriam thought. She thought about the hours and hours she'd wasted blaming herself. She felt as if she'd been unlocked from a pillory.

"Honestly," Hillary said, "my feet are killing me." Miriam heard Hillary padding off somewhere. The circle had gotten smaller by two. Miriam, Dan, and Cara could barely keep it together.

"Mrs. O'Brien," Aunt Chaia said, "I never had the blessing of a child." Her face twisted up and her hands crimped into claws. She looked as if she'd go mad again. But Chaia unclenched her hands and face. "Mrs. O'Brien, you should get down on your knees in thanks for having this daughter. You should open your arms to her. You should tell her that you love her."

From the corner of her eyes, Miriam saw Bubbie trembling with emotion. Miriam's mother was weeping, too. Everyone had thought that Chaia's life had been wasted, but here she was, dead, and being of great use to everyone.

"Kaylee, tell me it isn't too late," Mrs. O'Brien said, sniffing. "Tell me that you could love me again. I'm sorry. I'm so sorry. I just wanted you to be safe. I didn't mean to do you harm."

Kaylee's thoughts were as clear to Miriam now as images on Cara's huge digital TV screen. Miriam saw Kaylee thinking of being with Violet in Violet's room, the room looking like Eden, with all the stuffed animals and the flowers on the walls. She saw them whispering to each other behind cupped hands right at the dinner table while she herself was clicking and blinking to block Kaylee out. Oh, what fun Violet and Kaylee must have had to be able to be together without anyone else knowing. She saw Kaylee laughing with Violet in kindergarten, Kaylee looking more like a bigger kid than a woman. How would Kaylee give all that up to be with her blubbering mother? She wouldn't, Miriam thought, and felt hope seep out of her like air from a pricked balloon.

And then she saw Kaylee remember herself running home from the graveyard with Violet, trying to keep up with her as two cars sidled along the curb with strange men inside calling out to them. Kaylee's spirit swayed from side to side in indecision. She thought of what it must look like to other people when Violet just talked to her and no one else. Kaylee thought of how, before her mother had died, she had only really spoken to her mother. Kaylee had had no friends her own age. Kaylee thought of Violet growing up with only her as a friend, the way she herself had only grown up with only her mother at her side and what a freak that had made her. She couldn't go to a high school reunion because what could she tell people? "I'm still my mother's baby."

"I don't want to leave Violet," Kaylee said. "But I know I have to."

Miriam's eyes filled with tears. "Thank you for loving my granddaughter so well that you'd put her needs above your wishes."

"Kaylee, you're coming back to me," Mrs. O'Brien said, the hammocks of flesh swinging on her arms as she held them out to Kaylee.

"No, I'm not," Kaylee said. "I am not coming back to you."

Miriam couldn't bear it. Bubbie clopped her hand to her forehead. Miriam's mother said, "I can't take it anymore." Aunt Chaia twitched all over. "This is driving me crazy," she moaned.

"Miriam, is this going to be over soon?" Rory asked. She could feel him squirming with impatience. *Spilkes,* Bubbie called it.

"I will leave Violet," Kaylee said, "but not to be with you, Mother. I thought what I needed was your forgiveness to go on, but what I need is time by myself. I need to be able to make my own decisions. While I was on Earth, the only decision I truly made was to jump out my window. I love you, but I need to have you not looking over my shoulder. I need to be on my own."

Aunt Chaia reached out her bony hand to Kaylee. "I will guide you," she said. "I will take you up with me, and you can be free to go or to stay with me. You can be free."

Kaylee gazed at Aunt Chaia. "I can't leave Violet without saying goodbye to her, but if I am near her again, I don't think I'll be able to leave her." Kaylee wavered, a flame in a breeze. And then Aunt Chaia sent out a radiance of pink light from her bony chest to Kaylee, and Kaylee reached out her hand. There was a whoosh, and Aunt Chaia and Kaylee were gone.

"Give her time, O'Brien," Bubbie advised Kaylee's mother. "She'll be able to stand you someday."

"Let's all go have coffee," Miriam's mother said to Bubbie and Mrs. O'Brien.

"How many times do I got to tell you that coffee rots the insides?" Bubbie said, and within moments, they too went off with a whoosh. Miriam could still hear her mother and Bubbie arguing as they ascended with Mrs. O'Brien.

"It's over," Miriam cried. "It's over." She, Rory, Cara, and Dan, the only ones who had stuck it out, now huddled together, their arms around each other.

"Mom, what's wrong?" Cara asked.

"What do you mean?"

"I felt you shudder," Cara said.

"I was so happy that Kaylee left," Miriam said, "that I never thought about how Violet will feel now that Kaylee is gone."

From upstairs, they heard Violet call, "Kaylee? Kaylee?"

VIOLET NEVER HAD SO MANY RELATIVES IN HER ROOM at once: all her grandmas, grandpas, and Daddy and Mommy too. Violet was in her bed and they were all sitting on the floor, like story hour, but she didn't know what story to tell them.

"We didn't want you to be lonely," Mommy explained.

Lonely? Violet thought. Her room was as crowded as her toy chest. Grandpa Rory was so tall that he had to open Violet's closet and sit half inside it. And Grandma Miriam, who said she was "broad in the beam," had to twist herself to sit on one hip, which didn't look very comfortable. Grandma Hillary had on a tight skirt that she had to keep pulling down to cover her knees, and Mommy and Daddy sat in the corner like Jack Horner. But somebody was missing. Kaylee. Violet looked around for her. She didn't see her. Since Violet had first spoken to Kaylee in the hallway, Kaylee had been with her every day.

"Where's Kaylee?" she blurted out.

"Kaylee isn't here anymore," Grandma Miriam said.

"Kaylee wouldn't leave me," Violet said. She looked at Grandma Miriam. Grandma Miriam's face was very serious and she was nodding just a little bit. "She left?" Violet said, and Grandma Miriam nodded bigger. "Kaylee told me that she'd stay with me forever. She wouldn't leave without even saying goodbye to me."

"Kaylee knew that I would say goodbye for her," Grandma Miriam said.

Grandpa George bumped into Violet's standing lamp and caught it just in time.

"Be careful," Grandma Hillary told him. She was always worried about things getting messed up. Then all of them got quiet again, but they just kept watching her with spikes of worry shooting out of their heads that prickled Violet's skin.

Grandma Miriam got up from the floor and sat down on the side of Violet's bed. "Don't blame yourself for Kaylee leaving," she said. "It was nothing that you did wrong. You made her very welcome. She loves you very much, but she had to go."

"Why?" Violet said.

"She had to move on," Grandma Miriam said.

"Move where?" Violet asked.

Grandma Miriam squeezed her eyes closed and opened them again. Violet could hear Grandma Miriam thinking, *How am I ever going to explain this to a five-year-old?*

"You think I'm such a baby," Violet said. She looked around at all her family looking at her like she was still in a Pack 'n Play. "You all do. Kaylee is as old as Mommy, but she told me everything."

Mommy suddenly leaned against Daddy as if Violet's words had knocked into her.

Grandma Miriam let out her breath hard. "I'm trying to explain, Violet. You see, Kaylee needs to be with other spirits, and you need to be with other children and with your family. You were getting so far away from everyone that even Mrs. Oliver and Mrs. Vincent were worried about you."

"Kaylee is gone for good?" Violet said.

"Was she ever really here?" Grandpa George whispered to Grandpa Rory, and Grandma Hillary shushed him.

"Yes, Kaylee is gone," Grandma Miriam said. "That's what I've been trying to tell you."

Violet bunched her quilt in her hands. "You wouldn't even know if Kaylee was here," she yelled. "You couldn't see Kaylee or hear her. One time she jumped out and said 'boo' to you and you didn't even know."

"Don't be fresh to Grandma," Dad said.

"Where is she?" Violet demanded. "Where is Kaylee?"

"On your spring break we could all go to Disney World together," Grandpa George said. "Grandma Hillary and I haven't ever been there. When your father was little, we took him on tours of science museums. Think of all the rides at Disney World and think of seeing Mickey Mouse."

"Kaylee!" Violet called. She swung her legs out of bed and went around the house, looking everywhere. "Kaylee!"

Everyone followed her like a game of Follow the Leader. In the den, where Kaylee still wasn't, Grandma Miriam scooped Violet up in her arms.

"Violet, you're going to make yourself sick if you keep this up," Grandma Miriam said. "Kaylee had to go. She didn't mean to cause you harm, but she put you in danger when she took you to that cemetery."

"You made her go," Violet said. "You put her out."

"No, it wasn't like that," Grandma Miriam said. "We helped her on her journey."

"Kaylee wouldn't have gone if you didn't make her," Violet said. "I know it." The thought of Kaylee really not here made Violet feel like someone had put a dark hood over her head. "Kaylee is just hiding from you, from all of you. Put me down," she demanded.

"Violet, you don't understand," said Grandma Miriam.

Violet made her body as stiff as Play Dough that was left without the cover on. "I hate you," she said.

Grandma Miriam's face shook as though she was going to cry, but Violet didn't care. She twisted her body away from her. As soon as Grandma Miriam set her down, Violet ran toward the kitchen and everybody started after her.

"Don't come," she shouted. "You'll scare Kaylee away."

"Maybe she needs a tranquilizer," Grandma Hillary said. "They must prescribe something for kids."

"Shh," said Grandpa George.

"Let's leave Violet be for awhile," Daddy said.

Violet was glad to have them leave her be. She went into the kitchen and looked around. She looked with the front of her eyes and out of the sides of her eyes too. She looked underneath the table, where Kaylee once crouched, pretending she was a puppy. All through dinner Violet had heard her arfing. But Kaylee wasn't there. Violet looked up at the fan light on the ceiling, where Kaylee once held on and went round and round. "Whee," she'd said, her feet doing a jig in the air. Kaylee wasn't there either.

Violet went into the downstairs bathroom. She remembered Kaylee telling her to blow breath onto the mirror. Violet had climbed up on a footstool to do it. Her breath left a steamy circle. When Kaylee did it, nothing showed on the mirror. "That's the difference between us," Kaylee had said. Now Violet blew out her breath hard into her hands. It was like a warm wind. She wondered what it was like not to really and truly breathe. She held her breath. Her cheeks puffed out. She held it as long as she could, but it came out in a *pffft*.

"Kaylee, Kaylee, Kaylee, where are you? Kaylee, come back to me." Violet's throat felt scratchy, but she kept calling Kaylee's name. Each time she called her, it got harder to say her name, and her voice sounded like Mommy filing her nails.

"You'll hurt your throat with all that yelling," Grandpa Rory called, but Violet didn't listen to him. She had to find where Kaylee might be hiding. She went to the family room, where there were toys that didn't fit into her room. Violet opened all the cabinets, looking to see if Kaylee had scrunched herself up inside one. Kaylee could fit in the most crowded cabinet and Violet had seen all the Legos right through Kaylee, as if she was there and wasn't there. Like now. She would find her. She and Kaylee loved to play with the Dora the Explorer stove. Kaylee had said that in real life she'd never liked to cook. Violet looked all around the stove, even inside the oven. Kaylee wasn't there. Violet went back to her room where Kaylee always loved to be. She looked in their hiding places. She looked under her bed, but found only her bunny slippers and a crayon. Once Kaylee had hidden in the closet and heaped herself up with Violet's clothes that had come off the hangers. But Mommy had put all the clothes back, and now Kaylee wasn't there.

Violet threw herself onto her bed, her face in the pillow, and began to cry. She wouldn't go away without saying goodbye. She wouldn't.

The next day Kaylee still wasn't there and not the next either. Violet was so tired, but she couldn't stop looking for Kaylee. Even when she fell asleep for just a little bit, she heard herself saying, "Kaylee, where are you?" And then she'd wake right up and look around her room, but there was no Kaylee.

MIRIAM ALMOST FELL OVER DAN AND CARA AS THEY lay asleep in the hallway outside Violet's room. She could hear Violet inside, softly weeping. *Could Kaylee be watching Violet from above?* Miriam worried. If Kaylee saw Violet suffering like this, she wouldn't be able to stand it and she would come back. Then Violet would never have a chance at a normal life.

Miriam went into the guest bedroom, where Rory was asleep on the pullout couch instead of the bed. She gathered up her things and went down to the den to sleep so she wouldn't have to watch him not sleep with her. In the den she thought again about the possibility of Kaylee coming back to Violet and drew an afghan around her. *If only Violet would bond with all of us again, Kaylee might not be such a threat,* Miriam thought. But she could hear Violet mumbling, as if right in her ear, "I hate Grandma Miriam for making Kaylee go away."

VIOLET COUNTED OUT THE DAYS ON HER HELLO KITTY calendar, three whole days since Kaylee wasn't there. She walked around and around the house and couldn't stop, as if a fast train was inside her. She didn't talk to anybody, especially not Grandma Miriam, who had sent Kaylee away.

"Don't you think we should take her to a doctor already?" she heard Grandma Hillary say.

"If any doctor hears what's been going on in this house," Grandpa George said, "he'll put all of us away."

When she passed them again later, she was surprised to see her grandpas next to each other on the couch, Grandpa George's arm thrown behind Grandpa Rory.

"Looks like we won the battle, but we lost the war," said Grandpa George.

"At least we're trench buddies now," said Grandpa Rory.

Violet was glad they were happy together for once. If only Kaylee were here to see this, she thought, and then nothing else mattered to her except finding Kaylee.

"Kaylee, Kaylee, Kaylee," she called.

At dinner that night they ate in the dining room because there were so many people that it was company. "Eat, Violet, eat something at least," Grandma Hillary said. But Violet's belly was gurgle, gurgle.

Grandma Hillary ate a big, big piece of lasagna. "I'm eating like a pig here," she said. "I can't even button my slacks." She lifted her sweater to show that her button was open, and half the zipper too.

"I can lend you a skirt," Grandma Miriam said. They went off to another room.

Violet was glad. She was tired of her grandmothers trying to make her eat. It was too sad to eat without Kaylee there. Where was she?

"You don't have to eat if you don't want to," Mommy said. "I made you a shake. All you have to do is drink it. Just drink a sip." Mommy's eyes had dark rings under them. Violet had stubbed her toe on Daddy's head one night when she came out of her room, because he and Mommy were still sleeping on the floor in front of her door. Now Violet took a sip of the shake. It tasted like yogurt and strawberries and honey, but Violet held it in her mouth and didn't swallow.

"We're back," Grandma Hillary said. "You can cut me another piece of lasagna now."

Grandma Hillary was wearing Grandma Miriam's skirt. It was a skirt to the ground and had birds and leaves all over it. Violet was so surprised to see Grandma Hillary look like Grandma Miriam that she laughed and the yogurt, strawberry, honey shake came out her nose.

Mommy patted Violet on the back. "Are you all right?"

It felt bad to laugh when Kaylee wasn't there. Violet pushed the shake away. She didn't care that it spilled on the table. "Kaylee," she called.

"Not this again," Grandpa George said under his breath.

"There would be such peace in this house now if it weren't for that ghost," Daddy said.

Violet couldn't stand it. She couldn't stand that Kaylee had left without even saying goodbye. Where was she? Violet went upstairs two steps at a time. In the hallway, she stopped at the corner where she had first talked to Kaylee and told her that she could sleep in her room. She waited there, hoping to see her again, even if it was just to say goodbye. Violet plunked down in the corner, her back against the wall. She pushed her fists against her eyes, but still tears leaked out. Her knees, up under her chin, got wet.

"Should I go up and check on Violet?" she heard Grandpa Rory say.

"She needs time," Grandma Miriam said. "It's hard to miss someone as much as Violet misses Kaylee."

Violet stayed in the corner and stayed there until she couldn't stay there anymore. Kaylee wasn't coming back and she wasn't even going to say goodbye. Slowly, Violet got up and stamped the needles out of her legs. She went downstairs, one step at a time, toward the living room, stopping at the doorway, peeking in. Grandpa George and Grandpa Rory had fallen asleep, their heads on the back of the love seat, their mouths open.

"The grandpas are exhausted from worry," Grandma Hillary said. She was knitting fast, her needles clacking. "Knitting helps my nerves," she said.

Mommy and Daddy were doing a crossword puzzle together, Mommy sitting on the arm of the chair like you weren't supposed to. Mommy's worry line was deeper between her eyes than Violet had remembered. It looked like Mommy had gotten older. And Daddy kept pulling at his chin. Grandma Miriam was leaning forward on the couch to play Solitaire, slapping down the cards on the coffee table.

"Miriam," Grandma Hillary said, "maybe you can give me a reading some time."

"I wish someone would give me a reading," Miriam said. "I want to know if Violet will be all right. I want to know when she will join the living again."

Violet wanted to go around the house again looking for Kaylee. Instead, she took three steps into the living room.

Grandma Hillary put down her knitting and smiled, but her smile was pinched. Mommy's eyes were still worried-looking, but she smiled too.

Daddy nudged Grandpa Rory and Grandpa George. "Stop sawing wood and say hello to Violet."

"Violet," both grandpas said at once and got up to come toward her.

"Relax," Mommy told them. "Let Violet come in by herself if she wants to."

Violet hesitated, but then stepped into the living room. She came over to Grandma Miriam, who was the only one not gawking at her. Grandma Miriam just kept playing Solitaire. Violet looked at Grandma's cards. Grandma Miriam wasn't going to win the game with those cards on the table. Violet looked at the cards with her eyes open and then she looked with her eyes closed. "Grandma Miriam, I see an ace under this ten of hearts," Violet said, touching it. "If you take the ace out, you could win."

"Is she right?" Grandma Hillary said.

Grandma Miriam picked up the ten and turned over the card beneath it. It was an ace with black clovers on it.

"Of course she's right," Mommy said proudly. "Violet is psychic."

Even though it was cheating, Violet took the ace out from under the ten and set it out next to the other aces. And then, sitting very close to Grandma Miriam, Grandma's soft thigh against hers, Violet started building on the ace with a twosie and a threesie.

MIRIAM NOTICED THAT VIOLET SEEMED CHANGED. For a couple of days after the Solitaire game, she hadn't looked for Kaylee all the time. On the surface everything appeared okay, but in between talking to the living, Miriam heard Violet thinking, *Kaylee, Kaylee.*

"Violet's definitely out of the woods," George had said, and that night he booked a commercial flight back to Michigan for him and Hillary.

"Miriam," Hillary had said, putting her arms around her, "it's thanks to you that Violet is better. We're still not sure exactly what happened, but before Leeuwenhoek invented the microscope, who knew there were germs?"

Miriam didn't like her psychic ability compared to germs, but she knew that Hillary accepted her now.

Rory took Miriam aside. "You were right to interfere," he said. "I shouldn't have berated you for being you. I love you. Sure, you make trouble, but at least you know how to fix it. That's more than you can say for most people." Then he breathed into her hair. "I miss you, kiddo. Come back to Great Neck with me."

"I will, but not just yet. Rory, you might not be able to tell, but Violet isn't herself yet. Her aura is thin, not the vibrant rainbow it was before Kaylee left. I can't leave her until I see her happy."

"Mim, you can't stay here forever."

"Give me more time. I have to try."

"All right, but put some kind of time limit on it or Cara and Dan might not like it. You know the old saying about guests and fish stinking after a few days."

"I'll give it a week," Miriam said.

The next morning Rory and George and Hillary shared a cab to the airport. It arrived at the same time as Violet's school bus. Dan had wanted to drive her to school, but Cara had insisted that Violet needed to get back to her old routine as soon as possible. Everyone waved madly at each other. George, in his camel-colored cashmere jacket, held Hillary's arm. Hillary, also in a beige cashmere jacket, held onto the hem of the long, leaf-and-bird-patterned skirt that she hadn't taken off since she had borrowed it from Miriam. Miriam felt a fresh sparkle of fondness for them and a wham of love for Rory.

"You look so well rested," Miriam said to Dan and Cara. Neither of them had those dark rings under their eyes.

"Sleeping in our own bed instead of on the floor in front of Violet's door will do that for you," Cara said. She was out of sweat pants and wearing designer jeans with a red t-shirt that was gathered on one shoulder.

Dan, who usually went to work in a button-down shirt and khakis, had on a sport jacket and tie. "With everything going on," he said, "I didn't get a chance to get a haircut, so Cara blew out my hair this morning."

"I've always told him," Cara said, "what's the use of being a blond if you wear your hair so short? You look way cool like this," she added, winking at him.

"I'm going to make an appointment with the department chair today about my psychic research, Miriam," Dan said. "I put a tie and jacket on because who knows? He might have time to talk to me right away."

His "who knows?" had a special ring to it. He was asking her a psychic question, which he'd never done before. She understood that he couldn't very well have a reading with one of the psychics he was testing. It would muddy his statistics.

"I'm trying not to do readings for family," Miriam said, but she gave him a thumbs-up.

"Thanks, Miriam," he said, and went off with a confident swagger that tickled Miriam and Cara so much that they bumped fists.

"I'm getting back to work, Mom," Cara said. "I hope you'll be okay."

"Sure. I'm not the one who needs a babysitter around here." She went to the guestroom and phoned her business line. She had dozens of unanswered calls, one from Kaylee's husband, Tom.

"I'm so damn lonely," he said on her voicemail. "Do you think it would be okay for me to start dating with Kaylee only gone five months?"

Miriam wasn't going to call him back. Since she had helped his wife commit adultery, it felt wrong. But then she got a glimpse of a chubby-cheeked woman with graying blonde hair and a sweet smile. "I'm Natasha," the woman said.

Miriam called Tom. He was at work and on his cell phone. She could hear other men around him. "Tom, this is Miriam. I can't tell you what's right or wrong for you. All I can tell you is that I see a woman named Natasha with a Russian accent who might be for you."

"Jesus," Tom said, "she's living in my building. She just came from Russia. Do you think she's legal?"

"Tom, I can't know everything," Miriam said. She had certainly learned that through Kaylee's death. "All I can tell you is that I saw her. I'm not responsible for anything else. You find out whatever you need to."

"Is there any charge for this?" he asked suspiciously.

"No," Miriam said. "Good luck." After she got off, she got a quick flash of Tom and Natasha in church, Natasha in a white dress, Tom in the dark suit he'd worn to Kaylee's funeral. Miriam felt happy for him and for herself. She was excited about her work again, like she could do it and bring good to people instead of harm. She hoped Natasha wasn't just after a green card. She hoped that Natasha would love Tom.

When Violet came home from school, Miriam saw her looking around a moment and then pouting.

"Do you want oatmeal raisin cookies with milk?" Miriam asked.

Even though Miriam knew they were her favorite cookies,

Violet shook her head. She put her lunchbox on the table. In kindergarten they only brought snacks, but Violet liked her Holly Hobby lunchbox. The string cheese and box of grape juice were still inside it. So was the box of raisins.

Miriam couldn't let Violet sink into despair. "Let's play one of our special games, like we used to," she said.

"Won't Mommy get mad?" Violet asked.

"Mad at what?" Cara said, coming down the stairs.

Miriam's stomach clenched. She had forgotten to ask Cara if it would be all right. She had promised herself never again to act as if Violet were hers and not Cara's.

"I was just going to play a game with Violet," she said, her nerves making her speed-talk. "The game is that I draw something without showing it to her and put it in an envelope. She has to draw what she thinks the picture is inside it. And then we open the envelope to see how close her drawing is to mine."

"That sounds like fun," Cara said. "Can I play too?"

Miriam's stomach unclenched, and all the rest of her muscles too. "That would be great."

"How come you don't mind if we play this game, Mommy? You used to mind."

"Even grownups grow," Cara said.

Violet nodded solemnly. Miriam wanted to grab them both to her. Instead she said, "Go, you two. I'm going to make my picture now. Get some paper and pencils so you can draw what you think I drew. And don't look at each other's drawings, you hear?"

Cara and Violet went off giggling, holding hands,

swinging their arms. Kaylee had taught them all to be children again, Miriam thought. There was silliness in the air along with the aroma of pancakes from breakfast.

Miriam started simply. She drew a star. "Ready," she called out.

"Wait, wait," Cara called. "We haven't even started yet."

A few moments later Miriam heard Violet say, "Don't peek, Mommy."

When they came back in, Violet had drawn a star, not five-pointed like Miriam's, but a definite star.

"Oh gosh, I don't know if I should even show mine," Cara said.

"Mommy, it's just a game," Violet said. "It doesn't matter."

Cara held her drawing against her chest. It was a heart.

"Love is always right," Miriam said.

"Not really," Violet said, her dimple deepening. "A star isn't a heart, but that's okay, Mommy."

"This time I'll be the one who draws the picture," Cara said. "At least I know I'm good at that."

They played several times, Violet consistently doing better than Miriam. Then they all made dinner together. Miriam's own heart swelled along with the dough heating up in the bread maker. Just when she'd thought that everything was going better than she had ever thought possible, it got better still.

"When I was just your age," Miriam said, "my favorite place was Bubbie's parlor, where I watched her see her customers." She glanced at Cara, worried that she would object, but Cara just continued crimping the crust for a quiche. Miriam took a breath and went on, "Bubbie could tell them anything about their lives—who they would love and who they would hate, what spirits were around them, if they had some illness that she could cure by making them a potion or salve. So many people knew my bubbie and loved her. She helped the whole neighborhood. I still get calls from people who tell me that she saved their grandmother's life. Being a psychic can be a great blessing to yourself and others."

"But Grandma," Violet said, tearing lettuce into a bowl, "you get into lots of trouble for telling other people's secrets. Nobody likes you then. You can't go to Lisa Green's house anymore and her mother even takes her out of your class."

"That's true," Cara said, "but now if you find out something about someone, you can tell me or Dad or any of your grandparents. We won't tell anyone so you won't get into any trouble."

Violet looked as if she were thinking all of this over. "I decided that I don't want to do what Grandma Miriam does when I grow up. I want to be a writer like Mark Twain." Miriam saw her looking at her with hesitation. She knew Violet didn't want to hurt her feelings.

"That's a great idea," Miriam said, laughing with pleasure. She no longer needed Violet to follow in her and Bubbie's footsteps. Violet could be free to find her own way. Miriam was letting go of Violet just as she had managed to convince Kaylee to. Miriam felt as if she were already in heaven. Tomorrow she would take a train home and be with Rory again. Violet was all right. All the family was doing fine.

That night she heard Violet scream out, "Kaylee, Kaylee, come back." Miriam hurried to Violet's room, but Dan and Cara were already with her, so she left them to comfort Violet.

Miriam couldn't leave yet. When Violet came home from school, she just moped about, not doing much of anything, wandering here and there. Miriam was sure Violet was looking for Kaylee again. What could she do? Miriam couldn't stay here forever.

At dinner, Violet wiggled her top front tooth. "See how loose it is?"

"That's because you're going to be six in a week," Cara said. "It means the tooth fairy is going to visit you soon."

Violet wiggled and wiggled the tooth.

"Let it come out naturally," Cara said, but Miriam saw Violet pushing it with her tongue.

"Grandma told me Bubbie used to tie a string to a loose tooth and tie the other end to a doorknob," Violet said with a worried look. She pushed that tooth with her tongue until it came loose in her hand, like a small pearl.

"Put it under your pillow for the tooth fairy," Miriam said.

When Violet went upstairs, she called out, "Grandma, Grandma, look what I found!"

"Be right up," Miriam said. When she got to Violet's room, Violet was doing merry leaps, holding something to her chest.

"What do you have there?" Miriam asked.

"A picture of Kaylee! She left it for me so I would remember her. She left it like a goodbye."

"What?" Miriam said. "You have a picture of Kaylee?"

Violet held it out to her, and Miriam took it and looked at it hard. It wasn't Kaylee. It was the Madonna on the remembrance card that looked so much like Kaylee that Miriam had been startled by it at the funeral. She almost said, "I must have brought it from home," but thank goodness she kept her mouth shut. How had it gotten under Violet's pillow? *Maybe I took it with me and Violet found it in one of my pockets and put it under her own pillow.*

She took a deep breath. As long as Violet was okay, what difference did it make? Miriam didn't have to know everything. Just then she got a vision of her office in Great Neck, the crystals hanging at the windows casting shimmering rainbows on the white walls. On her white desk, right near her white phone, she saw a small card. And when her mind zoomed in on it, she saw it was Kaylee's remembrance card. *It's right where I left it,* Miriam thought. Prickles of astonishment rippled through her as she put the card back in Violet's hands. There was so much she didn't know, but right now, in this moment, she knew she loved her granddaughter, and whatever of her was inside Violet, connecting their futures, well, they'd both have to live to find out.

About the Author

Like Miriam Kaminsky, ROCHELLE JEWEL SHAPIRO is a phone psychic who lives in Great Neck, N.Y. with her pharmacist husband. Articles have been written about her psychic gift in such places as *Redbook*, *The Jerusalem Post*, the *Dutch Magazine*, *TV GID*, and the Long Island section of *The New York Times*. She's chronicled her own psychic experiences in *Newsweek* (My Turn), and *The New York Times* (Lives) which can be read on her website at *http://rochellejewelshapiro.com*.

Shapiro has won The Brandon Memorial Literary Award and was nominated for a Pushcart Prize in poetry. *Miriam the Medium* was also published in Belgium, Holland, and the U.K. and was nominated for the Harold U. Ribelow Award and appeared on the summer reading list of *The Hartford Courant*. Her poetry has appeared in such publications as the *Iowa Review*, *Moment*, *Harpur Palate*, *Inkwell Magazine*, and the *Los Angeles Review*. Besides her psychic practice, Shapiro teaches writing at UCLA Extension and writes for the *Huffington Post*.

Reading Group Guide

1. One of the themes of this book is how your gene pool shapes choices and family interactions. How did Miriam's gift, passed on to Violet, change all the relationships in the family? Is there something in your own gene pool that you have inherited, wish you've inherited, or dread that one of your children will inherit? Were you ever pushed to take lessons in things you weren't interested in or discouraged from pursuing something that felt essential to your being?

2. Another theme of this book is the immigrant experience. How did Miriam's family's escape from Russia impact on her even though she was born in the U.S.? Has the immigrant experience impacted you or other members of your family?

3. Haunting has many meanings in this novel besides the actual ghostly presence. What memories haunt Cara? Rory? Dan? Miriam? How do these memories shape their actions?

4. Because the author is also psychic, she was able to show how visions arise in a psychic's mind. All of us have had "coincidences," the uncanny way we think of a person and then he calls or a feeling comes over us, like a warning not to

drive down a certain street, and later we find out that there was an accident that our intuition helped us avoid. Have any of you had experiences like this?

5. Have you ever thought that you've seen a ghost? What were the circumstances?

6. Miriam lives in the present with her dead relatives, their opinions and arguments. Do you try, in your own way, to make contact with someone who is deceased? Do you find yourself calling out a person's name when you're in stress even though you have attended that person's funeral? Who do you sense around you, communicate with, unbounded by conventional ideas of space and time?

7. Some people are frightened by psychic experiences, but there are cultures where dreams are discussed at the breakfast table and everyone has a relative who reads tea leaves or tarot. What is the ESP climate of your family?

8. Shapiro addresses the issue of personal privacy. The only thing that's private anymore is what is in our own minds (provided we don't put it on Facebook or Twitter.) But Miriam, being a psychic, can be intrusive to those close to her. Have you had to set boundaries with people close to you? What were the circumstances?

9. The theme of mother/daughter relationships is strong in this novel. Cara has to rebel against Miriam in order to feel

as if she has her own life as Miriam had to with her mother. What price is Violet paying for her psychic gift in her relationship with her mother and both of her grandmothers? What have you done to try to break away from your mother? If you have children, how are they expressing this archetypal conflict?

10. In the novel, parents are shown to put too much pressure on their kids. How does this express itself in Dan's life? In Cara's? In Violet's? In Miriam's life? Have you been pressured by family or by teachers to fulfill something they wanted you to?

11. In Kaylee's Ghost, Violet's teachers don't understand her. Has there been a teacher in your life who really "got" you and helped you accept yourself or develop yourself in some way? In your children's lives?

Made in the USA
Lexington, KY
27 October 2013